Also by Kathryn Gualtieri

Murder Takes the Stage

The Laundryman's Daughter

Half Moon Bay: Birth of a Coastside Town

MURDER IN THE PINES

Kathryn Gualtieri

Murder in the Pines is a work of fiction, whose story-line and characters are the products of the author's imagination, but woven around incidents that occurred in early Carmel history. See Author's Note at the end of the novel.

Modified cover photograph and other photographs are credited to the Henry Meade Williams Local History Department, Harrison Memorial Library, Carmel, California

A Tin Lantern Publication
Post Office Box 1483
Capitola, California 95010

Book design by Dorothy Foglia,
Aptos, California

Printed in the United States of America.

ISBN 978-0-988-8563-0-1

January 2013

Dear Reader,

As a lifelong admirer of Julia Morgan, the first practicing woman architect in California, and best known for her design of Hearst Castle in San Simeon, I included her in this book and its sequel as a "friend and mentor" to my fictional heroine, Nora Finnegan. Morgan anchors both mysteries in time and plot.

Please indulge me in a bit of history. Julia Morgan is remembered on the Monterey Peninsula for creating Asilomar, originally used as a YWCA facility and dating back 100 years. She was commissioned by a group of influential women philanthropists who envisioned a safe, attractive place for young women to gather when away from home. By 1913, she had completed the Administration Building, named for its benefactress, Phoebe Apperson Hearst, followed by the Grace H. Dodge Memorial Chapel in 1915 and the Mary Crocker Dining Hall in 1918. All three buildings remain in use today, and were utilized in the early 1920s when my mystery novels take place. In 1956, the state of California's Department of Parks and Recreation acquired Asilomar and preserved it as a conference and educational center for all to enjoy.

When I first wrote the Julia Morgan character into Murder in the Pines, I never expected the book's 4th printing would coincide with the 100th anniversary of Asilomar. It is only fitting that I dedicate this print run to Julia Morgan and those outstanding philanthropists who made Asilomar a national historic treasure. May it continue to thrive for another 100 years.

Kathryn Gualtieri

ACKNOWLEDGEMENTS

I owe my deepest thanks to fellow authors, Dianne Day, Denise Osborne, Kay Holz and Gayle Ortiz, for their critiques of my manuscript, and especially to Kay, for her creative guidance on the cover artwork and for her unflagging advice and support. This novel was enhanced by Jacqueline Buie's editing skills and by book designer Dorothy Foglia's expertise in bringing my manuscript to print. Thank you to Carmel's local history librarian, Rose McClendon, for making available early issues of the *Carmel Pine Cone* and for giving me access to the library's collection of historical materials.

I would like to acknowledge Doug Thompson, former publisher of the *Carmel Pine Cone*, for accepting my book reviews and interviews with local authors and artists, as well as my articles on Carmel's history. Special thanks to former *Pine Cone* arts editors, Ivy Weston Hartman and Anne Papineau, for their guidance and for allowing me a close-up view into the world of journalism.

I am grateful to architectural historian, Kent Seavey, and to past and present City of Carmel planning staff, particularly Brian Roseth, Christi D'Iorio, and Sean Conroy, who provided me with a wealth of historical information. Also, I appreciate the support of Ralph Tober, former chairman of Carmel's Historic Preservation Committee, who shared his research on the Carmel City Council Meeting Minutes from 1916-1940.

Franklin Walker's *The Seacoast of Bohemia* and Sharron Lee Hale's *A Tribute to Yesterday*, plus the Harrison Memorial Library's photographs, included at the end of this novel, helped me visualize the setting and to develop the plot. However, I want to point out that this book is a work of fiction and a product of my imagination.

CHAPTER ONE

Thursday, November 11, 1921

Momentary doubts flashed through Nora Finnegan's mind as she closed her cottage's Dutch door behind her. This morning she was about to do something risky that she had been contemplating for the past week. It was possible that she would lose her reporter's job, and be forced to leave Carmel-By-The Sea. She took a deep breath to bolster her confidence and stepped onto the dirt path that led out to Monte Verde Street.

Her thoughts were interrupted when she came upon several neighbors in robes and hair nets who had gathered around one of the village's milk shrines. The women greeted her with smiles and nods. She gave them a perfunctory smile, took a pint of cold milk from her shelf, and left a buffalo nickel wrapped in paper for tomorrow's order.

It occurred to Nora that when she first came to live in Carmel, she hadn't realized the purpose of these open-air racks resembling oversized bookcases on every street corner. Aside from being a place where one heard the latest gossip, the shrines housed dairy products, delivered fresh each day from the nearby ranches in Carmel Valley.

Dropping her milk bottle into her purse, she continued walking at a fast pace until she reached Ocean Avenue, the village's main street and the location of the *Carmel Pine Cone*. She paused to check her reflection in the building's front window. Taller than most women at five feet, seven inches, she straightened her shoulders, adjusted the lapels on her suit jacket, and pushed open the door. Entering the empty reception area, she stored her milk in the ice box and hung her jacket on the coat rack, a routine that she had been following for the past three months. She walked over to the wall calendar where William Owens, the *Pine Cone's* publisher, posted the day's assignments. *Not again!* Her initials were next to two items that sounded dull and uninteresting. *You've waited far too long to assert yourself, Nora!*

Head down, she marched into the back room, where she found Mr. Owens standing in front of the only Chandler & Price flywheel printing press in the area. His eyeshade smudged with fingerprints and sweat marks on his shirt indicated that he had been working for hours. Nora knew it was an exhausting job, even for a strapping six-foot man. On the floor next to him lay stacks of already printed paper, some with notations circled in red ink. She recognized the pages as part of the new brochure that the Carmel Development Company had ordered last week.

"Excuse me, sir," she said in a loud voice.

Intent on inserting a blank sheet of paper into the press at the same time that he withdrew a printed one, Owens ignored her and continued pumping the noisy flywheel with one foot.

She had to interrupt him. She had made her decision.

"Mr. Owens!" she shouted over the din.

His foot stopped in mid-air. Turning around, he looked at her. "What is it?"

Her blue eyes flashing, she said, "I know you're very busy, sir, but I need to speak to you about my assignments." Her face reddened as she went on, "I've been working here since September, Mr. Owens. I'd prefer to have a meaningful story to write about . . . " Hesitating, she blurted out, "for once."

When he didn't answer, Nora held out the list she had torn off the wall calendar. "Who will be interested in the grocery store's latest shipment of turkey basters, roasting pans and ovenettes? And why are the Pine Inn's Thanksgiving table decorations so important?"

Looking irritated, he shut down the press, stretched, and then walked over to his desk in the far corner. Forty year-old William Owens was clean shaven with dark brown hair that was beginning to gray at the temples. "Sit down, Honora," he said, and pointed at the chair opposite him. Having been a fellow classmate of her father's at the University of California at Berkeley, he had known her since childhood and always called her by her given name.

Nora took a seat and hid her trembling hands in her lap. She had come this far and she wasn't about to back down. She began, "I'm aware of the upcoming holiday and that you have advertising pressures to factor into your decisions for feature stories. However, since I started working at the *Pine Cone*, you've yet to assign me one significant news article. I know that I'm up to the task."

Owens frowned. "Last time I checked, young lady, I was still in charge of this newspaper. That gives me the right to decide what articles to run, based on our readers' preferences." Picking up a sheet of newsprint from the top of his desk, he passed it over to her. "Did you happen to read this story in last Sunday's paper?"

Nora frowned as she scanned the lead article in their competitor's daily. The slick illustration on the newspaper's front page featured a smiling woman wearing a striped apron. Her open hands encircling a turkey that she had just stuffed, she looked poised to put the bird into one of those new cooking gadgets called an "ovenette." Nora wasn't impressed, but she kept quiet. She knew the publisher was making his point.

"Women prefer reading about the latest methods of cooking a turkey," he said, "especially at Thanksgiving time. Now think about why I agreed to hire you. Despite your limited writing experience, you're a woman, and I distinctly recall explaining to your father that I wanted an assistant with a female point of view."

She had to admit that what he was saying was true, but it angered her that he had deflected her request for more meaningful assignments by bringing up her father. For years, both men had remained friends, even after John Finnegan was promoted to the editor's post at the *San Francisco Call* and Mr. Owens relocated his family to Carmel to publish its first newspaper. Before she could think of a response, she heard the telephone ring in the outer area at the same time as the office's front door banged open.

Mary Lee Owens, the *Pine Cone's* receptionist, called out, "I'll get it," followed by, "Stay, Dasher!" Before the publisher's wife reached for the telephone, she released a small dog that was bent on ignoring her command. True to his moniker, the Welsh corgi skidded across the floorboards and raced into the back room. He jumped up on Owens, who was standing and about to return to his printing press.

"Down!" he yelled at the dog. "We'll discuss this another time, Honora. I have an important deadline to meet by this afternoon."

She had been dismissed. However, Nora determined that his decision would only be a temporary setback. On her way out to the reception area, she bent down and rubbed Dasher's head where he liked being petted. She had no argument with the Owens' family dog. At her desk, she reached into one of the drawers and selected a fresh pad of writing paper. Stuffing it into her purse, she went to the coat rack and put on her jacket. Mrs. Owens was still negotiating the demands of an irate telephone caller, but she smiled at Nora as she left the newspaper office.

The sun had disappeared behind the clouds and a cold breeze was coming up Ocean Avenue from the beach. Nora headed for Leidig Brothers Groceries. She would write about those boring ovenettes and do her best to make her article sound topical, as well as informative. After all, Mr. Owens was the boss.

Watching her go, Mary Lee Owens left her desk and hurried to the back room. She found her husband at the printing press, where she knew he had been working since sun-up. She tapped him on the shoulder. "Please stop for a minute, dear."

During their 20 years of marriage, William Owens had valued his wife's opinions. He suspected what she was about to say next. Shutting down the press, he asked, "What's gotten into that girl?" Then he walked over to his desk and waited for his wife to settle into the same chair that Honora had vacated. "Do you think she's becoming a problem? I'm giving her a chance that most reporters would envy, and there were men that I could have hired in her place. I was simply doing Honora's father a favor."

Mary Lee usually deferred to her husband when it came to business decisions, but she wouldn't this time. She had listened to his frequent complaints over Nora's supposed shortcomings and had hoped that he would come to see her in a different light over time.

But that hadn't happened yet. She said, "It's true that you've given Nora an opportunity, William, but I don't think you understand her goals. She's bright, industrious, and at 21, a young woman — not a girl, as you often refer to her. She wants more of a challenge. While her job here gives her experience, I think you've been holding her back."

"Nonsense! She'll soon tire of her journalism career, return to San Francisco and marry a nice boy — someone her parents approve of. They'll start a family. If you ask me, that's every girl's ambition."

Mary Lee shook her head. "You aren't sure what Nora intends to do with her life. Why did she work so hard to attain a college degree if she didn't plan to use her education? As for marriage and children, she isn't thinking about those choices now."

"Isn't marriage what all parents want for their daughters? At least that's what I see ahead for our Sally."

"Sally is only ten years old, and by the time she's Nora's age, the world will have changed. If I have anything to say to Sally then, it will be to encourage her to follow her heart. We're giving her the right values. I'm confident she'll make good decisions."

Owens snickered. "Since you women won the right to vote, you want to change everything to suit yourselves. I don't understand you. As a wife and mother, aren't you happy with the way things are?"

"Of course I am, but it's my belief that Nora would like more options to choose from than the ones my generation had." Getting up, and with Dasher racing ahead, Mary Lee retraced her steps to the front reception area. For now, the corgi sided with her. A moment later, she heard the printing press start up.

Having worked on her ovenette assignment all afternoon, Nora was surprised to look up and find Mr. Owens hovering in front of her desk. She stood up and handed him her finished article. "I hope I've covered the subject adequately, sir," she said. "I also want to say how sorry I am to have spoken the way I did this morning."

He shook his head. "That isn't what I came out to talk about, Honora. I'm sure your story will be fine. I wonder if you have made any plans for tomorrow evening."

"If the weather's decent, I usually take a walk on the beach after work. Then I fix an early supper. I can easily rearrange my routine."

The smile on his face surprised her. "Good! I admire flexibility in an employee. One must be able to adapt, especially in our business."

As she listened to him, Nora wondered what was coming next.

"Sit down, will you," he said, as he turned a nearby chair around and straddled it. "I'd like you to join me at the Board of Trustees meeting. They're taking up a new and controversial topic that I'm convinced will have a major impact on Carmel's future. I think you would benefit from hearing the Trustees' opinions."

Nora's spirits rose. "I'd like to attend the meeting. Can you tell me something about the subject they're going to discuss?" She waited, knowing that he always told a story from the very beginning.

Owens drummed his fingers on the top of the back of his chair. "In the fall of 1916 — the year after I started publishing the *Pine Cone* — the residents here voted 113 to 86 to incorporate Carmel-By-The-Sea as a city. At the same time, we also elected five Trustees to govern us."

"Who leads the group, sir?"

"A Board President. I'll make sure to introduce you to Ben Fox, as well as the other Trustees. They're the ones who will decide whether or not to allow a hotel to be built on our beach."

Nora thought the topic sounded intriguing. "What time shall I be there?"

"Mrs. Owens wants you to come by the house for supper at 5:30. I'll tell you more about the proposed development while we eat. Then we'll walk over to City Hall together." Getting up, he added, "Mind you, Honora, we're having leftovers. I hope that suits you."

Nora smiled. "I live on leftovers."

Owens headed around the front counter. Turning to look at her, he said, "Don't forget about your other story on the Pine Inn's Thanksgiving decorations."

"I won't, sir." As she retrieved her purse from her bottom desk drawer, she could hear the printing press start up again. Excited by his unexpected invitation, Nora felt like celebrating. After supper, she would have a piece of apple pie from the Blue Bird Tea Room, and for once, she wouldn't fret about her figure.

Putting on her jacket, she headed out the door. She had no idea what Mr. Owens had in mind for her tomorrow evening. Perhaps it would turn out to be her first challenging assignment.

CHAPTER TWO

Night had already fallen, and it was only 5:30. Nora lit her lantern before leaving the Blue Bird Tea Room. Picking up the paper box with an apple pie that she had just purchased, she stepped outside onto Ocean Avenue. Because the village lacked street lights, she was obliged to use her homemade lamp, a tin can with a wire handle and holes punched in the sides to allow candlelight to shine through. The heavy fog that had swept in from the ocean in the afternoon still lingered.

Walking home along the wood sidewalk, she noticed a light from another lantern. It was attached to a tall man in an odd tartan plaid overcoat. He appeared to be looking for something. As he drew closer, she could smell his cigar's aroma and see its intermittent glow as he inhaled.

"Pardon me, miss," he called out, "but do you know the Shamrock Garage? I'd be grateful if you'd point me in the right direction. I can't find a thing in this fog." He exhaled a plume of smoke and mumbled, "In this day and age, why Carmel doesn't put in street lights is beyond me."

Nora studied the stranger's deep set eyes and his neatly trimmed beard. He wasn't anyone she had seen in the village before. She said, "Peter Quinlan's garage is on this side of the street where Ocean Avenue intersects with Junipero. You're headed straight for it."

He tipped his hat and smiled. "Thank you, miss. I'm much obliged."

As they passed each other, Nora could almost feel the man's eyes appraising her.

When Martin Fields reached the place where the sidewalk ended and the road began its vertical climb to the top of Carmel hill, he spotted an older model Buick parked at the corner. A "FOR HIRE" sign was propped up on the wind-screen. Lifting his lamp, he made out the words on the hand-printed sign on the adjacent building: "Shamrock Garage, P. Quinlan, prop."

He knocked on the garage door. Getting no response, he pressed his ear against the wood surface. Hearing a clanking sound from somewhere inside, he yelled, "Hello. You in there! Quinlan!"

Nothing.

Using his fist, Fields hammered on the door, and jumped backwards when it suddenly flew open.

A broad-shouldered man somewhere in his twenties filled the entrance. Fields noted the black eyebrows that came together above his fleshy nose. Muscled arms were straining the seams of his coveralls. Having himself been a boxer in college, Fields thought that the fellow would make an excellent pugilist.

"So you're Quinlan," he said. "I'm here to rent a motorcar." On his walk from the hotel, he had been envisioning something like the Twin-Six Packard parked in his Long Island garage across the country. "I assume the manager at La Playa telephoned you."

Quinlan nodded, as he wiped his hands on a grease-stained towel. "She did, but as you can plainly see, it's after hours. Shop's closed for the day."

Fields frowned. "That so? Well, I need transportation tonight, not tomorrow." He pointed at the Buick. "Do you have anything in better shape than that run-down wreck?" He moved forward and started to enter the garage.

Stepping in front of him, Quinlan grabbed Fields' forearm in a vice-like grip. "Whoa!" he said. "Leave your lantern outside and put out that danged cigar. Are you crazy? There's gasoline in here."

Unused to being ordered about by the likes of a common workman, Fields swore under his breath, but blew out the candle in his lamp and set it down on the sidewalk. He ground his cigar under his boot and entered the garage.

Trailing behind, Quinlan muttered, "I told the lady from La Playa that five o'clock is when I close. She should've explained that to you."

Fields glanced around the cluttered workshop. "What

makes you think I run by your schedule? From the looks of this place, you could use my business. And I'm not in the habit of being turned down."

An habitual poker player, Quinlan's face revealed little emotion. He could raise the ante with the best of them. "You're new in town, mister, which means you don't know the roads here. This fog's unsafe to drive in. If you were to crash one of my Buicks, I'd be out my investment. How do you propose to cover that?"

Fields' blood pressure went up as he checked the handwritten price list nailed to the back wall. "I'll pay you twice your going rate of two dollars a day. And I know my way around." Pulling out his wallet, he laid a ten dollar bill on the workbench. "Now give me your best motorcar."

Quinlan jerked his thumb at another Buick, its hood up, in the center of the shop. "That's a better machine," he said. "Problem is, I'm working on it and the job won't be done for a day or two. Only thing I got at the moment is the one you saw outside."

Fields groaned. "Well, I guess it will have to do. Let's settle the bill, but be quick about it. I don't have all night."

Grabbing a printed form from a shelf, Quinlan held out a pencil. "Sign here. And mind you, I want a good-sized deposit, in case you wind up in a ditch."

Opening his wallet a second time, Fields took out a fifty dollar bill and laid it on top of the ten. "Ulysses S. Grant ought to take care of it." He scrawled his name on the form and ignored the mechanic's hand to seal the deal. Then he strode to the exit and stepped out to the sidewalk, where he picked up his lantern.

Quinlan decided he could play the stranger's game too. He let his customer wait while he pocketed the sixty dollars and filed the rental form in a cigar box. Coming outside, he pushed past the man and got into the Buick. "I'll start her up for you," he said. "Here's where you turn on the headlamps." He swung the motorcar around. Getting out, he said, "Take it slow. You can't see but a few feet ahead of you." Turning abruptly, he stalked back inside the garage and slammed the door behind him.

Fields shook his head in disgust, climbed into the driver's seat, and drove west down Ocean Avenue toward the beach. Luckily, there were no other vehicles to distract him. When he came to the coast road where the Avenue ended, he turned north.

The Buick lumbered along a route that, in some places, consisted of nothing more than two muddy troughs.

Shifting a fresh cigar from one side of his mouth to the other, he noticed the headlamps begin to flicker. Probably a loose wire, he thought. Then the wipers quit. Moisture condensed on the wind-screen and seeing the edges of the road became problematic. Without warning, the motorcar's rear end started to slide off onto the shoulder. Pulling hard on the steering wheel, he was barely able to keep the Buick in the middle of the road. He stuck his head out to assess his whereabouts as he let the motorcar crawl ahead. That only resulted in the fog dampening his hair. He still couldn't get his bearings.

At the next bend, he braked and came to a stop. Opening the driver's door, he lifted himself out of the seat and stood on the running board. Had he missed the turnoff to Bella Vista? To his relief, he spied a familiar landmark, a stand of cypress trees up ahead on the left. Inching the motorcar forward, even with only the flickering light from the headlamps, he caught sight of two stone columns bracketing an open gate that led to a circular driveway. He pulled in, and minutes later, parked behind another motorcar under the *porte cochere*.

Set back from the road, the mansion perched above the sand dunes at Carmel's outskirts and the start of 17-Mile Drive. The first time Fields had visited the place, he had taken a dislike to Bella Vista. In his opinion, its stucco walls, tile roof, and iron grill-work were too rustic for his taste. The design couldn't begin to compare to the classic, columned East Coast manor that he lived in.

After turning off the ignition, he stepped onto the gravel path and headed for the front entry. Stopping next to the other motorcar, a black Pierce-Arrow, he admired the uniquely styled headlamps that the designer had sunk into the front fenders. He bet they wouldn't flicker. Why wasn't he driving something like this? He would lay into that fool Quinlan for passing off an unsafe motorcar when he brought the Buick back to him in a few days.

Climbing the front stairs, he ignored the brass knocker, since David Chatham was expecting him. The oak door opened easily into a high ceiling foyer. Looking around, he remembered the mansion's stodgy interior and simple oak furniture. In the library off the hall, he found his host seated in an armchair next to the fireplace. The young man greeted him with an arm wave.

"Never like to keep a man waiting," Fields said, as he removed his overcoat, dropped it on a chair, and walked towards his host, his hand outstretched.

Chatham didn't get up. He let his guest's hand hang in the air. Eyes glazed, he hoisted his brandy snifter in the air and said, "What took you so long, Marty?"

On hearing the man's slurred speech, Fields stiffened. "We'd better get something straight if we're going to work together, David. I want you to stay sober. We're dealing with some heavy opposition. Today I spoke to Ben Fox, the Board President. He assures me I'll get a fair hearing at the Trustees' meeting tomorrow night."

Swallowing the last of his drink, Chatham stood up and walked unsteadily to the liquor cabinet. "That so, Marty? Then you don't know the first thing about politics."

Fields snorted at being criticized. "Just what are you implying?"

"I'm talking about how much time it's going to take for me to persuade our elected people to vote the way we want them to, Marty, not to mention the time spent convincing the residents. I'll need a lot more money than you originally gave me."

Body swaying, Chatham poured himself a generous helping from the bottle.

Fields fumed. "Drop all this money talk and don't call me Marty. I don't like it." He edged towards Chatham, but held himself in check by turning away when he saw the French doors leading out to the terrace. Strolling over, he pushed one open and took a deep breath to stem his anger. The house didn't impress him, but its proximity to the ocean captivated him. He wasn't sure if the pounding in his ears was his beating heart or the surf on the beach below Bella Vista.

Stepping out onto the terrace, Fields immediately felt less agitated. He was glad that he had made an effort to see Chatham tonight because his visit confirmed that the man was going to be a problem. Calmer now, he returned to the library and forced a smile. "We have some things we need to settle on."

Chatham took a sip of his drink. "Know what, Marty? We have to settle on you paying me enough to do my job properly. With what I know about you, I might talk."

Before he could stop himself, Fields lunged at Chatham, sending his glass flying. Grabbing the man around the neck, he wrestled him to the floor. When he saw his face turning blue, he let go. "Mind you, David, no more liquor and no money demands," he hissed. Pushing the gasping man away, he stood up and straightened his jacket.

Walking back to the open French door, Fields could hear the sound of the breaking waves, even though he couldn't see them through the fog. He found they had a comforting rhythm. His goals were clear. The Board of Trustees would approve his hotel project on Carmel beach. Afterwards, he would demolish this ugly house, build a new vacation home on the spot where he was standing and rid himself of David Chatham. Everything was going to fall into place.

Seated in the kitchen of her wood-framed cottage, Nora Finnegan thought about the stranger she had met on her way home from work. His observation that Carmel was a backward town because it lacked street lights had annoyed her. As a resident, she knew the reason for this was that the majority of the villagers wanted to keep their environment natural looking. She would comment on it the next time she wrote in her journal, but she was too tired to pen anything tonight. Pushing back her chair, she got up and pulled a sweater off a peg on the wall. Draping it over her shoulders, she opened the door leading to her back yard.

The fog had lifted. Standing on the porch, she was surprised to hear the noise of an approaching motorcar. Someone had to be lost. At this time of night, the hotel guests who were staying at La Playa a few blocks away had already tucked themselves in for the night. Taking the path along the side of her cottage, she headed to the grapestake fence that separated her front yard from the road. She was eager to see who it was.

A motorcar, its headlamps flickering, moved slowly down Monte Verde Street.

Nora made out the driver's face as it passed. It was the stranger who had asked her for directions earlier. He must have found the Shamrock Garage.

Standing in front of her cottage, she took in the familiar soothing sounds of night in Carmel: lapping waves on the nearby beach, and rustling branches of the Norfolk Island pine alongside the cottage. Her parents had planted the tree 16 years ago when they had first bought the property. She looked forward to seeing it decorated with Christmas ornaments again this year.

Turning to go into the house, she hoped that joining Mr. Owens at the Trustees' meeting would be the start of more fulfilling assignments at the *Carmel Pine Cone*. If not, it probably meant that she would need to make a career move and find another job.

CHAPTER THREE

Friday

When Nora and Mr. Owens arrived at the two-story Carmel City Hall at 7:00 P.M., they found an overflow crowd. The upstairs meeting room facing out onto Ocean Avenue was packed. In addition to those who were already seated, residents clustered in groups at the back of the room and down the staircase. Latecomers had to remain outside under their umbrellas at the building's side entrance on Lincoln Street. The rain had deterred no one.

The heavy turnout hadn't surprised Owens. He expected the residents to be cantankerous, considering the importance of the topic. Turning to Nora, he said, "I hear nothing but complaints from people who object to being jammed together on these hard benches. Yet nobody ever thinks of getting up and leaving."

After entering the room, Owens introduced Nora to Ben Fox, the Board of Trustees' President. A man of medium height with a potbelly and red suspenders, Fox seemed jovial and polite. Nora knew of his penchant for fixing things. On those occasional visits to Fox's repair shop, she couldn't help but notice the sign over the entry: "I can mend everything but broken hearts." Would the Board's President be successful tonight in bringing the disparate crowd together, she wondered.

Before taking the reserved seats for "Members of the Press" in the first row, Nora said, "If it's all right with you, sir, I prefer to sit next to the center aisle."

Owens nodded, removed his hat, and went in first. As he sat down next to her, he said, "Are you aware that Carmelites fall into many different cliques, Honora?"

"I haven't lived here long enough to know much about the town's diversity."

He raised his voice so that she could hear him above the commotion. "First we have the thespians. They spend most nights at the Forest Theater and the Arts and Crafts Hall, practicing their lines for the next play they're putting on. Generally, these folks ignore city politics, unless an issue arises that might deprive them of a stage on which to perform."

Nora grinned, but decided not to interrupt him with questions.

"Then there are the literati. Most evenings, they gather over at Holiday House and listen to the latest music or recite poetic odes to one another. They only care about local issues when something threatens to affect their life style."

Just then, a man whom Nora didn't recognize came up and handed Owens a piece of paper. "Here are my thoughts on the hotel project," he said. "I hope you print this in your letters from readers."

Nora watched him return to his seat a row behind them and across the aisle.

Owens leaned over and said, "That was Carmel's resident poet, Robinson Jeffers. It looks like he's taking an interest in tonight's discussion. This is a rare occasion. Normally Jeffers doesn't leave his home on Carmel Point." Tucking the man's note into his pocket, he added, "Now, where was I?"

"You were telling me about Carmel's different cliques," Nora offered.

"That's right, I was. Our most powerful group is made up of the artists. They call themselves Bohemians. They will opine on everything. I'm sure we'll be hearing from Carlotta Fleming. She's their most outspoken member."

Having listened to his opinions, Nora had no difficulty guessing which of the village cliques would show up tonight.

The pounding of Fox's gavel reverberated through the chambers. "Criminy sakes. Quiet down, folks," he shouted. "I want everyone to come to order!"

Nora sensed that "Mr. Fix-It" was in no mood to be challenged. Glancing sideways at Mr. Owens, she felt a little smug at having complained yesterday about her dull assignments. Her forwardness had paid off. Earlier, during supper, he had told her in a friendly way that covering Trustees' meetings was his responsibility. Nevertheless, he wanted her to be here tonight to assist him by writing down quotes when people got up to speak. 'Everyone likes to see his or her name in print,' he had said, 'so be sure to spell their names correctly.'

She had already taken down the names of the three Trustees who were present and had left space to write down what they would say later. Mr. Owens had mentioned that two of the Trustees were absent, but had valid excuses. Thus, the Board might not come to a final decision tonight. She couldn't imagine why the two men hadn't arranged their schedules so that they would be present for such an important local issue. She wondered if the Trustees served without pay.

Her proximity to the Trustees' table allowed her to observe the remaining three men up close. To the right of President Fox sat Trustee Roland Milliken, a portly man with muttonchops and a handlebar mustache. Nora recognized him as one of Carmel's two barbers. Earlier, to her amusement, Milliken almost fell out of his chair when Fox banged the table with his gavel. She guessed that he had been dozing. Now wide-eyed, the barber pulled a handkerchief from his pocket and blew his nose with gusto. Rearing back in his chair, he raised his fingers and carefully twisted his mustache ends. She wondered if his silly affectations perturbed those who had voted for him in the last election.

The Trustee who puzzled her most, however, was the man seated on President Fox's left. Mr. Owens had identified him as Doctor Arthur Taylor. This was his first term of office. She had no idea why a physician would want to be a politician. He was handsome and better dressed than his fellow Board members. Yet he seemed uncomfortable and self-conscious. He never looked up. Nor did he acknowledge the crowd's presence. Shuffling his papers and fidgeting, he alternated between checking the wall clock and studying his notes. Nora decided that he probably would rather have been tending to a sick patient.

Order restored, President Fox checked the speakers' signup sheet. "Let's see. The first name is Joseph Levy. Why don't you tell us what's on your mind, Joe."

Nora stared at the white-haired man in the front row across the aisle from her. Levy was gabbing with the man seated behind him. Apparently, the proprietor of Carmel's general store hadn't heard Fox's invitation. Nora saw the woman who was sitting next to the shopkeeper prod him in the ribs to get his attention.

Levy jumped up. "As I was just telling Mr. Jeffers, I don't see what's wrong with building a hotel on our beach. He disagrees, but I said there's plenty of space and it will help us attract visitors and paying customers to Carmel. I'm all for the idea and so's the missus. Right, Mildred?" Leaning over, he patted his wife's shoulder.

"Levy's for it," coursed through the room and snaked down the crowded staircase, like backyard gossip. Nora took down Levy's statement on the notepad in her lap. It had been short, but to the point, she thought. Nonetheless, she wondered what Mrs. Levy's opinion would have been, if she had been asked to give it. Why was it that wives rarely spoke up and always deferred to their husbands?

Fox called out another name that Nora recognized. The middle-aged woman in a dark raincoat and felt hat had just come in the room. Her hat brim dripped with moisture, its feathers limp and sagging. She looked drenched. Undeterred, she strode up the center aisle to address Fox and his fellow Trustees.

"That's Paulette Villard," Owens whispered. "Do you know her, Honora?"

Nodding, Nora wrote down the name of Hotel La Playa's manager. She had met Mrs. Villard on her evening walks, while passing by the hotel to admire its stone tower, and entering the lobby to get warm before returning home. She was anxious to hear a woman's viewpoint, even though she imagined Mrs. Villard would probably consider a new Carmel hotel as a competing business.

To her surprise, as the innkeeper approached the Trustees, she paused in the aisle and shook her fist at Mr. Levy! "Shame on you, Joe," she shouted. "I'm opposed to another lodging place, especially one right on the sand dunes." Turning to the Trustees, she said, "My inn is set back from the beach, so it doesn't spoil anyone's view. Mr. Levy and his cronies want to drive La Playa and the Pine Inn out of business. I don't support a project that affects existing hotels. I know you Trustees will do what's best for the community and the existing businesses. Turn down this project!"

Nora wasn't surprised by Mr. Levy's reaction. Already out of his seat, he appeared ready to respond, but Mrs. Levy restrained him from confronting the hotel manager. The Villard woman seemed to enjoy the discomfort that she was causing the man. Hat feathers swishing like a peacock's tail, she grinned at him and sashayed to the back of the room, all the while acknowledging the crowd's applause.

"Quiet down, people," Fox warned, "or we'll be here all night. The next person to speak is Rob Jacklin. Come on up, son."

At the sound of the name, Nora turned in her seat, but she couldn't locate Jacklin. However, she did notice Doctor Taylor leave his seat and walk over to speak to a young man leaning on a cane on the far side of the room.

Craning her neck, she caught sight of Jacklin emerging from an animated group near the stairs. She remembered his lean frame, auburn hair and angular features. He still reminded her of the heroes she had imagined in her childhood adventure novels.

As he walked up the aisle towards her, she recalled last summer's 4th of July picnic, when she and her parents had first met the decorated war veteran. Nora knew that Jacklin held strong convictions, based on listening to the discussion between him and her father on the nation's post-war problems. Her father had made a point of thanking Jacklin for his exemplary service under General Pershing. Later, she had fantasized about spending time with the former army lieutenant and current elementary schoolteacher. She hoped to have a chance to meet Jacklin again, and wondered if Mr. Owens might agree to let her interview him for an opinion-piece in a future *Pine Cone*.

Jacklin waited without speaking until Trustee Taylor resumed his seat at the front table. Then he began his remarks by conceding the heavy responsibility being placed on Carmel's elected officials. He went on to say, "All of us know the value of our unspoiled beach. We mustn't compromise its natural beauty for unchecked development. The price is too costly."

A few naysayers responded with groans. Jacklin turned around and glared at the men. "I'm talking to imprudent residents like you." His words brought more protests.

"Calm down, everyone," Fox interjected. "Please address the Trustees, Rob."

Jacklin shrugged and continued, "A beachfront hotel will destroy what we cherish most about living here. Approving it would set a dangerous precedent. Other buildings will be built and the beach will be sacrificed. I urge you to vote against the proposal. As for me, I'll do everything in my power to kill it."

Loud shouts erupted on both sides of the argument. Some Carmelites cheered, while others booed. The clamor was deafening. Nora admired the teacher's directness, but she was sure that many in the crowd had been taken aback by Jacklin's use of the word 'kill.'

"Time for the next speaker," Fox yelled. "Remember, we set this meeting to end by ten o'clock." He pointed to a man seated in the middle of the room. "There you are, Reverend Seagraves. According to my list, you're up next."

Nora stopped writing in order to study the man who was coming up the aisle. His gray hair curled in waves above his white clergyman's collar. When he reached the front, he adjusted his frock coat and faced the audience. One hand fondled a jeweled cross on a chain around his neck. Bowing his head, he cast his eyes downward. The crowd hushed.

Mr. Owens whispered, "He's doing that for effect. I doubt that he's praying."

"I'm Charles Evans Seagraves, spiritual head of the Reformed Bayside Church," the clergyman intoned. "Heed my words, fellow Carmelites. This development is God's way of helping you survive. You should embrace the hotel because it will bring this place out of its moribund existence." He turned and faced the Trustees. "A hotel will revitalize the community, improve its standard of living, and make Carmel a first-class travel destination. I implore each of you Trustees to support the new hotel. Amen."

Nora heard a few scattered 'Amens.' Her pencil raced across the paper, as she took down the minister's entreaty.

"Go back to Boston, preacher," someone shouted. "You don't belong here."

President Fox silenced the miscreant with several sharp raps of his gavel.

Thinking back on Mr. Owens' words doubting the clergyman's sincerity, Nora wondered if he was already counting the extra money in his church's collection plate.

"I supported Ben Fox when he ran for a second term," Owens whispered. "I wrote an editorial praising his leadership. It's apparent tonight."

"Pardon me for saying so, sir, but the reason you endorsed Mr. Fox was because he's favorable to the business interests," Nora suggested.

When he frowned, she wondered if her comment had been too pointed. Then he laughed, and she was relieved.

"I'll admit to that, Honora, but so far, the speakers seem to be favoring, not opposing, the new hotel."

Fox wrapped his gavel. "Time for the next speaker. Come on up, Carlotta."

"Carlotta Fleming speaks for all of us," a male voice called out from the back of the chambers. Immediately, cheers and whistles erupted on all sides.

As Nora waited for the artist to step forward, she considered Mr. Owens' earlier observations of Carmel's residents. He had said that Carlotta Fleming was the leader of the Bohemians, the town's most powerful clique. If Nora had to choose a social group, which one would it be? She didn't see herself as part of any group. She was a writer, but she wouldn't feel comfortable with the literati. And she had no formal training as an actor. She would need more time before she could side with any of them.

Nora focused her attention on Carlotta Fleming as she moved to the front of the room. The woman had tied back her gray tresses to disclose an unblemished complexion and piercing blue eyes. A pair of silver earrings dangled from her lobes, while a large, metal starfish had been pinned to the collar of her floor-length purple cloak. Its velvety material fell away in folds as she glided forward.

Carlotta waved at her noisy admirers and stood in front of the Trustees' table. Then she turned around and looked down at Nora. She smiled, revealing perfect white teeth. "Hello, Miss Finnegan. I've been meaning to thank you for your story about the opening of my Cypress Gallery. We artists love being appreciated. You're a perceptive reporter and have a marvelous future ahead of you."

Nora blushed at the compliment and the mention of the feature article that had appeared in last week's *Pine Cone*. It carried her first byline.

Turning to face her audience, the artist brought her arms up and held out a gold-lacquered box about the size of a cigar box. Everyone fell silent. Carlotta's strong voice reverberated to the corners of the room. "I want to tell all of you something important," she stated. "We're fortunate to live here. Carmel must remain the way it is forever."

A noisy stamping of feet erupted. The crowd yelled "Yes!

Yes!"

Then she turned to face the three Trustees. "President Fox, you have to work hard to preserve our beach and protect it from ill-conceived tampering by these outsiders. This is your sacred duty as our leader. Each of you Trustees is the caretaker of the one thing we cherish most." Pausing, she said quietly, "our beach."

Nora looked up in amazement as the artist suddenly began twirling, causing her cloak to fan out in a circle. As she moved, she raised the gold box overhead for all to see.

In one fluid motion, she pulled it down across her body, opened it, and with a sweeping hand, broadcast sprays of fine white sand in all directions. Sand particles landed on the floor in front of Nora, Owens, and on the Trustees' table.

"Save our glorious beach," Carlotta cried out. "Save our beach now!"

Electrified, the audience jumped up and chanted in unison, "Save our beach! Save our beach! Save our beach now!" Some of them climbed on the benches and continued shouting, until the message was carried to those huddled on the stairs and outside the door. Fox hammered his gavel, but this time he was unable to quell the noise.

Nora felt Mr. Owens nudge her arm. "Did you take down her words, Honora?"

She nodded and said, "The woman's simply magical, isn't she?" Nora could tell that the publisher, like everyone else, had been caught up in Carlotta's performance.

Midway down the center aisle, the artist swayed to the crowd's rhythmic chant, moving first to one side and then the other, her cloak continuing to spiral out.

Nora got up and climbed on top of her bench to get a better view of the woman, who, by now, had spread white sand down the entire aisle. She shuffled it along with her black slippers, as she made her way out of the chambers.

Owens stood up, struggling to hold his emotions in check. He'd observed the woman's behavior and the crowd's reaction to her. "I'm afraid Carlotta has carried the day," he muttered to Nora.

Jumping down to stand next to him, Nora thought about Carlotta's message about the significance of Carmel's beach. It occurred to her that the proposed hotel project could be in serious jeopardy.

CHAPTER FOUR

For the next two hours, the speakers went on at length about the merits of preserving the beach. Nora counted only a handful of residents who spoke in favor of the proposed hotel.

"I'm ready to call for a continuance," Trustee Milliken said. "It's nearly ten o'clock, and some of us have to go to work tomorrow. I say we make our decision on the merits of the hotel project when the rest of the Board is present."

"Our side demands equal time," a male voice shouted.

Trustee Taylor's hand shot up. "I agree with Davey Chatham. I object to the suggestion that we adjourn. We need to listen to everyone who came out tonight."

As Chatham limped to the front, Nora realized that he was the young man with the cane whom Doctor Taylor had spoken with earlier.

"You're not allowing those of us in favor of the hotel enough time, President Fox," Chatham said. "Don't forget, we all had to sit through Carlotta's antics."

Fox checked the sign up sheet and made his decision. "All right, Davey. We'll listen. Besides, there's somebody else I'm waiting to hear from. The hotel developer came by my shop yesterday and told me that he wanted to speak. Don't see him yet."

Trustee Milliken let out a long sigh. "It's late, Ben, and it's raining. After we hear from this speaker, I vote to go home."

"Say what you came to say, Davey," Fox grumbled. "Then we'll adjourn if no one else shows up."

Trustee Taylor smiled and settled back in his chair as Chatham began speaking.

"David's my real name, but everyone around here calls me Davey. I support Mr. Fields' hotel. Some of you who spoke against it are just plain wrong to talk it down. I've got a few things to say and I want them put into the record."

Owens tapped his pencil on the edge of his notebook. He looked at Nora. "I think young Chatham's stalling for time until Mr. Fields arrives."

"I agree with you," she whispered back. "But President Fox is going along. He probably wants to keep his promise to the developer."

Loud voices from the back of the room caused them both to turn around. A man was pushing his way through the crowd and up the center aisle. As she watched him approach, Nora remembered where she had first seen his rain-soaked plaid overcoat. They had met while she was walking home after work last night, and she had seen him again when he returned by motorcar to Hotel La Playa.

As he reached the front and the Trustees' table, each Trustee stood up, leaned over, and shook hands with the stranger. To Nora's surprise, Trustee Milliken even slapped him on the shoulder.

"Looks like the hotel developer has friends in high places," Owens whispered.

"Here's the man who'll put Carmel on the map, you ungrateful Bohemians," Chatham shouted. He and the newcomer shook hands and Chatham returned to his place next to the wall. Some in the audience jeered.

Martin Fields removed his hat and set it on the front table. Nora thought that he would likely receive a favorable opinion from the ladies in the audience. Over six feet tall, with salt-and-pepper hair and a trimmed matching beard, he had a friendly face. What bothered her, though, was the cigar he was smoking. When he dropped the smelly cheroot into a glass of water sitting in front of Ben Fox, she flinched. She was horrified at such boorish manners.

"Thanks for holding my place, David," Fields said. "Mr. President, as you know, I'm Martin Fields. The hour's late, so I'll only say a few words to the folks. I'm happy to fill in the details and answer their questions at a later date, when all the Trustees are present to make the decision."

"Go ahead, sir," Fox replied. "I'll give you five minutes."

Nora's dislike of Fields grew as she watched him remove his wet overcoat and dump it next to his hat directly in front of Trustee Milliken. Then, facing the audience, the developer loosened his tie. "This collar button's biting into my neck," he said, with a grin on his face. "You men know what I'm talking about."

Cupping her hand in front of her mouth, Nora whispered to Mr. Owens, "Poor Trustee Milliken. He's barely visible behind that mound of clothing. Why doesn't he ask Mr. Fields to clear it off?"

Owens chuckled. "I heard that Fields has his beard trimmed daily at Milliken's barber shop. Roland probably doesn't want to embarrass him and lose a customer."

As she watched Fields fold his arms across his chest and step away from the Trustees' table, she had to admit that the man radiated self confidence, if not defiance.

"I'm not from this area," he began. "I live in New York. But that hasn't stopped the merchants in your charming village from getting to know me and supporting my hotel. Why shouldn't they? If you Trustees go along with my proposal, it's going to improve everyone's business. My project pencils out financially. My investors are rock solid. And we all know there's nothing sinful about making money."

Allowing time for his words to sink in, Fields continued, "My plans also call for a new public bath house to be built nearby on the sand dunes. It's my donation to the town. Construction will begin in January, weather permitting."

Nora saw Trustee Milliken's head pop up from behind Fields' clothing. He said, "Mr. Fields, as long as it makes us money, we're very interested in your hotel."

A loud groan came from those in the audience who objected to the barber's obvious bias.

Fields turned and waved at Milliken. "I'd like you and the rest of the Board to take a look at my numbers, Roland. A hotel on your beach means a bright future for generations of Carmelites to come." Fields then turned to face Owens directly. "Mr. Publisher, you can quote me on that."

Nora could tell by Fields' facial expression that he had expected not only Mr. Owens, but the audience as well, to applaud. But after hearing only random mutterings, he concluded with, "Thanks for your kind attention." Then he strolled over to stand next to Davey Chatham.

Ben Fox pounded his gavel. "Well, it seems we've heard from everybody. Mr. Fields makes a useful suggestion. This project's too important to be decided by only three of us tonight. With the concurrence of the rest of the Board, I'll continue this discussion to our next Trustees meeting. Are we all agreed?"

Trustees Taylor and Milliken nodded and stood up to leave.

Fox rapped his gavel. "We're adjourned."

As the crowd filed out, Nora was surprised at how quiet they had become. Owens went up to the front table to get comments from the Trustees. She headed for the door to ask individuals for their views on the hotel proposal. Some residents refused to state their opinions. Others wanted 'to think things over.' A few said that they didn't want their names printed in 'that biased newspaper.'

Hearing disparaging remarks from several people, Nora had to assume that Mr. Owens' frequent editorials advocating the paving of Ocean Avenue and his support for more tourism had irked residents. Just this past week two of her neighbors had told her that they preferred the existing compacted dirt roads and disliked the idea of paving any of Carmel's streets. It would only encourage more visitors who would come and disrupt their quiet lives, they said.

Outside City Hall, the rain hadn't let up. When the publisher caught up with her, Owens asked, "Shall I walk you home, Honora?"

She shook her head and unfurled her Chinese-red umbrella. "That's not necessary, sir. Pine Log is only a few blocks away, and, as you can see, I have my lantern."

Owens tipped his hat and joined a man who was going the opposite way.

Nora spotted a small group of people gathered in a circle in front of the tea room across the street. She heard a woman's voice, one that she recognized. "We'll meet at Oak Bower Monday night and develop our strategy. Rob, why don't you bring along some of your young friends with like minds?"

Nora hadn't heard of a Carmel cottage with the name of Oak Bower. However, she knew that Carlotta Fleming had just extended an invitation to Rob Jacklin to come to a meeting there.

Looking down to avoid the puddles, she stepped off the sidewalk and crossed Ocean Avenue.

The artist was waiting for her when she reached the other side of the street. "Hello again, Miss Finnegan," Carlotta said. "I must say, you have excellent taste in umbrellas. I'd like you to attend our Monday meeting as well. Bring your notepad and come at eight o'clock. Hopefully, the article you'll write afterwards will explain our group's position on Mr. Fields' hotel." Not waiting for Nora's reply, the artist put up her umbrella and walked off with another woman.

Having been delayed, Nora knew that she had no chance of catching up with Rob Jacklin, who, by now, was a block away. She had hoped to talk to him after the meeting ended. A missed opportunity, she thought, but she would speak to him when they met again at Oak Bower.

Resuming her walk, her tin lantern swaying, Nora steadied her umbrella against the driving rain. She felt very much alive. Good things were coming her way. Thanks to Carlotta Fleming, she had been invited into an elite circle, one that included Rob Jacklin. She thought back to Mr. Owens' words about Carmel's diverse social groups. Without having to choose from among them, she had been included in the most dynamic one — the Bohemians — and she would have a significant story to write up. *Would Mr. Owens print it?*

The smell of Martin Fields' cigar overwhelmed the Buick's compartment. He inhaled and felt himself relaxing, although he knew the smoke was causing his passenger to suffer another fit of coughing.

Luckily, he had discovered the perfect spot for their rendezvous, one where they wouldn't be disturbed. He had driven here this afternoon to set things up. It had been daylight then. Now, in the dark, and with the rain coming down in sheets of water, the unfamiliar bends and curves of 17-Mile Drive seemed hazardous. Funny, he thought — Carmel was either foggy or rainy. Every few moments, he had to apply the brakes, then steer the Buick back onto the road, which, in some places, had become a quagmire. Peering through the blurred wind-screen, he noticed a peculiar assortment of ramshackle buildings — the remains of a fishing camp, he'd been told. Some rickety tables leaned at odd angles in front of the shacks, as if they'd been abandoned in a hurry. Hotel La Playa's concierge had said that the site was where the Chinese once sold polished abalone shells to the tourists. He was glad that he didn't have to fend off some hawker who was peddling an iridescent souvenir.

About a mile beyond the camp ruins, he saw the secluded building through the overhanging pines. When he had come here earlier, he thought its log walls resembled an army fort. It didn't look like a place where people lounged after playing a round of golf. He understood why its owners had replaced this old lodge with a new one in a much better location. Bringing the Buick to a halt, he parked in front of the unimposing entrance and turned off the ignition. Opening the driver's door, he stepped out and crushed his cigar in the wet gravel. He and his companion entered the lodge together.

Earlier in the afternoon he had placed candles on the fireplace mantle and left a bottle of champagne and two flutes for their use. Taking some matches out of his pocket, he moved across the dark space and lit the tapers. The cavernous room was devoid of furnishings.

Fields was eager to celebrate the favorable reception he'd received from some of Carmel's Trustees a short time ago. "Hand me those glasses," he said, as he snatched up the bottle, undid the wire covering the cork, and popped the champagne. "You know, I can see a role for you in my brand new venture."

The only response to his words came in the form of a deafening gunshot. Pain exploded through his chest. He fell backwards onto the bare floor. Broken glass and a bubbly liquid quickly began mixing with his warm blood.

CHAPTER FIVE

Saturday

On arriving at the *Pine Cone* a little before noon, Nora found Mr. Owens reading the mail at the receptionist's desk. "It looks like there could be a downpour any moment, sir," she said, as she put her umbrella by the door. "Shouldn't we be going?"

"In a few minutes," Owens said. He got up and went to the back room.

Last night, to Nora's surprise, he had told her that he wanted to introduce her to the business side of running the newspaper. Today, for the first time ever, she was going to accompany Mr. Owens on his rounds. Usually the office was closed on Saturday afternoons, so that he could pick up the merchants' advertising copy, collect past due bills, and gather ideas for future news articles.

Looking out the window, she realized that they might get soaked if they waited much longer. Foreboding clouds overhead threatened more rain.

The telephone rang. Nora went around the counter and picked it up on the first ring. "*Carmel Pine Cone,*" she said. "Miss Finnegan speaking. How may I help you?"

"I want to place an ad," the agitated voice said. "It's urgent."

After taking down the man's name and post office box, Nora asked, "What do you wish the advertisement to say, sir?"

"Here goes, and make sure you get it right. I want the first part in bold letters: LOST DOG. $5 REWARD. Follow with: Mixed breed terrier. Blind in left eye. Missing left rear leg. Right ear half gone. Broken tail. Answers to the name of Lucky. That's it."

Nora couldn't help but wonder how an animal with so many physical problems could be called 'Lucky.' She said, "The ad will run next week. I'll put your bill in the mail."

"I'm much obliged," he said, and hung up.

As she placed the new order in Mrs. Owens' in-box, she saw Mr. Owens coming back to the front reception area.

Hat in hand, he said, "Let's go."

Posting the "Closed" sign in the front window, Nora grabbed her umbrella and followed him out the door. After locking it, he took her elbow and helped her negotiate the rain puddles that had accumulated since last night.

"Why aren't the residents behind my campaign to pave this infernal street?" he groused, as they walked along Ocean Avenue. "Just look at it — it's a muddy swamp. And with these scrawny trees running down the center, it's inefficient as well. People here howl about keeping things natural looking, but this is ridiculous. Where's the progress, I ask you?"

Nora studied the young pines that had been planted in the center of the road. "When these are fully grown, they'll make Ocean Avenue more attractive. Without them, Carmel's drivers would park their motorcars in the middle of the street."

Ignoring her comment, he stepped between the trees. "I'll have to try harder to convince our readers that the city needs to pave it."

Nora frowned at the thought of what he called progress. "I respect your views," she said, "and the business people agree with you about the need for more parking, but neighbors of mine tell me they want the village to remain unchanged. I agree with them."

He looked over at her. "I wasn't aware that you held an opinion on the road paving issue, Honora."

"It's only that I like Carmel the way it is, sir."

They had arrived at Levy's General Store. While Mr. Owens held the door for her, Nora could see that the place bustled with noontime customers. She attributed this to two things: an ideal location on the main street, and the unique merchandise Mr. Levy carried: cameras, sailing ship models, cutlery, curios, and even rare stamps and coins. For the past ten years, the wood-framed building's white false front and covered overhang shading the sidewalk had attracted travelers and residents alike.

Stepping inside, she spotted the shopkeeper standing next to a glass counter filled with souvenir bracelets and other handmade jewelry. Attired in his trademark short white coat and bow tie, she thought Mr. Levy's rosy cheeks gave him a healthy look, no doubt acquired by his twin passions: fly-casting and outdoor photography. Despite his reaction to Mrs. Villard last night, she liked his kind demeanor. With a white beard, and round spectacles, he was the perfect Father Christmas in the village's annual parade.

"Be with you two shortly," he said. Then he went to help a customer who wanted to examine his assortment of handmade Italian stationery and colored inks.

After waiting for several minutes, Owens became impatient. "I'm going to the magazine rack to see if the latest *Camera Craft* is in." He headed to the rear of the store.

Nora moved past another display counter filled with fishing flies and lures, which caused her to think of her father. He always came into Levy's to buy fishing gear when the Finnegan family arrived in Carmel for their summer vacation. His excuse was, 'local flies attract local fish.' Lately, her father had been too busy to spend his leisure time angling on the Carmel River.

Meandering past the postcard rack, she remembered the times when her mother, a compulsive correspondent, had visited Levy's to purchase postcards. Created by the local photographers, the scenic shots piqued her mother's interest in the area's natural beauty, especially around Big Sur.

Nora continued browsing, until she heard voices drifting towards her. While pretending to examine the postcards, she peeked through the rack's open spaces. Mr. Owens was conversing with the young man who had spoken in favor of Mr. Fields' hotel last night. Wearing the same old army jacket, Davey Chatham seemed excited. He was waving his cane up and down and speaking rapidly. She couldn't quite catch what he and Mr. Owens were talking about.

Owens broke away from Chatham at the same time Mr. Levy finished serving his customer. Walking back to the front, he motioned at Nora to join him. "Joe, you remember Miss Finnegan," he said. "Mary Lee and I count her parents as our closest friends. Though they live in San Francisco, they've been summering here for years."

As Nora shook Levy's hand, she was surprised by his gentle handshake, despite his burly frame carrying almost twice her 125 pounds.

"A gracious couple, your folks," he said, "and friendly too. Didn't I hear that you're living alone in your family's cottage, Miss Finnegan? That must worry them."

Nora said, "Yes, they do worry, Mr. Levy, but they rely on Mr. and Mrs. Owens to watch out for me."

Owens glanced at her and smiled, but didn't add anything. Picking up a fishing reel and rod that someone had leaned against the counter, he flipped it a few times. "I'm hoping for better weather tomorrow," he said,

Levy motioned them over to a waist-high counter. "Take a look at these, William. My new camera lenses arrived. Since we don't have to work tomorrow, how about a picture-taking trip over to Abalone Cove?"

"I'd like to, Joe, but the workload at the newspaper's beginning to pile up. So are some of my other personal obligations. I'm feeling a bit overwhelmed."

Nora wondered if her request for more challenging assignments had also placed an extra burden on him. While it made her feel guilty, she knew that she had done the right thing. Otherwise, she would never have been asked to help him cover the Trustees' meeting last night, and she wouldn't be with him on his rounds today.

Changing the subject, Owens asked, "Have you heard what's been proposed for the vacant acreage across from the cove? Young Chatham was just telling me about it."

"What's he know anyway?" Levy said, lowering his voice. "I don't trust him."

"Well, Davey says eastern capitalists want to put houses around the golf course. He plans to sell his place to Martin Fields. He claims the man's eager to buy Bella Vista. Davey wants to invest in Fields' new hotel with the money from the sale."

"Outsiders always see a way to make their money here," Levy said. "As for Davey putting in with Fields, well, he doesn't own Bella Vista. His mother holds the deed, and she's not selling just because Davey wants to." Shaking his head, he went on, "Remember that scrape he got into, when he tried selling used army equipment? Went broke. Mrs. Chatham put him on a tight leash after that. He has no capital of his own."

"I heard about that too," Owens said. "But back to the golf course. It's an ideal setting for new houses. I like the idea. It would bring new business to our stores."

"So would a hotel on our beach," Levy said.

Nora recalled his speech in favor of Fields' proposal last night. She felt certain that he and Owens would back what in her mind was unchecked growth. She listened, but didn't voice her opinion, as the two men continued talking about a photography excursion tomorrow, if the weather permitted.

Back out on the sidewalk, Nora realized that she had forgotten her umbrella.

"I'll go get it for you," Owens said. "Where did you leave it?"

"It should be next to the postcard rack."

As she waited at Levy's front door for his return, she was nearly knocked over by some boisterous children who were running around and chattering to one another. After counting eight of them, Nora realized that they were all boys. Then she spotted Rob Jacklin walking towards her.

"Hello," he called out. "Aren't you Nora Finnegan, the *Pine Cone* reporter?"

She nodded. "Hello, Mr. Jacklin."

"Do you work on Saturdays, Miss Finnegan?"

Years ago, Nora's journalist father had taught her a useful technique to deflect attention away from herself. Question the questioner. "Is this a school outing, Mr. Jacklin? If it is, then where are your fourth grade girls?"

He smiled as he rounded up the boys. "This is a Carmel Boys Club field trip, not one for my class. I'm the group's sponsor, but I hadn't counted on the possibility of rain." He looked up at the sky. "We're in luck, as it seems to be clearing. Say, would you like to join us? The boys and I will be exploring and photographing the flora and fauna in Pescadero Canyon."

Earlier, Nora had seen his pictures of a canyon by that name on Levy's postcard rack. Before she could reply, Owens came out of the general store, her umbrella under his arm.

"Hello, Rob," he said, and put out his hand. "I hope my Sally's arithmetic scores have improved since our last parent-teacher conference."

"She's doing better, sir."

"I'm glad. I couldn't help but overhear what you asked Miss Finnegan. She's not officially working." Handing Nora her umbrella, he said, "Go along with Rob, why don't you? I'll handle the bakery and barber shop appointments. You can come along next week. Being outside in the fresh air, enjoying nature, will do wonders for you."

Although Nora felt he was teasing her for her earlier remark about protecting Carmel's natural beauty, Jacklin's invitation did intrigue her. Then she realized that she couldn't traipse through a canyon in her good suit and pointed shoes.

"I'd like to come along, Mr. Jacklin," she said, "but first I'll need a change of clothing. May I join you and the boys on the beach in fifteen minutes?"

Jacklin grinned. "Excellent! They'll need watching over. I'm counting on you to help me keep them in sight at all times. We can't have anyone getting lost in the woods. And call me Rob, won't you?"

"All right, Rob, but only if you call me Nora." She could feel the flush in her face and neck. Pointing up at the sky to divert his attention, she stammered, "Those rain clouds seem to be disappearing. That's a very good sign, isn't it?"

"Lucky for us, the change in the weather has helped to convince you to join us, Nora."

"I'm really looking forward to it," she said.

On her way back to her cottage, Nora realized she had been affected by Jacklin's presence. She had no doubts that she would enjoy spending the rest of the day with him. He was someone she would like to know better. The field trip would also be a chance for her to speak to him about that opinion-piece she had thought of writing.

CHAPTER SIX

In the time it had taken Nora to scurry home and put on a different outfit and walking shoes, Rob had purchased the makings of a picnic: boiled ham sandwiches, sweet pickles, chunks of cheddar cheese, winter pears, and bottles of ginger beer. She caught up with the group on the beach and helped the boys remove their oilskin jackets and use them as makeshift tablecloths on the sand. They gathered around and ate and drank everything in sight.

Rob's students couldn't remain still for very long. He had his hands full, trying to get them together to pose for a picture. Then he said, "Boys, we came here to do some hiking. So let's line up and start walking."

Nora led the young explorers marching Indian file along Carmel beach. Rob brought up the rear. The wind flicked salty spray in their faces as the waves tumbled ashore and broke at their feet. They headed north along the shoreline. She had never hiked here before, but in the distance she recognized Pescadero Point, one of the area's natural landmarks. The towns of Monterey and Pacific Grove were out of sight beyond the outcropping.

"Are you all right up there?" Rob shouted to her above the noisy surf.

She turned and waved. "Everything's fine," she yelled back. Removing her jacket, she tied it around her waist. Looking down at her young companion hiking with her, she noticed that he was shouldering a cloth sack tied on a stick. The boy was small in stature, compared to the others. A brown hat with a yellow band covered his blonde hair. His tan slicker hung loosely over his brown shirt and pants. There was a red kerchief around his neck.

He was also kicking up sand as they walked.

Nora looked down at his scuffed high-top shoes. "What's your name?" she asked.

"Frederick Woodward, miss."

"I'm Nora Finnegan. Have you hiked on this beach before with your dad or your friends?"

He shook his head. "My dad's dead, and I'm not a member of the club. Me and my mom moved here last summer. Mr. Jacklin told Mama he wanted me to come today. I've never hiked here before."

"I'm sorry about your father, Frederick."

"Call me Freddie, miss. Everybody does."

"All right — if you call me Nora." Although she was interested, Nora didn't pursue the boy's personal loss and ruin his outing. "Well, Freddie," she said, "what do you think Mr. Jacklin has in store for us when we reach the canyon? Are we going to find frogs and lizards?"

He shrugged. Reaching for the bundle tied to the stick resting on his shoulder, he undid the knot and extracted a notebook and pencil. "I'm supposed to write down what I see today, so Mr. Jacklin knows what interests me. He told us to look for unusual leaves, plants and maybe animal tracks. But what I want to find is a bird nest — one with a speckled egg in it."

Nora watched him sketch an oval with a few dots on it. He held it up for her to see.

"Wouldn't that be a treasure," she said. "I'll help you look, if you like."

His face lit up. Eyes on the water, he saw something and ran towards a nearby tide pool. A few moments later, he ran back to where Nora was standing.

"Look at this, Nora!" he shouted.

She made out the remains of a starfish in the palm of his hand. Enmeshed in a brownish glop of dried kelp, the creature had been dead for days, she suspected. "You have very good eyesight," she said. "That's quite an unusual specimen. I'll bet you can sketch it."

Hearing the boy's excited voice, Rob moved up to join them at the front of the line and complimented Freddie on his find. The trio trooped one behind the other along a foot trail until they came to a wood gate.

"Let's stop here until the rest of the boys can catch up,"

Rob said. "This is the toll booth where 17-Mile Drive begins."

Nora saw that the access to the private forest road was controlled by a uniformed guard.

"Good afternoon," Rob said to the man as he walked up to the booth's open window. "I'm Robert Jacklin from Sunset School. You should have my name on your list. My Boys Club has received permission to hike into the canyon today."

Studying his ledger, the guard found the entry. "I got it," he said, and stepped out of the booth. "Be careful about the fast motorcars speeding through here. My boss don't want nobody run over, 'specially some helpless female or a little kid. That'll cost me my job."

Nora looked up and down the dirt road. There wasn't one motorcar in sight. She appreciated the guard's warning, but not the part about being 'some helpless female.' She wanted to say, 'We're not as weak as you think when we're bearing your children.' Instead, she kept quiet and waited for Rob's response.

"Thanks for the warning," he said. "We'll be careful." Without a backward glance, Rob lifted the gate and shepherded Nora and his charges across 17-Mile-Drive to a wide area in the road where another hiking trail began.

Entering Pescadero Canyon, Nora looked up and saw that the tree branches were weighted down by the recent rain. Shadows gave the filtered light a purplish cast. The boys raced forward and scoured the terrain. They outshouted one another as they made their way along the trail running parallel to the road. Nora watched them point out plants, exchange information and scribble entries in their notebooks.

Staying close to her, Freddie didn't join in with the others. He and Nora lagged behind. He poked his hobo stick in the underbrush and scanned the tree branches. Nora's favorite wild lilac, the purple ceonothus, grew everywhere in low sprawling clumps at the bases of the Monterey pines and coastal live oaks. She showed Freddie a type of fern that she had never seen before. He drew a sketch of it in his notebook. She found that she enjoyed his company. Would he discover that elusive bird nest, she wondered? He seemed comfortable, traipsing along with her, but she was troubled by his reticence in mingling with the other boys. Later on, she would speak to Rob about getting him to socialize more.

Somewhere up ahead, she heard Rob calling out the names of youngsters who must have wandered off. Due to their meandering, she and Freddie had lost sight of the teacher. He was preoccupied, which meant that Freddie was her responsibility. She stepped up the pace and turned to tell the boy to hurry. But he had disappeared.

Suddenly, to her left and behind her, she heard him shout, "Help, Nora. Come quick!"

Ignoring the fact that her good jacket had snagged on a buckhorn sage growing beside the trail, she plunged through the bushes in the direction of Freddie's voice. After several long minutes of plowing through thorny overgrowth, she finally saw him.

He was standing at the top of a rise and pointing at something. She felt relieved that he didn't appear to be hurt. Maybe it was nothing more than his finding a bird's nest, she thought.

As she caught up with him, she could see the boy's discovery. An overturned motorcar, all four wheels in the air, rested at the bottom of a ravine near the place where the road formed an S-shaped curve. Like some giant primordial beetle, its undercarriage glistened from the reflection of water droplets mixed with oil.

Then Nora spotted a familiar-looking plaid overcoat on the ground next to the motorcar. Part of the cloth was caught in a manzanita bush, but most of it was covering a person who was lying on the ground. The garment was stained with a reddish-brown substance.

Grabbing the boy, Nora held him close, perhaps to calm herself, as well as the frightened child. Before he could ask her any questions, she shielded his eyes with her hands. Turning him around, she said, "Come with me, Freddie. Let's find Mr. Jacklin right away."

CHAPTER SEVEN

Nora kept her eye on Freddie and the other boys as Rob scrambled to the bottom of the ravine to check the overturned motorcar for signs of life.

When he returned, he took her aside. "The driver's dead. I'd better head back to Carmel and notify the sheriff to get out here."

"Is it Mr. Fields, the hotel developer?" Nora asked. "I recognized his overcoat."

"Yes, I'm afraid so. Will you take charge of things while I'm gone?"

Though she felt apprehensive about it, Nora agreed immediately. She knew that she would have to divert the boys' attention away from the accident scene. Gathering them around her, she asked, "Who would like to hear a good story about a very courageous dog?"

Whoops exploded from the group.

"The person who wrote the story was a man named Jack London," Nora continued. "He visited this area several times." Settling the children in a circle at a distance from the ravine, she began, "Once upon a time, there was a brave, sturdy dog named Buck who . . . ."

"What kind of dog is Buck, miss?" a boy interrupted.

"He's part German Shepherd and part Saint Bernard. One night Buck is kidnapped from his California home and sold to some men who want a strong animal to pull a dog sled for the gold miners in a place called the Klondike."

"Where is that?" another boy asked.

"In Canada, where it's very cold. Buck has a hard time learning to become a sled dog. He had been a family pet who slept inside at night. Now he had to sleep outside under the snow pack, and had to fight off other dogs for food. But he wanted to be the best sled dog in the team. Does anyone know how many dogs are in Buck's team?"

The children shouted out various numbers, but not the correct one. Then Freddie, who had said nothing up to this point, raised his hand.

"Can you tell us, Freddie?" Nora said.

"It's nine, Miss Finnegan. My mom read me this story."

"You're right. Now I'm sure the rest of you want to hear how Buck becomes the lead dog."

"Yes!" they chorused.

For the next hour, Nora filled their young ears with London's tale of Buck in *The Call of the Wild.* Even Freddie seemed to enjoy listening to the story a second time. She had just reached the end when she noticed two police vehicles come up the road, each displaying "Monterey County Sheriff" in white letters on their sides. In the lead was a black patrol wagon, followed by a four-door sedan with Rob in the passenger's seat.

A tall, broad-shouldered man with a bushy mustache stepped out of the sedan. Even from a distance, Nora saw the star-shaped Sheriff's badge pinned to his uniform. He wasted no time in taking charge.

Speaking to a younger man in a lawman's uniform who was getting out of the patrol wagon, the sheriff said, "Deputy Connery, have the young lady help you figure out how to escort those children home."

Connery nodded. "Will do, Sheriff Terry. And I'll make sure the youngsters don't go wandering off."

Nora watched the sheriff lead Rob down the embankment. Jacklin had his camera slung over his shoulder. A second lawman, carrying a canvas stretcher, followed them. The trio slid down the incline in order to reach the victim. Nora told the boys, who were watching anxiously, to stay seated in the circle while she went to meet Deputy Connery.

As she came up to him, he tipped his Stetson. "I'm Deputy Jimmy Connery, miss. And who might you be?"

"My name is Nora Finnegan." Judging him to be in his

twenties and just under six feet tall, she didn't care for the way his blue eyes swept over her figure.

"Rob's told me all about the girls he meets in Carmel," he said. "But he's never mentioned one as attractive as you, Miss Finnegan."

Annoyed by his flattery, Nora said, "Let's get started. I'll help you figure out the routes to get the boys home."

"Look, I'm sorry if I offended you." He smiled and softened his voice. "I should have said at the start that Rob and I were high school friends ten years ago."

"First you need to write down their names and where they live."

"I do know that Carmel doesn't have any street addresses. I'll need your help with directions. Let me get a pad and pencil." He headed for the patrol wagon.

When he returned, Nora said, "I'll introduce you to the boys." She led the way to the waiting children. They had remained in a circle, but were jabbering to each other. Clapping her hands, she said, "I'd like your attention, please. This man is Deputy Sheriff Connery. I want you to give him your names and tell him where you live. He's been put in charge of driving all of us home."

As Connery began taking down information, Nora caught sight of Sheriff Terry.

He had just appeared at the top of the embankment. Rob and the other deputy were following him. They were struggling with the stretcher they were bringing up from the canyon floor. Nora remembered that Fields had been stocky. Grunting and perspiring, the two men took the body to a spot near the patrol wagon where the sheriff was waiting.

She had never seen a dead person. Perhaps it was time for her to take a look at one. Coming up to the men, she overheard the sheriff say, "Set him down, and after you rest a bit, load the stretcher into the back of the wagon." Stamping his feet to dislodge some mud that had accumulated on his boots, Terry pointed to the deputy and said, "Jensen, I want you to make arrangements to pull the Buick out. You'll need strong rope and a team of horses."

Jensen nodded and walked back to the edge of 17-Mile Drive where the Buick had gone into the ravine. Squatting, he studied the tire marks in the dirt. "Hold on, Sheriff," he yelled. "A second motorcar must have pushed the Buick over the side."

"Take a picture of those tire tracks, Rob," Terry said.

Nora remembered her father's favorite piece of advice: 'Always be on the lookout for an exclusive story.' She had to act now or lose the opportunity.

"Excuse me, Sheriff," she said. "We haven't met. I'm Nora Finnegan. I'm a reporter for the *Carmel Pine Cone*. I'm curious. What fatal injuries did the victim sustain in the accident?"

"Nice to meet you, miss, but it's beginning to look less and less like an accident," Terry said. "You're welcome to see what I mean — that is, if you've the stomach for it." Reaching down, he pulled off the covering on the dead man. Then he moved aside to give Nora room.

As she came forward, an unpleasant odor of death filled her nostrils. Fields lay on his back, partially hidden under dried leaves and grime. His face looked blotchy and purplish-red. Flies buzzed around, lighting on his nose and lips. Dried blood stains had spread over the front of his clothing.

Terry put his hand on Fields' abdomen and lifted his shirt. "Here's the wound that bled and killed him. He was shot point-blank by someone standing in front of him. Must have hit his aorta, which resulted in massive internal bleeding."

Nora leaned over to see better and brushed away flies hovering around the body. She shuddered. Feeling dizzy, she began to sway.

Terry put a hand on her shoulder to steady her as she backed away. "Sorry you had to see this, miss," he said.

Just then Deputy Connery joined them. Kneeling down next to the body, he emptied Fields' pockets, then stood up and handed some papers to Terry. "It appears he died face-down, Sheriff. That made the blood rush to his face and head. Judging from the rigor, I'm guessing that the time of death was sometime during the night."

Terry perused the papers and said, "This shows the Buick belongs to Pete Quinlan. He rented it to our victim two nights ago. Connery, you head for the Shamrock Garage after you take Miss Finnegan and the boys home. Let Quinlan know what's happened. Jensen, you and I will drop Jacklin off at his place and then head back to Monterey to visit the coroner. And Rob, I appreciate all your help. At the inquest, I'll present the crime scene pictures that you took. I'll need the negatives also."

Rob nodded. Using a rock as a table, he packed up his camera.

The sheriff continued examining the dead man's papers. "Says here his name is Martin Fields. Address is on Long Island, New York State. Must be a visitor."

Having recovered from her lightheadedness, Nora waited for Rob to say something about Fields' identity, but he kept silent. She imagined there would be time to provide details later.

Deputy Connery had gone back to the patrol wagon to retrieve a cloth bag. He returned and handed it to the sheriff, who put the dead man's papers and wallet inside.

Nora wished she could read some of the documents, but she knew in a murder investigation, that information was privileged.

"Time to get moving," Sheriff Terry said. "Everybody ready to go?"

At six o'clock that evening, Nora hurried along Mission Street to the Owens' cottage. Nestled under the oaks, the family had named it *La Selva*, meaning the forest in Spanish. A few blocks from her own home, she often visited here during daylight hours. Tonight her tin lantern revealed the landmarks she counted on: a stand of coastal live oaks growing at the corner of Eighth Avenue.

Although her visit was unscheduled, it was important to her. She was eager to let Mr. Owens know about Martin Fields' murder. As she ran up the porch steps, she spotted the Owens' 10 year-old daughter, Sally, peeking out through the front window. Nora knocked on the door.

When Owens opened it, she guessed she had interrupted his reading. A book was tucked under his arm. "I'm sorry to disturb you, sir," she said, "but I have urgent news."

Moving away from the door, Owens said, "Come in, Honora. What's wrong?"

Setting her lantern down, she stepped inside. After he took her coat, she entered the front room and walked over to the fireplace to warm her hands. The sounds of female voices and clattering dishes came from the kitchen at the rear of the house.

Owens gestured towards the dining room. "Have you had your supper? We just finished, but Mrs. Owens hasn't put all the food away."

"That's kind of you, sir, but no thank you," Nora said. "I

thought you should know what happened this afternoon." Pulling out her notes from her purse, she handed them to him. "It's all in here." She moved over to the piano bench and sat down to wait as Owens went to the sofa and searched for his glasses among the cushions.

"You're being quite mysterious," he said, as he sank back into the sofa. "What's this all about?"

"As you know, I spent the afternoon with Rob Jacklin and his fourth grade boys, sir. We hiked into Pescadero Canyon, which was very pleasant, but sad to say, we found a body. Actually, young Freddie Woodward discovered it."

Owens looked surprised. "Whose body was it? Anyone from around here?"

"It was Martin Fields, the hotel developer. He'd been thrown out of a motorcar, one of Pete Quinlan's."

"Fields is dead? I'm shocked. He seemed healthy when he spoke at the Trustees' meeting last night. But there isn't any rush to discuss his death with me now, is there? I'll have plenty of time on Monday to put together his obituary."

"I'm afraid his death wasn't an accident. He was murdered."

Owens sat up straight. "Are you sure?"

Nora nodded. "Fields died from a gun shot wound. The sheriff allowed me to view it and I've written an eyewitness report. It's all in those notes. I'd like to develop the story further if you assign it to me. I'll be careful not to make any errors."

Owens shook his head. "I can't allow you to cover a murder. It's not appropriate for a young woman to get involved in sordid details of that sort."

"But you haven't read what I've written."

"I don't need to, Honora. You say that you were permitted to view a dead body. What will your parents think of me if I let you write about it? And don't forget your Thanksgiving feature article, which you haven't even started."

"I can easily do both, sir. I'm not going home to San Francisco for the holiday."

Owens thought for a moment. An exclusive story wasn't something that his Monterey competitor would have. He said, "I'll tell you what. Let me read your notes and talk it over with Mrs. Owens. I'll give you my decision in the morning after church."

Nora shut the Owens' front door behind her and bent down

to pick up her lantern. It was still glowing. The candlelight lifted her spirits. She hoped she had persuaded Mr. Owens to let her write the Fields' murder story. As she headed home, she thought of ways to expand it.

For one thing, when Sheriff Terry had looked at the papers he'd taken from the dead man's pocket, she had read them too. One was a hotel reservation form. At the top were the words, La Playa, and underneath was a sketch of the star-shaped tower that Nora saw on her evening walks. It was clear that Mr. Fields was a guest there.

Tomorrow she had an appointment with Paulette Villard, the hotel's manager, to gather material for her feature story on La Playa's upcoming Thanksgiving activities. Mr. Owens had just spoken of it, and for the first time, Nora looked forward to writing it. While there, she would steer the conversation to Fields' comings and goings. She knew that Mrs. Villard had objected to his proposed hotel at the Trustees' meeting. The woman might be willing to say something revealing about the dead man.

Pine Log lay straight ahead. As she pulled open her cottage's front door, Nora wondered who in Carmel disliked Fields enough to kill him. Many, including Mrs. Villard, hated the developer's hotel project. Would that be a motive to murder him?

CHAPTER EIGHT

Sunday

A ringing telephone awakened Nora from a sound sleep. Rolling out of bed, she grabbed her robe from the closet and hurried across the cold floorboards to the front room. Parting the curtains to let in the sunshine, she snatched up the telephone. "Hello. This is the Finnegan residence."

"Good morning, dear. Did I wake you?"

"I've been up for hours, Mother," Nora lied.

"You haven't telephoned us this week. Your father and I were getting concerned about you."

"I'm sorry. I've been busy at the *Pine Cone*." Nora didn't elaborate on her issues with Mr. Owens' dull assignments or her recent request to cover the story about Martin Fields' murder. She thought it prudent not to give her parents any more to worry about.

"Is your reporter's job taking up all of your time?"

"No, not entirely," Nora said, keeping her voice light. "I'm having a bit of a social life." She knew that her mother would welcome any sign of progress in that department.

"Do you mean you've met someone?"

Rather than reply to a question with so much meaning behind it, Nora deflected her mother's curiosity. "Do you remember the Prestons, that nice couple from South Carolina that you and Father met here last summer? Well, they were in town this week, visiting their son Keith."

"Of course, I remember them. Keith is the young man who runs the library."

"They invited me to go out one evening. Keith hired a motorcar and drove the four of us out to Carmel Point along the beach road to the Carmel Mission."

"It must have been a pretty drive, especially if it was a clear night."

"It was, Mother, but I was surprised when I saw the mission's plain-looking interior. The place is in serious need of repair. Yet, despite all that, the musical program we were treated to was unforgettable. You and Father would have enjoyed it."

"It was nice of the Prestons to include you, dear."

Seeming satisfied that all was well with her only daughter, and hearing a hint of a possible romance, Alice Finnegan said, "Your father and I would be happy to return the Prestons' favor, Nora. Why don't we invite Keith to come up to San Francisco for a visit while you're home at Christmas? Surely the library gives him time off from his duties."

Nora thought it best to dampen her mother's enthusiasm. "Let's think about that, shall we? I've got to go. Will you tell Father I love him and that I'll call soon?"

Since she had some time to spare, Nora took a stroll before heading to All Saints Episcopal Church. She passed the colonnade of young Monterey pines running down the center of Ocean Avenue. They looked more like bushes at this point, she thought. Despite Mr. Owens' opinion, when fully grown, they would make an attractive separation of the motorcar lanes in both directions.

All the shops were closed. Carmel's residents were either sleeping in, or worshipping at their churches. Her mood was upbeat as she admired the window displays. The village had taken on a festive air for Thanksgiving. Orange pumpkins and baskets filled with apples were clustered among straw bales and cornstalks. She paused in front of one store and smiled at the pen-and-ink cartoon of a fat tom turkey being chased by an ax-wielding grocer. The prankster who had drawn it on butcher paper must have tacked the sketch onto the grocery store's front door during the night.

Turning south onto Monte Verde Street, she arrived at the wood-shingled church that the Owens family attended. Some faithful souls had strung cypress boughs over the church's double doors and decorated them with dozens of seashells. A bell was tolling the end of the service. Organ music drifted out to the street.

As she admired the decorations, the church doors parted, and a stream of parishioners emerged, with Reverend Hatch leading the way. Nora spotted Mr. Owens behind the minister with Mrs. Owens and Sally. She hoped the publisher's wife had converted her husband's old-fashioned ideas about women not being allowed to cover a murder story. She was about to find out if progress or hidebound tradition had prevailed.

The publisher waved at Nora as he came down the stairs. His wife remained chatting with some of the parishioners.

"Good morning, Honora," Owens said. "It's a beautiful day, for a change."

"It is, sir." To her surprise, he seemed happy to see her.

Pulling some papers from his coat pocket, he handed them to her. "I've read your notes. Your description of the crime scene was thorough. I've made up my mind. You have the assignment."

Nora's face brightened.

"However," he added, "no physical danger must come to you. You're to take no foolish chances with anyone connected to the murder. Furthermore, you'll apprise me of your movements every step of the way."

As she considered his admonitions, Nora could hardly contain her excitement. When he had finished, she said, "I don't intend to interview anyone other than the sheriff at the present time. And I'll have a completed article on the Fields' murder, as well as the Thanksgiving feature story you assigned me, by tomorrow morning."

"That will be fine. Be sure I get them by the one o'clock deadline. I won't be going to the office this afternoon. Mr. Levy and I are driving out to the lighthouse to do some picture taking. This weather is ideal." Owens turned his head and glanced up at his wife, who was still standing at the top of the stairs. He couldn't be sure of it, but it looked to him like she had just winked at Honora.

After they said goodbye, Nora continued on her way to her appointment at Hotel La Playa. With a spring in her step, she headed downhill to the road that had been nicknamed Professors Row. During Carmel's formative years, she knew that professors from Stanford University and the University of California at Berkeley had built their summer homes along here to be close to the ocean. Beyond the houses, to the west, sunlight filtered through a windbreak of cypress trees at the top of the sand dunes.

Breathing in the fresh air, Nora listened to the waves and thought back to Mr. Owens' decision. She felt certain that his wife had tipped the scales in her favor. But her conscience bothered her about some other matters. She remembered her earlier conversation with her mother. Why had she deliberately omitted any mention of her desire to write about the Fields' murder? She had to find a way to make amends. Once her article appeared in the *Carmel Pine Cone*, she would send a copy to her parents.

There was also the matter of the romantic interest between her and Keith Preston. It was true that they were good friends, but it hadn't progressed beyond that. If she had been truthful, she would have told her mother that she did feel attracted to Rob Jacklin. He had initiated what Nora interpreted as an interest in her yesterday when he had placed a comforting arm around her at the crime scene in the canyon. She should have pulled away, as that would have been the proper thing for a young lady to do. But she hadn't. Was she encouraging Rob to become involved with her? *Enough of this behavior! Tell the truth, Nora, no matter how hard that might be, especially to your mother.*

Having achieved what she perceived to be an act of contrition, she proceeded down Professors Row until she reached the hotel grounds. La Playa's front gate was open and welcoming. Perhaps there was something within these walls that would point her to Martin Fields' murderer.

CHAPTER NINE

Entering the lobby, Nora passed by several departing guests who were standing in line in front of the hotel's reception desk. Paulette Villard was behind it, processing their bills. Having witnessed the innkeeper's combative demeanor at the Board of Trustees' meeting on Friday night, Nora saw that today the woman seemed very affable with her guests. Since it might be some time before she could sit down and chat, Nora headed for the reading alcove off the lobby.

Taking an armchair where she could keep an eye on Mrs. Villard, she noticed a petite, middle-aged lady seated in a matching armchair on the other side of the fireplace. The woman wore a tailored suit with a black silk scarf loosely tied around the collar of her white blouse. Her upswept hair framed an oval face. Nora recognized her. Julia Morgan, the San Francisco architect, was sketching in a notebook. Although she suspected that the woman preferred her privacy, Nora decided to introduce herself. "Excuse me, Miss Morgan," she said. "My name is Nora Finnegan. I have the utmost regard for you."

The architect looked puzzled.

"Allow me to explain," Nora continued. "I'm a graduate of Mills College and I happen to know that you designed our library and bell tower. Your picture has been featured in our school yearbook ever since I was a freshman."

Closing her sketchbook, Miss Morgan smiled and said, "I'm pleased that someone your age appreciates my work, Miss Finnegan."

Nora grinned. "However, what I valued most about Mills

was the natatorium you designed for us. If it weren't for your pool, I'm afraid that I wouldn't have learned how to swim so well."

"Thank you for those nice compliments."

"May I ask you a question, Miss Morgan? I heard that the school's administration had to be coerced into constructing our swimming pool, since it was for women. Is that true?"

"I'm afraid so. Personally, I think athletic endeavors are an important aspect of anyone's education, whether male or female. We know that women are capable of becoming superb swimmers with the proper training. The Olympic trials confirm that." Leaning forward, she asked, "Are you by any chance a San Francisco Finnegan?"

"Yes, I am, and I was born there. Perhaps you know my father, John Finnegan. He's the editor of the *San Francisco Call*."

The architect's eyes studied Nora's features through her round-rimmed wire glasses. "I knew it. I see the resemblance. I met your father years ago while he was working as a reporter for the newspaper. He came to interview me after the '06 earthquake and later wrote an article on my first major project, the restoration of the Fairmont Hotel on Nob Hill."

Nora smiled. "Father always says that he enjoyed his years as a news reporter. He met so many interesting people. Now he has many administrative responsibilities that take up most of his time."

Julia nodded. "Matter of fact, I'm also acquainted with your mother. She and I served for years on a volunteer board in Chinatown."

Familiar with her mother's support of the orphanage called Cameron House, Nora said, "She remains on that board to this day. Did you design that building as well?"

"Yes, I did, and it turned out to be one of my favorites."

The stories Nora had heard about the architect's reclusiveness were mistaken. The woman was very approachable. She said, "If you haven't made any plans for this evening, would you care to join me for supper? I live up the street in one of our typical Carmel cottages. I would be happy to show it to you, and if its design sparks your interest, I'm sure our *Pine Cone* readers would enjoy reading your comments. Oh, I forgot to tell you," she added, "I'm working here as a reporter for Mr. Owens, the newspaper's publisher."

Julia's face brightened. "I accept your kind invitation. Your father must be very proud that you're following in his footsteps."

Nora beamed. "Shall we say six o'clock then? My cottage's name is Pine Log." It used to be a canvas tent cabin. My father had it redone with walls, windows and a proper roof. We used it as a temporary home for a year after the '06 earthquake." Tearing a sheet of paper from her notepad, she wrote down the directions. "If I'm not being too inquisitive, Miss Morgan, what brings you to Carmel?"

"This morning I'm presenting a design proposal to a client. We were supposed to meet in the lobby at eleven. He's late."

"Is your client planning to build a new residence here?"

"Yes, it's to be a second home for him and his wife. Perhaps you know the gentleman? His name is Martin Fields."

Nora put her hand to her mouth to stifle a gasp, as she heard a shriek from Mrs. Villard at the front desk. The woman was within earshot and must have overheard their conversation.

Hurrying over to them, she said, "Miss Morgan, if you had told me that you had an appointment with Mr. Fields when you came downstairs for breakfast this morning, I would have explained that the poor man was found murdered yesterday."

"What happened to him?"

"According to the sheriff, his body was found in a ravine in Pescadero Canyon. Sheriff Terry and his men were here last night, questioning me and my staff."

Julia shook her head. "This is terrible news. What a tragedy."

"Mrs. Villard," Nora interjected, "I'm covering the Fields' case for the *Carmel Pine Cone*. I'd like to speak with you about him."

Giving Nora a withering look, the manager said, "It's *MISS* Villard, young lady, and our discussion today is supposed to be about my Thanksgiving activities, as I remember."

"That's correct," Nora said, "and I intend to get that information from you as well. But I'm also writing a feature story about Mr. Fields' murder."

Julia Morgan stood up. "I'm sure you two ladies want to discuss matters privately. I'll return to my room and place a few calls in light of what's occurred." As she headed for the stairs to La Playa's second floor, she looked at Nora and said, "Miss Finnegan, I'll see you at six o'clock this evening."

"Miss Morgan is such an accomplished lady," Paulette Villard said, as she tucked in a few strands of hennaed hair that had somehow escaped from her French roll. "She's done well in what most people would consider a man's field." Then, snatching up two throw pillows from a nearby loveseat, she placed them on the fireplace's raised hearth. "Let's talk here, where I can keep my eye on the front desk."

Nora sat down next to her. "Tell me, Miss Villard. Is Mr. Fields' family here with him?"

Their backs to the fire, Paulette Villard shook her head, and then looked around to make sure that no one was listening. "When he checked in several days ago, he told me that his wife was taking a later train from New York. Sure enough, the poor woman arrived today. They don't have children. They live in Manhattan and have a second home out on Long Island." Lowering her voice to a whisper, she added, "It's the missus' side of the family that has the money."

Nora listened to the woman's words, which were intermixed with loud popping sounds from the freshly cut logs in the fireplace behind them.

"I'm not a gossip, mind you," the manager went on, "but Sarah Fields is a real snob. When she stayed with us last time, she ordered everyone around like servants."

"Why didn't she accompany her husband on this trip?"

"I think Mr. Fields had his reasons. If I had to guess, it was because he wanted her out of the way."

Paulette Villard's heavily-ringed fingers clutched Nora's wrist. Her grip was firm; as if to emphasize that her secret had to remain between them. Nora decided not to pull away, thinking that might cause the woman to stop talking.

"I'll share a little tidbit with you, Miss Finnegan, but if you tell anyone that it came from me, I most certainly will deny it."

"Trust me to keep your name out of it, Miss Villard. I never divulge my sources."

The innkeeper seemed satisfied that Nora would keep a confidence. "La Playa has a fine reputation and what happens within these walls is nobody's business. I go out of my way to protect my guests' privacy, but if you ask me, Mr. Fields purposely didn't bring his wife this time."

"Why would he do that?"

"Let's just say that I observed his behavior last Thursday

evening. He came down to the lobby a little before dark and went out to the garden, then back upstairs to his room. He did this two or three times. Finally, he came in here to the library alcove and took a seat by the fire."

"It sounds like he was waiting for someone," Nora prompted.

"Like I told Sheriff Terry last night, he could have been expecting the woman whom I've seen him with once or twice since he checked in."

The revelation surprised Nora. "Do you know who she is?"

"No, but I've seen her around the village. Anyway, after a time, Mr. Fields got tired of waiting. He pulled a flask out of his pocket and took a few swigs from it. That concerned me. Earlier, I had arranged for him to rent a motorcar from Quinlan's garage. I began to worry that he would be in no condition to drive. Besides that, he was imbibing alcohol. That's illegal."

"Did he say where he planned to go?" Nora asked.

"No, but I found out later from my concierge. He wanted a motorcar to take him to Bella Vista, that big mansion on 17-Mile Drive."

"I'd like to talk to the concierge if he's available."

Paulette Villard's eyes narrowed. "Oresto Santoli didn't come to work today. He had to take care of some family business." Pointing at a tall, olive-skinned young man in a beige uniform, who was standing at the front desk, she added, "That's his cousin, Rudolfo. He's filling in for him."

"You've been most helpful. Will you ask Mr. Santoli to call me when he returns?" Scribbling her name and telephone number on a slip of notepaper, she handed it to the woman. "Would you give this to him, please?"

Tucking the paper into the waistband of her skirt, the manager said, "Let's go into the dining room and discuss what I've been planning for the hotel's Thanksgiving celebration. That's why you're here, isn't it?"

"That's what I came to La Playa to find out," Nora fibbed. Getting up from the hearth and replacing her pillow on the loveseat, it occurred to her that she had just broken her vow to always tell the truth, and worse yet, within an hour of having made it.

In the dining room, Nora took notes as Paulette Villard plied her with details of the holiday meal, table decorations and after-dinner entertainment. She would have more than enough material to write her article about La Playa's Thanksgiving Day activities. Mr. Owens would be pleased. But more important, she had learned a great deal about Martin Fields for her other story. There were questions that needed answers. For instance, who was the woman that Miss Villard had seen with Fields before his death? Why had he rented a motorcar, and who drove the one that had pushed the hired Buick into a ravine? Did the murderer intend it to look like an accident? Putting her notebook in her purse, Nora prepared to leave.

Getting up, Paulette Villard said, "If you've nothing planned for the holiday, Miss Finnegan, you're welcome to join us here. There will be no charge to you. I have always enjoyed having the residents take part in our festivities."

Surprised by her offer, Nora thanked the woman and left through the lobby. As she closed the front gate behind her, she couldn't help but think that Miss Villard's offer might have been extended to entice her into writing a favorable article that would encourage more business. Was she being overly suspicious? Then again, perhaps the woman was merely being friendly.

The interview had taken longer than expected, but she had time to spare before her next appointment at the Pine Inn. Hiking through Professors Row, she made her way back to the village and at the same time, thought about her menu for tonight's supper with Miss Morgan. She regretted not having accepted last summer's offer from the Finnegan's housekeeper to learn a few cooking tips. She was on her own. Poached local fish, mashed parsnips and Brussels sprouts from her next door neighbor's garden would be easy to prepare and she could warm up the leftover pie from the tea room for dessert.

After supper, she would bring up Martin Fields' name and try to get Miss Morgan's impressions of the dead man. However, she really didn't expect the architect to say anything that would be considered unprofessional.

Then Nora remembered something. She hadn't found out the location of Carlotta Fleming's cottage. The artist had invited her to a meeting there tomorrow night. She also needed a means of getting to Oak Bower. She could have rented a motorcar from Quinlan's garage if her father had taught her how to drive before she left San Francisco. To her great disappointment, he had remarked, 'You needn't fret about driving, Honora. Your husband will take you where you want to go after you marry.'

As she approached Carmel's business district, she recalled one of her father's little wisdoms: 'Look upon your problems, not as obstacles, but as opportunities.'

The Fields' murder story had to be her biggest opportunity to date.

CHAPTER TEN

Keith Preston looked up as the library's front door opened. "What a nice surprise, Nora," Carmel's librarian said in his Southern drawl. The clean-shaven transplanted South Carolinian was sitting at his desk, stamping dates on white cards and stuffing them into the pockets of some library books that were lined up in front of him. A slender man who was about the same height as Nora, he stood and piled a load of books in his arms.

"Don't stop what you're doing," she called out. "I know what I'm looking for."

"I'm supposed to help the patrons."

Every time she visited here, Nora marveled at how Keith had changed the library for the better. What had begun as a voluntary effort had been transformed over time into the village's social hub. She enjoyed hearing him brag that the original book collection of 400 volumes had swelled since 1905 to 5,000. She thought much of the credit went to the Carmel Development Company, the firm that had donated the brown-shingled cottage and moved it free of charge to a lot at Lincoln and Sixth Avenue. Especially on a cold day like this, she was glad that the house's original Franklin stove heated the rooms and made them a comfortable place to read.

And there was an extra bonus. Keith kept the library open on Sunday afternoons to the delight of residents like her who had to work during the week.

"It's no trouble, really," he said, as he came around the desk.

Heading for the bookshelf where the city directories were

kept, Nora stopped short when she heard a commotion behind her. Turning around, she saw Keith down on one knee, retrieving some books that had fallen on the floor.

"You should really pick up your big feet, Mr. Preston," she teased.

Bathed in sunlight streaming through the front window, his wavy blond hair, as always, was sprinkled with paint flecks. Today they were a combination of white and yellow. She never commented on them, not wishing to embarrass him. She knew the flecks were a result of Keith's part-time work as a house painter, although he had come to Carmel to be a plein-air painter. Unlike many of Carmel's struggling artists, Nora knew that Keith's jobs helped him survive. His $19 a month librarian's salary paid the $7.50 rent on his cottage, with the rest going for food, clothes and incidentals. His house painting money covered the cost of his passion: canvases, oil paints and fine brushes.

As he shelved some books, he said, "I saw you last Friday night at the Trustees' meeting. I was sitting behind you with some friends."

"I saw you too, but have you heard what's happened to Mr. Fields?" Nora told him about the discovery of the developer's body in the canyon.

The news shocked him. "I wonder if someone was angry enough to get rid of him. I'm all for stopping the beach hotel, but I draw the line at killing a man over it."

"I feel the same way, but I'm here on another matter." Studying the city directory page that listed residents' names starting with 'F,' she found what she needed. "Miss Fleming has invited me to attend a meeting tomorrow night," she said. "According to this entry, her home is on Carmelo Avenue on the outskirts of town."

"I'm going too. Want me to come by for you? I can find Oak Bower, even in the dark. This is going to be an important meeting, especially with Fields turning up dead."

"That sounds fine, Keith."

"Then I'll stop by for you a little before eight."

About to leave, Nora thought of something. "Are you familiar with a house called Bella Vista?"

"You mean the large house at the north end of town? That's the Chatham place. Why does it interest you?"

"I'll tell you while we're walking to Miss Fleming's."

"Aren't you the coy one," he said, as he opened the front door for her. "Have some tea with me later. I take my break at three o'clock."

"All right, I'll meet you at the Blue Bird," Nora said over her shoulder as she ran down the path leading out to the street. It had been hours since her meager breakfast. She could do with something more than tea.

A cool wind had come up from the beach, as Nora arrived at the front entrance of the Pine Inn. Her appointment was for 2:00 P.M. and it was nearly that time. Entering the lobby, she saw the hotel manager behind the reception desk. No guests demanded his attention and it was past the busy lunch period. The innkeeper greeted her and showed her to a table in the empty dining room.

For the next hour, they reviewed his plans for Thanksgiving. Together with the notes she had taken earlier on Hotel La Playa's holiday activities, she had more than enough material for a multi-column feature story that she knew would satisfy Mr. Owens.

The clock in the lobby struck three times. Nora put away her notes and said goodbye to the manager. Leaving by the side door, she detoured past the candy store to gaze at its delectable fare. For someone who was trying to watch her weight, she felt fortunate that it was Sunday. The shop was closed.

Making her way across Ocean Avenue, she spotted Keith at one of the tea room's window tables. As she entered, he stood up and held the chair out for her.

"Thank you," she said, as she sat down. With its lace curtains, white tablecloths and napkins, the Blue Bird always felt homey to Nora whenever she came here. Each of the tables held a Chintzware teapot with matching cups and saucers. Placing her napkin in her lap, she said, "I especially like the way someone has embroidered these cloths with a blue chick on toothpick legs."

"Whoever sewed them has a good sense of humor," Keith added. "She's also stuffed a big fat worm in the chick's beak."

They both laughed.

Studying the menu board, Nora said, "I think a piece of the mince pie will go nicely with our tea. What about you?"

Keith nodded at the hovering waitress. "We'd like two good-sized wedges of warmed homemade mince pie, miss."

The waitress wrote it down on her order pad. "Right away, Mr. Preston."

While they waited, Nora lifted the teapot from the trivet,

refreshed Keith's cup, and then filled hers to the brim.

In a few minutes, the waitress returned and set generous slices of pie in front of them. Nora used her fork to separate off the tip of her piece. "I'm making a wish and eating this end part last, in hopes that it comes true," she said.

Keith, who had already sampled his dessert, shrugged. "I've never had any luck come from that custom." Waving at their waitress, he said, "Miss, I'd like a little brandy sauce to go with the pie."

The young woman smiled and said, "I'll be happy to get some for you, sir."

Nora ate a few bites of her pie, put down her fork, and took a sip of the aromatic Earl Grey tea. As her eyes roamed the room, they lit on a striking woman seated at one of the back tables. Turning to Keith, she said, "Who is that with Rob Jacklin?"

"Aren't they a handsome couple? She's Claudia Woodward. That's her son, Freddie, seated next to her."

Seeing Rob in the company of a beautiful woman upset Nora. She wondered if she had misinterpreted his invitation to join him and the Boys Club members yesterday. More important, had she also misunderstood his embrace at the Fields' crime scene? "I can't believe that she's old enough to be Freddie's mother," she said.

"Well, she is. The two of them moved here from San Francisco before school started."

Nora remembered Freddie telling her the same story as they hiked together yesterday in Pescadero Canyon. "When did you meet her?" she asked.

"I guess it was about a week later. She and Freddie came into the library one afternoon. She wanted an adventure story to read to him. I picked out several books that I thought would appeal to his age group. After talking to the boy, I found him to be an intelligent lad, and there's no doubt that his mom's a stunner."

Nora didn't respond.

Catching Freddie's eye, Keith waved at him. The boy got up from his chair and waved back.

The only thing that Nora saw was Rob reaching across the tea table and taking Mrs. Woodward's hand. Sliding her pie plate towards Keith, she knew that she couldn't possibly eat the tip now. Her wish would never come true. Feeling a jealous knot forming in the pit of her stomach, she said, "Why don't you take this? I've lost my appetite."

"Are you sure?" Before she could answer, he took a bite of her pie. Nora watched as a piece of buttery crust dropped on the front of his white shirt. Leaning over, she flicked it off with her napkin, but not before a grease stain appeared.

Looking down at it, Keith frowned. "I'll need to take this to Ki Mee first thing in the morning."

Freddie had left his seat and was running towards them. "Hi, Mr. Preston and Miss Finnegan!" he shouted. He came to a stop, and at the same time, grabbed the back of Nora's chair for support.

"I should be going," Nora said, and reached for her purse.

Keith looked surprised. "Why so soon?"

Claudia Woodward had caught up with her son. Grasping his shoulder, she said, "Use your inside voice, dear, and please be more careful. You're disturbing these people." She pulled him away from Nora's chair.

"He's no bother," Nora said. She stared at the young woman's navy blue dress, emphasizing her trim figure. She couldn't deny her sense of style. The paisley scarf covering her shoulders gave Mrs. Woodward an exotic East Indian look.

Keith scrambled to his feet. "Remember me, Mrs. Woodward? I'm the librarian, Keith Preston. How nice, to see you and Freddie again. Oh, forgive my manners. This is my friend, Nora Finnegan."

Claudia Woodward looked down at Nora and smiled.

She has dimpled cheeks.

"I'm pleased to meet you, Miss Finnegan."

And her voice is as soft as silk.

"Freddie has told me all about you. You were very kind to watch over him in the canyon yesterday. I'm ever so grateful."

"Freddie must be a treasure to you," Nora said, as she got up from her chair. *We're the same height, but my looks are ordinary. Her high cheekbones, brown eyes, and long chestnut hair frame a heart-shaped face. It's no wonder that Rob chose her over me.* Determined to escape, she tried to edge toward the tea room's front door. She hoped that Keith would take notice and escort her out.

However, Claudia Woodward continued to hold everyone's attention. Glancing at Rob Jacklin, who had come up to join them, she said, "I'm thankful that you and Miss Finnegan were with Freddie yesterday." Taking the teacher's hand, she went on, "You both kept him safe. Freddie's all I have in the world, and I'm very worried about him."

"Why is that?" Keith said.

"Last night he woke up after having a nightmare. He was crying and mumbling something about blood on a man's overcoat."

Freddie, who had been listening to his mother, began trembling. "I was scared, Mama. But Miss Finnegan covered my eyes so I didn't see anything bad."

Rob knelt down on one knee. "Freddie, do you remember that strange-looking hat that Sherlock Holmes wore in *The Hound of the Baskervilles?* And how about that silly pipe that was always dangling out of one side of his mouth?"

Rob jumped into a crouch, pulled his wool cap down over his ears, and took a pipe from his pocket. Stuffing it in his mouth, he looked up at Freddie and mimicked the famed detective. "And how are you, my dear Watson?"

Freddie burst out laughing. Nora could see that Rob's clowning had dispelled the boy's bad memories. She respected the teacher's skill in handling young children and wondered if she would ever feel comfortable enough to compliment him.

Growing more impatient to leave, she heard Rob say, "Keith, you'll recall that I checked out several of Sir Arthur Conan Doyle's mystery stories from the library at the beginning of the school term. I've been reading them to my fourth graders during our lunch periods. Holmes' adventures hold their rapt attention, especially on rainy days, when we have to stay indoors."

"I'm happy that the library's collection is serving you well," Keith said.

Hopping about on one foot, Freddie said, "My favorite one's 'The Speckled Band.' I like the scary part where the snake comes down the bell rope next to the man's bed!"

The adults, with Freddie in the midst of them, stood around the tea table, discussing Carmel's unpredictable weather and "Polly with a Past," the motion picture that was showing at the Manzanita Theater. Finally, to Nora's relief, the group moved outside, where they said their goodbyes. Nora stood back as Rob and Claudia headed down Ocean Avenue on their way to the beach. Freddie was skipping along between the couple, holding onto their hands.

Keith's eyes were studying Nora. He said, "Will you walk me back to the library?"

She nodded, but didn't reply.

Once they arrived, he said, "Let's sit for a minute. Is something bothering you, Nora? At the tea room it seemed to me that you were a little envious of Mrs. Woodward. I'd like to tell you about her background and maybe you'll think more of her."

Averting his gaze, Nora perched on the library's bottom step. She stared out at the row of Monterey pines running down the middle of Ocean Avenue.

"Claudia's an accomplished person," Keith began, as he sat down next to her. "She studied photography for a year in New York before she married. When she returned to the West Coast, I was told that she exhibited her art prints at one of San Francisco's prestigious photographic salons. She is serious about her work, just as you are about your journalistic career. I would think that's a trait you'd admire in another woman."

Nora couldn't keep her annoyance to herself any longer. "Gushing over Mrs. Woodward is getting tiresome. Both you and Rob have been taken in by her good looks. You're fawning over her." Nora shook off his hand on her arm, got up, and started walking towards the street.

"I don't understand you at all," Keith shouted, as he stood up. "I hope you're in a much better mood tomorrow night for the residents' meeting." Spinning around, he pulled open the library door and went inside.

Feeling miserable, Nora headed down Ocean Avenue. Seeing Rob with Claudia Woodward had been painful for her. But why did she care so much? She knew she didn't have any claim on him, nor did she have time to get involved in a romantic relationship. She had to find a way to get past her disappointment.

More important, why had she lashed out at Keith just now? Her angry outburst had nothing to do with the librarian. He had been a perfect gentleman at the tea room and had even paid their bill. She, on the other hand, hadn't remembered to thank him. She had better call and apologize to him for her unacceptable behavior.

For now, though, she had other worries. Today all the grocery stores were closed, but she wanted to buy fresh fish for this evening's supper with Julia Morgan. Keith's remark at the tea room about giving his soiled shirt to Ki Mee reminded her that the unmarried Chinese man who did the village's hand-laundry always went fishing on his day off. Usually he returned with a much larger catch than he could consume. She would go and knock on the back door of his laundry where he lived, and buy some fresh snapper or whatever he had caught this morning.

Then there was tomorrow. She had an important deadline to meet. Her articles on Carmel's Thanksgiving events and her story on Martin Fields' murder had to be ready by one o'clock. She would be up all night.

CHAPTER ELEVEN

Monday

Nora awakened at seven, dressed, and headed out her cottage's front door. She was thankful that Mrs. Philbrook's Banty rooster hadn't started its noisy crowing under her bedroom window at sunrise. Nearing the newspaper office, she suddenly realized that in her haste, she had forgotten to stop for her milk order at the corner shrine. Now she was not only weary from getting only five hours of sleep, but hungry as well.

However, she was pleased about one thing she had done. After Miss Morgan departed for La Playa last night, she had telephoned Keith and apologized for her behavior that afternoon. She also thanked him for paying her share of the tea room bill. The call had made her feel much better about herself.

Unlocking the front door to the *Carmel Pine Cone*, she wondered why Mrs. Owens wasn't at the office at this hour. She raised the window shade in the reception area and started planning her day. The holiday feature was completed, but she was having difficulty with certain aspects of her story concerning Fields' murder. She recalled Mr. Owens' instructions to her on her first day on the job: 'I want you to make your articles detailed and accurate, Honora, but please don't overwrite them.'

Sitting down at her desk, she began reworking her lead paragraph, but stopped when she heard a loud voice coming from the music studio next door. Carmel's voice teacher was in full throat, going through her vocal exercises. Nora couldn't concentrate, due to the woman's repetition of the same phrase from *'Un bel di.'* She wasn't enjoying 'One fine day!' Of all the Puccini arias to bedevil her with, it had to be that one from "Madame Butterfly."

Dissatisfied with what she had written so far, she took a fresh sheet of paper and began all over again. Remembering last night's conversation after supper with Miss Morgan, she recalled how she had purposely brought up Martin Fields' hotel project. The architect hadn't wanted to comment on it and had not spoken a word against Fields or his widow, whom Miss Morgan said she had met at La Playa that afternoon.

The telephone's ring interrupted her musings. Picking up, Nora said, *"Carmel Pine Cone.* How may I help you?"

"It's Mr. Owens, Honora. I'm glad you came in on time."

Nora ignored his reminder that she had arrived at the office after eight o'clock on two occasions last week. "I've been working on the Fields' murder story," she said. "But it surprised me that you and Mrs. Owens weren't here when I came in."

"We've been delayed by that darned cat of ours. Plato's stuck in one of the oak trees in the front yard. Sally refuses to go to school until he's been rescued. I've been trying to coax him down, but he keeps climbing higher. He's up about thirty feet now."

"What are you going to do?"

"I called the fire department, and wouldn't you know, their ladder doesn't reach that high. They said they'll need to climb the tree the rest of the way. I want you to cover things and answer the telephone calls until Mrs. Owens and I get there."

"I will, sir." Nora crossed her fingers and went on, "But does this mean a delay in your afternoon deadline?"

"I'm afraid it does."

Masking the relief in her voice, Nora said, "In that case, I'll put my Thanksgiving story on your desk and follow up on some loose ends on the Fields' article."

"That's fine. Have everything turned in to me by 3:00 this afternoon. I'll start typesetting your Thanksgiving feature as soon as I get in."

As Nora put down the receiver, her spirits lifted. It might turn into *'Un bel di'* after all.

Mary Lee Owens came into the *Pine Cone's* reception area an hour later. The publisher's wife had her corgi in tow.

"How's Plato doing?" Nora asked, as she leaned down and petted Dasher. The dog licked her hand and then plopped down at her feet.

Mary Lee went around the front counter and sat down at the receptionist's desk. "Actually, that cat handled his problem better than I did. I was amazed when he came down the tree all by himself at the same moment the fire truck drove up. As a gesture of our gratitude, I fixed coffee for the firemen and put cream in a bowl for that darned cat."

"It sounds like a memorable morning," Nora said. "I'll bet Sally was happy to have her kitty back."

Mary Lee laughed. "Mr. Owens has taken her to school, despite her claims of an upset stomach."

Now that Mrs. Owens was here, Nora was free to contact the concierge at Hotel La Playa. Also, Claudia Woodward had made reference to Fields' bloodstained overcoat. It appeared to Nora that Freddie's mother might know more about the hotel developer than she had let on. There was enough time before Mr. Owens' revised afternoon deadline to talk to both of them.

"I'm going to interview some people for a story, Mrs. Owens," she said, as she picked up her notepad and purse. "When Mr. Owens gets in, please tell him that I'll be back by three. But just in case, I left my other article on his desk." Getting up, she headed for the front door.

Entering the lobby, Nora peeked into La Playa's dining room. She spotted Miss Morgan at one of the tables. Across from her was an older woman whom she didn't recognize. She wanted to stop and chat, but with her deadline looming, she couldn't afford to waste any time. Walking past the reception desk, she came to a smaller desk with a cardboard placard with the word "Concierge" on it. The young man standing there was reading a foreign magazine.

Going up to him, she asked, "Are you Mr. Santoli?"

His dark features were similar to Rudolfo's, the young man whom she had seen here yesterday, and who was now lounging next to the entry.

Santoli snapped his fingers. "*Si, signorina.* You want help with luggage, yes?" He shouted, "Rudolfo! *Vieni*! *Subito!* Come here!"

As the man hurried over to them, Nora could see the family

resemblance. Miss Villard had told her that he was Santoli's cousin. Putting up her hand, she said, "Thank you, but no luggage." Rudolfo shrugged and returned to his post.

Oresto Santoli said, "Then what you want, *signorina*?"

"I'm Miss Finnegan from the *Carmel Pine Cone*. We spoke on the telephone."

"Ah, *si*. I remember."

"My newspaper would like answers to a few questions I have regarding one of the hotel's guests. I need to ask you about the late Martin Fields."

Santoli shook his head. "A sad thing that was. *Che peccato*. What a pity for the wife. But I know nothing. We don't suppose to be friends with the patrons." Pointing towards the staircase up to the second floor, they could hear the manager's voice, berating someone. Santoli shook his head. "Miss Villard no allow it."

"Where did Mr. Fields want to go last Thursday night?" Nora prodded. "I was told that you gave him some directions."

"I tell him the way to the garage, then how to get to a house on 17-Mile Drive. *Signor* Fields, he left the hotel after that, but he say nothing to me. That's all I know."

"Was anyone with him that night?"

"No, this time, he was alone."

"What do you mean, 'this time,' Mr. Santoli?"

"*Signor* Fields, he not always by himself. I see him with a pretty *signorina*. He brings her here a few times." Putting his fingers to his lips, he made a soft, kissing sound. "*Bellisima*. Oh, *scusi*. She not so beautiful as you."

Their voices had drawn Paulette Villard's attention. "Who are you talking to down there, Oresto?" she called out from the second floor landing.

Nora had to learn more before the manager came down. She said, "Who was this woman with Mr. Fields? Do you know her name?"

Before Santoli could answer, Nora heard scuffling sounds and a series of shouts from the vicinity of the hotel's entrance. She turned to see Rudolfo fending off three men, all of whom were wearing uniforms. Their gold badges gleamed. Holstered revolvers hung from their belts. One lawman pushed past Rudolfo and headed towards Nora. She recognized him as Sheriff Frank Terry.

Pointing to the bellman's cousin, he yelled, "Are you

Oresto Santoli?"

The concierge looked bewildered. "*Si*. What did I do?"

"I'm the sheriff, son. I need to question you. You'll have to come with me."

Without warning, Nora felt Santoli's arm grab her around the waist and pull her up against his body. Breathing rapidly, Santoli pressed a sharp object against her throat.

"No closer, Mister Sheriff," he shouted, "or the pretty *signorina*, she is dead!"

Sheriff Terry froze and watched Santoli keep the knife blade at her neck. Half-pushing, half-dragging her across the lobby, the concierge made it out the front door. When he reached the garden, he put a hand on Nora's back and shoved her into some prickly bushes before running off.

Nora put her hands to her face as she felt herself falling. Raising her head above the thorny branches, she felt relieved that she had escaped with only a few scratches.

Meanwhile, the concierge had catapulted over the low fence. Two police officers, their guns drawn, scrambled after him.

Nora climbed out of the bushes, reentered the lobby and headed for a bathroom. The incident had left her shaken, but her instinct to protect her face had served her well. If only the scratches on the backs of her hands would stop stinging. Standing at the sink, she splashed water on her face and hands and dried them with a towel. She took a comb from her purse and fixed her hair, using the mirror over the basin.

Terry's voice penetrated the bathroom door. "You all right in there, miss?"

"Yes, I'm fine, Sheriff." Nora said, as she brushed off leaves from her wool serge suit before stepping out to the lobby. A crowd had gathered around Miss Villard, who must have fainted. She was lying on the floor. Sheriff Terry's senior deputy, Jimmy Connery, whom Nora had met in Pescadero Canyon, was bent over the innkeeper and was rubbing her wrists.

Connery looked up as Nora approached them. "You had a narrow escape, Miss Finnegan," he said. "Are you sure you're all right?"

"Yes, thank you," Nora said, and headed over to the sheriff, to ask why he was arresting Santoli. She had to wait while Terry and the other lawman, Deputy Jensen, pushed the handcuffed concierge into the back seat of the police wagon parked in the middle of Camino Real.

Overhead, two black crows perched on a pine bough made loud, cawing sounds. To Nora, they seemed upset by the commotion going on below their nest.

Assured that Santoli was under control, Sheriff Terry walked over to her. "I remember you," he said. "Do you realize that you could have been killed? You'll want to file an assault charge against the man. I'll need your statement."

Nora shook her head. "I don't intend to press charges, Sheriff. I wasn't hurt. I think he behaved that way because he was frightened."

"Why are you here, Miss Finnegan?"

"I told you in the canyon that I am a reporter for the *Pine Cone*. My boss, Mr. Owens, assigned me to cover the Fields murder." Nora reached into her purse and brought out her pen and notepad. "I came here to talk to the concierge about him. I'd like to know why you're arresting Mr. Santoli."

"I'm surprised that the publisher is allowing a young woman to cover a heinous crime like murder."

"I'll have you know I'm quite up for it, Sheriff."

Frank Terry shook his head. "O. K. Here's what I know. Oresto Santoli is a suspect in the Fields case. He knew the developer, and he obviously had access to his room. We've learned that Santoli deposited a large sum of money at his Monterey bank just recently. I don't think he came by that much cash honestly."

"Are you suggesting that he stole the money from Mr. Fields and then killed him to avoid being found out?"

"We're investigating that possibility. Normally, Santoli makes monthly deposits of five or ten dollars at a time. Yet this past Friday, he deposited the sum of five hundred dollars. A suspicious bank manager called me this morning. I sent Deputy Connery to Santoli's home to question him about the deposit, but he wasn't there. We thought he might have left town, but we were lucky to find him here. We came to question him."

"So you think that robbery was the motive for Mr. Fields' murder?"

Terry nodded. "I have no proof of his culpability yet, but La Playa attracts a well-to-do clientele. In his position, Santoli can identify guests with money. And as you saw, he tried to run. An innocent man doesn't take a woman hostage at knifepoint to help him make his escape. That is, unless he's done something criminal."

"There could be other reasons why he would avoid talking to you," Nora said. "Perhaps he is in the country illegally. Have you looked into his citizenship status?"

"That's all I'm going to tell you, Miss Finnegan. We have a suspect in custody. We'll prove whether or not he's guilty."

Nora put away her notepad. "I'm going to telephone you later, to see if you have any more information about Mr. Santoli. Also, I want to interview him while he's in jail."

Terry's face looked grim. "I'll say it again, little lady reporter. Don't interfere with official police business."

"I don't intend to, sir. I'm only seeking information."

Nora remained standing at the front door as Terry returned to the police wagon. She could see the concierge's frightened face peering out the back window. She waved at him and imagined how awful Santoli must feel at this moment. He was not only losing his freedom, but he could also lose his job. She hoped the sheriff would allow her to interview him. She wanted to know more about the mystery woman he had seen with Mr. Fields.

Then she remembered Paulette Villard. Heading back to the reception desk, she spotted Rudolfo, the bellman. "How is Miss Villard?" she asked.

He shrugged and pointed to the closed door in back of him. "She's resting in her *letto* — her bed."

"I want to leave a message for her." Tearing some paper out of her notebook, Nora wrote: Please call me at the *Pine Cone*. She folded the sheet and handed it to Rudolfo. Hopefully, Miss Villard would be able to describe Mr. Fields' female acquaintance if Nora couldn't get anything from Santoli.

As the bellman took the paper from her, Nora thought of the first paragraph for her article:

SHERIFF ARRESTS SUSPECT IN MURDER
Monterey County Sheriff Frank Terry arrested a prime suspect, Oresto Santoli, the concierge at Hotel La Playa, for the murder of Martin Fields, the eastern capitalist who planned to build a hotel on Carmel beach.

Nora was determined that her article would have only solid

information. She recalled Mr. Owens' own words, which were printed at the top of the front page of each issue of his weekly newspaper: 'If you read it in the *Carmel Pine Cone*, you may safely repeat it.'

She turned to leave, and saw someone waving at her from across the lobby.

CHAPTER TWELVE

As she left the dining room, Julia Morgan noticed Nora standing at the reception desk. The young woman looked upset. "Miss Finnegan," she called out, as she walked up to her. "Are you all right?" Seeing Nora's injured hands, the architect opened her arms and enveloped her new friend in a hug. "What happened to you?"

"I can't tell you how glad I am to see you," Nora said. "I was involved in a police incident a few minutes ago and was pushed into some bushes. I'm perfectly fine now."

"You don't look fine to me. Come up to my room. I have some medicine to stop those nasty-looking scratches from becoming infected."

Pleased with the offer of help, Nora said, "That's sweet of you. Besides, I want to tell you what went on."

The two women climbed the stairs. It was the first time Nora had visited the hotel's second floor. The hallway walls were covered with clear heart redwood. Thick carpeting cushioned her steps along the corridor. As she passed by the heavily varnished guest room doors, she noticed the small brass plaques at eye level. Each commemorated a particular naval achievement. Now she knew why visitors came to stay here. The ambiance evoked a quiet elegance.

Reaching the corner unit at the west end of the building, Julia stopped and unlocked the door to Room 2C. Nora read its plaque: "*The Beaver. First Steamship in Pacific Waters. Entered Carmel Bay in 1838.*"

Inside, the suite consisted of a tiny hallway, sitting area, and an adjoining bedroom and bath. Studying the nautical furnishings, Nora imagined that she would find the same quality décor if she were traveling first-class on an ocean-going vessel. Two portholes opened onto the rear garden and admitted sunlight. A tripod equipped with a brass telescope dominated the bay window facing the ocean. All the teakwood furniture had been upholstered in navy blue sailcloth. There was a roll-top desk on one wall. Above it hung an oil painting of the steamship "Beaver." Through an archway leading into the bedroom, Nora could see a four-poster bed covered with a counterpane dotted with small white anchors.

"Make yourself comfortable on the sofa," Julia said. Walking to the bedroom, she took a medicine bottle out of a suitcase. Returning to Nora, she took her hands and daubed the aromatic liquid on the abrasions. "I always carry 'wintergreen' with me in case I accidentally cut myself," she said. "It soothes and heals at the same time. I had it made up by a Chinese herbalist in San Francisco."

Sitting down next to Nora, Julia continued, "Let's talk while your hands dry. I heard the commotion from the dining room, but I had no idea what was going on."

Nora described how she had come to see the concierge and had been taken hostage by him when the sheriff tried to arrest him. "I don't think Mr. Santoli intended to harm me. He used me as a shield while he tried to get away from the police."

"Do they believe he's involved in Mr. Fields' murder?" Julia asked.

"The sheriff thinks that he robbed him of five hundred dollars. I wonder how Mrs. Fields is taking her husband's death."

"Fortunately, Miss Villard notified her by telegram before she arrived in Carmel. Her train was approaching San Francisco when the cable finally caught up with her. So she was prepared."

"When did you first meet the Fields?" Nora asked, probing for anything about the couple's relationship.

"It's funny, but prior to yesterday, I had only met him once. He came alone to my San Francisco office and asked me to prepare some sketches for a house he wanted to build here in Carmel. I told him that my custom was to visit a new client's residence first, to ascertain the family's living preferences. I wanted to meet his wife and discuss her likes and dislikes."

"Did he agree?"

"No, he objected, saying that he would make all the decisions for both of them. Reluctantly, I agreed. I was here last month to look at his proposed home site. During our meeting this time, I was to present him with my ideas."

"Have you talked with Mrs. Fields about her husband's plans?"

"We met this morning. As I expected, she was distressed by his death and said that she had no interest in building a house here. She offered to pay me for my efforts."

"What was your impression of her?"

"I would say that Sarah Fields is used to getting her way. She explained that she and Mr. Fields had separate interests, but that she was going to pursue his application to build a hotel on Carmel's beach. She wants it to be a memorial to her late husband."

"You know, Miss Morgan, I think I mentioned last night at supper that most of the residents don't want the shoreline touched. The beach is off limits to any buildings."

"I told Mrs. Fields what you said. She knows she will be facing serious organized opposition from the group being led by Carlotta Fleming."

Nora was quiet for a moment. Then she said, "When I spoke to the concierge before his arrest, he claimed to have seen Mr. Fields with a local woman. Did his wife give you any indication that she knew he was involved with someone here?"

"No, she didn't. We didn't talk about personal matters. My role was to develop architectural plans for a new residence that would replace an older one." Julia paused, and then said, "There was one thing that did seem odd, though."

"What was that?"

"I received a surprising telephone call from Mr. Fields earlier this week. He asked me to modify the house design to include a small studio and dark room. It was to be for 'a possible tenant,' as he put it."

Nora was puzzled. "What would prompt him to request those changes?"

"I couldn't speculate on his reasons."

Just then the ship's clock on the desk struck the hour.

"My goodness, is it eleven o'clock?" Nora said. "Before I leave you, Miss Morgan, may I ask one last question? You said that you visited Mr. Fields' proposed home site. Can you tell me the location of the old house that he was going to tear down?"

"I was told the place was called Bella Vista. It's above the beach at the north end of town."

Nora was surprised to learn that Fields intended to demolish Bella Vista. She was pleased that now the place wouldn't be destroyed. Looking at her hands, she said, "These scratches feel so much better. Thank you. I'm glad we talked, but I really should go, if I want to make my boss' afternoon deadline." Nora stood up and said goodbye.

As she walked along the hall corridor, she was startled to see a man waiting for her at the top of the landing. His breathing sounded labored, as if he had run up the stairs.

"*Signorina* Finnegan," he said. "You know me —Rudolfo Daneri. I come to ask you don't write nothing bad about my cousin, *per piacere*. He hurt nobody."

"I'm sorry, but I can't help you, Mr. Daneri. My obligation is to report his arrest."

"This thing shames our family. We come here to this country to work. We're not criminals."

"If your cousin is innocent, as you say, then the sheriff will let him go."

Rudolfo lowered his voice. "Maybe you change your mind if you look around *Signor* Fields' room. Maybe you find something to help Oresto. I have the key." Reaching into his uniform pocket, he brought out a heavy ring with multiple keys dangling from it.

Nora felt sure that Sheriff Terry would consider any such action as breaking and entering. Then again, Mr. Fields was dead. It would be impossible to get his permission.

"I guess that would be all right."

As she and La Playa's bellman headed down the corridor in the opposite direction from Miss Morgan's suite, Nora heard footsteps coming up the staircase. Giving Rudolfo a worried look, she asked, "Who's that?"

He grinned. "It's only my little sister, Angie. She does the dusting. No worry." He inserted a key into the lock of Room 2A.

As the door swung inward, Nora's eyes scanned the text on its brass plaque: *"Louis Gasquet, French Consul. Arrived in Monterey on the Primavera in March 1845."*

"I leave you alone," the bellman whispered, as he closed the door.

Nora stepped into the darkened guest room and noticed that its velvet curtains were drawn. The gloominess of the space put her on edge. She could see that the room was furnished with fine mahogany bedroom pieces, but everything reeked of cigar smoke. Pulling aside the drapes, she opened a window on the hotel's street side.

The room hadn't been aired or serviced for several days. Nora thought the sheriff must have insisted that things be left as they were. The double bed was unmade. A suitcase filled with men's socks and underwear lay open on the seat of a nearby chair. A pair of silk pajamas was draped over the back of it. She went to the desk and found a postcard propped up against the lamp. The building pictured on the front of the card looked familiar, but she couldn't quite place it.

Crossing the room, she opened the armoire, removed a dressing gown from an inside hook, and checked the pockets. Nothing. She returned the garment to its hook.

At the bottom of the closet lay some leather slippers next to a pile of dirty laundry. She pulled out a dress shirt, held it up to her nose, and detected the scent of a woman's perfume. Dropping it back on the pile, she removed a pair of tweed trousers from a hanger and went through the pockets. Finding nothing, she replaced them on the hanger. A handful of brown needles dropped out of the cuffs onto the carpet. *That isn't unusual. Fallen pine needles are everywhere one walks in Carmel.*

Returning to the desk, Nora opened a brown leather binder. Inside was a folded watercolor sketch labeled: *Carmel Beach Resort. Designed for M. Fields, 1921.* Closing the binder, she wondered if Mrs. Fields would really follow through on her husband's project.

She picked up the postcard and studied it again more closely. The photograph showed a hawk perched on a signpost at the entrance to a one-story building. Then she remembered the building. It was the old Pebble Beach Lodge, a place that had closed two years ago. She turned the postcard over, in hopes of discovering the photographer's name, but it wasn't there. Nora had to assume that the postcard was from the collection at Levy's general store. Fields probably had purchased it recently. She returned it to its place by the desk lamp.

Making sure that she left everything the way she had found it, she closed the window, pulled the drapes, and shut the door behind her.

Walking towards the stairway, she thought about the floral perfume on Fields' soiled shirt. Without a doubt, it had to belong to his unknown female companion. Mrs. Fields obviously had not taken up residence in her husband's bedroom, and the dress shirt had been worn before he was murdered last Friday evening.

Who was the mystery woman?

Nora had no idea.

CHAPTER THIRTEEN

Wood smoke from the neighboring stoves and fireplaces filled the night air. Nora stepped across some pine needles piled up at the edge of the road. "Thank heavens for this lantern," she said to Keith. "I can barely see where we're going." Lifting her lamp, she studied her friend's profile. In the watch cap and woolen scarf that his mother had knitted for his last birthday, Keith was unrecognizable.

Taking her elbow, he steered her around a fallen tree branch. "Oak Bower's just ahead," he said. "See those lights on your left?"

"I thought they were fireflies," she joked. "Seriously, what are they?"

"Tin lanterns — each one filled with a candle stub, just like yours."

"I didn't realize that so many people were coming to Carlotta's meeting. It shows the commitment of those opposing Mr. Fields' hotel."

"You should hear my library patrons' conversations. Everyone's against it. They wonder what's going to happen, with the developer dead."

"I have some news in that regard that I just learned today," Nora said.

Keith chuckled. "Being a reporter, you hear twice as many secrets as I do."

"Perhaps so, but you remember my telling you about meeting Julia Morgan? She said that Fields wanted to buy the Chatham mansion. He was planning to demolish Bella Vista and build a vacation home that Miss Morgan was in the process of designing."

"What a foolish man. Bella Vista's a magnificent place."

"She also told me that Fields' widow isn't the least bit interested in buying the mansion. But she's going ahead with her late husband's hotel."

Keith stopped walking and looked at Nora. "Really? That's all the more reason for us to organize against her!"

A few moments later, they had arrived at Oak Bower, the Fleming cottage. All its windows were aglow, but the front door remained closed.

Nora couldn't get over the size of the crowd. "By my count, there must be two dozen people here in Carlotta's front yard."

Keith could see that Nora was shivering. Removing his scarf, he put it around her neck. "Keep this on, at least until we get inside."

Hugging herself to stay warm, she said, "Thank you. As we've been standing here, I've been studying Miss Fleming's home. I can't figure out what that brownish material might be on the exterior walls. It looks like the bark of a redwood tree."

"That's exactly what it is. Carlotta told me that it never needs painting."

Nora was impressed. "It's very unusual. By the way, how did you two meet?"

"I introduced myself to her one afternoon at her art gallery. I took an immediate liking to her. As a fellow artist, she's given me good advice to improve my plein-air technique."

Nora was glad that his relationship with Carlotta was on solid ground, and not the type where a young man becomes infatuated with an attractive, older woman.

Suddenly a loud cheer went up as the cottage's door swung open. Clad in a Japanese kimono, Carlotta stepped out, waved, and placed a kerosene lantern on the porch railing to light her visitors' way. Blowing out their candles, the crowd, including Nora and Keith, filed up the front steps.

When she entered the main room, Nora stared up at the high-pitched ceiling with its exposed redwood beams. They made the space seem even larger than it was. Tall bookcases flanked Carlotta's Carmel stone fireplace. Her landscape paintings hung on every wall. Nora was reminded of the fairy tale cottages that had been illustrated in her childhood books.

Following Keith to the far side of the room, she squeezed past some of the other residents who were already seated. She had to step over a small dog that was stretched out on the room's braided rug. Except for the twitching of its tail, the animal remained motionless. Nora thought its long, silky ears were a bit too large for its body, but she liked its brown and white coat.

"What kind of dog is that?" she asked Keith as they sat down on a bench.

"I don't remember, but I've heard Carlotta boast that she's a pure-bred."

Just then, their hostess came up with a tray of pottery mugs filled with coffee. As Nora reached out to take one, the dog got to its feet. Pattering over to her, it sniffed at her boots and leaned into her legs. "She probably smells Dasher, the Owens' corgi," Nora said, while she petted the animal's head. "Look at her, Keith. Isn't she beautiful?"

"Maisie obviously wants to meet you, Miss Finnegan," Carlotta said, as she offered Nora the cream pitcher and sugar bowl.

"What kind of a dog is she, Miss Fleming? Her brown eyes are amazing."

"Maisie's a Cavalier King Charles spaniel, a gift from my late husband. And she's a far better companion than he ever was, if I may say so."

Taken aback by the woman's indelicate remark, Nora covered her embarrassment by asking, "Is she a good watchdog?"

"Yes, she is. Her best feature is her ability to hear the raccoons running on my roof before I do."

The dog wagged its tail and then plopped down next to Nora's feet.

When Carlotta had finished passing out the mugs, she set the tray on a table against the wall and walked over to stand in front of the fireplace. "We have a large crowd here tonight," she said. "I want to thank you for coming, and I'd like to introduce some people before we get started. Across the room from me is one of Carmel's most outspoken activists. Everyone say hello to Perry Newberry."

People applauded until Carlotta held up her hand. "Perry will be a major asset to our cause. I'm also delighted that so many of our literary friends have joined us. The MacGowan sisters are over there on the sofa. Fred Bechdolt and Jimmy Hopper are sitting in the row behind them. These authors support what we're doing. I want to thank the artists too, especially Mary De Neale Morgan and George and Catherine Seideneck, who have brought their out-of-town guest, Mayotta Brown. We're pleased to have you with us tonight. Lastly, I'd like to recognize the news reporter for the *Carmel Pine Cone*. Nora Finnegan is seated in the back, next to one of our promising plein- air painters, who also happens to be our librarian, Keith Preston."

The group responded by applauding once again.

Carlotta paused and looked around. "I don't see Rob Jacklin, but I know he wouldn't want us to wait. He'll be along soon."

Crossing the room to stand next to Newberry, Carlotta went on, "Perry, before you address us, I want to say that Mr. Fields' recent death isn't going to put an end to his proposed hotel. I know this, because I received a telephone call before the meeting from his widow, Mrs. Fields. She informed me in no uncertain terms that she will be pushing the Board of Trustees to approve a hotel on our beach. The project is very much alive."

The crowd groaned in unison.

Carlotta continued, "I told Mrs. Fields that we residents are united and will do everything possible to stop her hotel from being built. Now, Perry, why don't you share your views with us?"

Nora looked over at the square-jawed man who was standing on the opposite side of the room. He was dressed in workman's attire. Nudging Keith's arm, she whispered, "Has he just come from a job site?"

"He builds cottages all over Carmel, but don't let his appearance fool you, Nora. He's as good with words as he is with a hammer. What Perry says carries weight."

Nora took paper from her purse, readying herself to write down the builder's words as Newberry removed his khaki-colored cap and ran his fingers through his hair.

"I'll start out by describing some of the good things the Carmel Development Company has done for our community," Newberry began. "After providing us with a free library building, J. F. Devendorf and Frank Powers arranged the use of an entire block of land so that we could establish a performing arts theater under the pine trees. Since then, most of you have worked hard to develop our Forest Theater, where, over the years, plays have been presented for everyone's enjoyment. We're going to go to the Company again and tell them that we, the residents, want to purchase Carmel beach."

Cheers went up, especially from a small group sitting on the outside patio beyond the open French doors. They had arrived late and hadn't been introduced by Carlotta. Nora knew they were playwrights, like Newberry, and sympathetic to his cause.

After taking a sip of coffee, he said, "We've fought off greedy commercial interests for years, and our vigilance has paid off. We've preserved the forest we live in. Our coastline looks the same as it did when the first explorers set foot on our beach."

Those seated on the patio stamped their feet on the fieldstones in agreement.

One man sitting near Nora jumped up. "That's all to the good, Perry. All of us want to keep our beach intact, but how can struggling artists, writers, and residents outmatch rich developers with big money. You could tell last Friday night at the Trustees' meeting that Fields' message was resonating with our elected officials."

Several people booed at the mention of 'elected officials.' Nora was surprised by their reaction, since most had likely voted the current Trustees into office.

Newberry swayed from side to side, as he sensed the crowd's frustration. "You're correct, Fred, but we have to fight them. We'll go to Mr. Devendorf and ask him what the Company will take for the beach property. We might not be able to outbid the price that was offered by Fields and his investors, but we'll try to convince Devey to keep the beach in its natural state and in the public's hands. Now, how many of you are ready to help, besides my good friend, Fred Bechdolt?"

Dozens of hands went up. Voices shouted, "Aye! Aye!" The loudest came again from the writers seated on the patio. Apparently satisfied with the response, Carlotta and Perry raised their joined hands in the air. The crowd continued whooping and clapping. Nora watched in amazement as Carlotta attempted to curtsy in her tight-fitting kimono.

As the artist struggled to straighten up, Keith put his hand over his mouth and stifled a laugh.

Nora frowned.

"But she looks so funny," he mouthed.

A pounding noise interrupted the group's enthusiasm.

Recovering her balance, Carlotta walked over to the front door. Before she could get there, it swung wide open. With Maisie at her side and barking, Carlotta confronted the intruder.

Someone shouted, "Were you eavesdropping outside, Chatham? Get out!"

Davey Chatham scowled at the artist and used his cane to ward off the dog. "Why didn't you invite me here tonight, Carlotta? I want to know what you and your friends are saying. Why can't we all come together on this hotel?"

One artist closest to the door grabbed Davey's free arm and tried to shove him out to the porch. Keith rose and ran over to assist him. The duo wound up pushing Chatham up against the wall.

"Let go," he yelled, as he broke free. Picking up his cane and pointing it at Carlotta, he said, "I have a message for you silly Bohemians. The beach will be built on. You can't stop us. I'll tell Mrs. Fields what you're plotting!"

As Chatham was forced out the door, Carlotta slammed it shut and locked it.

Newberry waved his hands to restore order. "Carlotta and I, Rob Jacklin and Fred Bechdolt will go to talk to Mr. Devendorf tomorrow afternoon. We'll ask him to help us buy Carmel beach."

As the crowd got up to leave, Nora looked around and thought that everyone seemed pleased with the decision. Newberry's parting words would make a perfect introduction to her story on the residents' meeting.

"Just a minute," Carlotta called out. "I want to remind everyone that, at the next Trustees meeting, when they take up the hotel issue, Perry and I will be speaking for our side. I'll also contact Rob and let him know what was decided tonight. No doubt he will also want to address the Trustees. And before she leaves, I want to thank Miss Finnegan for joining us at this important meeting. We will need her help too."

The crowd cheered.

After saying goodbye to their hostess, Nora and Keith headed out to the street. "I wonder what happened to Rob Jacklin," she said. "He was very excited about saving the beach at the Trustees' meeting. I thought nothing would have kept him away tonight."

"He must have had a passionate date with Claudia Woodward," Keith teased.

"Don't be impertinent."

As the two friends made their way back to Pine Log, Nora felt energized. "I'm so glad that Carlotta invited me," she said. "With her leading us, I know we can save the beach. Hopefully, my article will generate more support for not building a hotel there. Of course, I'll be fair-minded in my writing."

Keith smiled as he pulled his watch cap down over his ears. "I never doubted you for a minute," he said.

Nora was lighting her tin lantern when she heard Keith begin to sing:

> "Some stick to biz, some flirt with Liz,
> Down on the sands of Coney.
> But we, by hell, stay in Carmel,
> And nail the abalone."

"Did you make that up?" she asked.

"I wish I had, but I'll have to credit Sinclair Lewis for that particular stanza of 'The Abalone Song.' And I know another one by Carmel's poet, George Sterling, that I think is even better."

"Let's hear it."

Taking his arm, Nora listened, as his baritone voice rang out:

> "Oh, some like ham and some like jam,
> And some like macaroni.
> But our tom-cat he lives on fat
> And juicy abalone."

CHAPTER FOURTEEN

Tuesday

W hen Nora arrived at the *Pine Cone* a few minutes after eight o'clock the next morning, she was surprised to see Billy, the black stallion belonging to Carmel's one-man police force, tethered out in front. Once inside, she was even more surprised to see Marshal Gus Englund. Leaning on the front counter, he was idly flipping through the pages of the newspaper's current issue.

Tall, with broad shoulders, and wearing a tan uniform and riding boots, the former army cavalry officer and Pinkerton detective seemed pleased to see her. He tapped his cap's visor and said, "Morning, Miss Finnegan. No rain for a change."

"This has been a wet November, hasn't it?" What Nora really thought was, had someone left the office door unlocked last night? Otherwise, why was the policeman here? Not only that, but where was Mrs. Owens this morning? Going to the front window, Nora turned over the "Closed" sign and headed to her desk. "Is there something I can help you with, Marshal?"

"Thanks, but I've already been waited on by your boss."

Just then, William Owens walked out of the back room.

"Hello, sir," Nora said. "I'm sorry I'm a few minutes late, but I'll have that story about last night's meeting at Carlotta Fleming's place finished within the next hour."

"That's fine, Honora. I'm not ready to set the type anyway."

"Excuse me, Miss Finnegan," Englund interjected. "One of Miss Fleming's elderly neighbors telephoned me at home last night. She was complaining about some loud noises next door. I sort of assumed it didn't amount to much. Was I right?"

"One could say it was an enthusiastic crowd, sir. You know how that happens in Carmel, when a controversial issue is hotly discussed. It all ended amicably."

"I'm glad to hear it from you."

Owens came over to stand next to the marshal. "As I was telling you, Gus, we're grateful. Mary Lee was upset at that dog when Dasher ran off last night after a raccoon. She was worried when he didn't come home. That's why I called you. We're relieved that you found him and brought him back."

Englund chuckled. "That raccoon turned into a cornered skunk and your dog got sprayed real good. He stunk to high heaven, but the smell will disappear once the missus gives him a tomato juice wash." Closing his incident book, he added, "Finding lost pets is a lot more fun for me than handing out speeding tickets and collecting unpaid taxes."

"All the same," Owens said, as he pulled out his wallet, "Mary Lee and I are indebted to you. If there's a charge for what you and your horse did, I'd like to pay it."

"No need for that. My $110 monthly salary covers my duties. But the next time you see us, offer an apple to my partner outside. He'd appreciate it." Heading to the front door, Englund reached to open it, when it unexpectedly swung inward.

The President of Carmel's Board of Trustees took off his bowler and stepped over the threshold. "Glad I found you, Gus," Ben Fox said. "Of course that horse is a dead giveaway. I need to talk to you about the Fleming group that's opposing the new hotel. They're planning to demonstrate during next week's Trustees' meeting when we will decide the project's fate. I'm getting concerned that things could get out of hand."

Englund snickered. "What would Carmel be without a contentious dispute, Ben? Don't worry. I'll handle it, but thanks for the advance notice. I'll be at the meeting."

Both men tipped their hats to Nora as they left the office together.

Facing Mr. Owens, Nora said, "I'm sorry I wasn't here on time, but I just couldn't get to sleep last night. Then I overslept. It won't happen again, sir."

Standing at the open door and gazing out at Ocean Avenue, Owens didn't answer. Then he closed it, walked around the counter and sat down in the chair next to Nora's desk. He said, "After hearing Ben, I started imagining the trouble that this hotel project might cause us, and how Gus is going to deal with it."

"Do you think the marshal might have a problem controlling things?"

He nodded. "Perhaps — if one considers what happened a few years ago. We were holding an important city election, and Ben told Gus to post the public notices all around town, to make sure that the residents were made aware of the measure they were about to vote on."

"What was the issue, sir?"

Owens stared up at the ceiling. "It was quite a news story, Honora. And it's about my favorite topic — paving Ocean Avenue."

Thankful that he didn't seem concerned about her tardiness, Nora relaxed. "I'd really like to hear what Gus Englund did that caused the city a problem."

"After the polls closed, I was at City Hall when they counted the votes. I was so excited when I learned that the majority of the residents had voted in favor of paving our main street. However, this wasn't the result that Perry Newberry was hoping for. A few days later, he and an attorney went to a judge in Monterey to contest the election results. I still can't believe what happened next. The judge nullified the vote."

The news surprised Nora. "It sounds like Mr. Newberry had justifiable grounds."

Owens shook his head. "None of us thought so at the time. Later we found out the reason for the judge's decision. It seems our marshal had ridden around town on Billy and had posted election notices on every block, just as Ben Fox had instructed him. The problem was, Gus never once got off his horse. The notices were up so high that people couldn't read them! It was an honest mistake on his part, but the judge declared the election invalid, due to improper posting."

Happy to learn that the primary road through the village's business district had been left unpaved, she said, "That's quite a story."

Owens nodded. "I'm sorry that the residents' will didn't prevail. The decision to overturn the vote was decided on a legal technicality and Gus' error."

The telephone rang at the receptionist's desk.

"Answer that, will you," Owens said, as he stood up. "I'd like you to fill in until Mrs. Owens gets in." Then he disappeared into the back room.

For the rest of the morning, Nora answered telephone queries and in between, worked on her assignments. At noon, she brought out a hard-boiled egg, some carrots, and an apple from home. As she was finishing her lunch, the telephone rang. She picked up the receiver and said, "*Carmel Pine Cone.* How may I help you?"

The voice on the other end of the line sounded excited. "Hello, Nora. This is Julia Morgan. Are you free to come over to Hotel La Playa right away? It's urgent."

"I'm afraid that I can't leave the office, Miss Morgan. I'm filling in for Mrs. Owens until she arrives. What is this about?"

"I don't think Mrs. Fields will wait much longer. She called my room half an hour ago and said that she had come upon a suspicious item belonging to her husband. When she told me what it was, I urged her not to contact the sheriff until she discussed it with you. It appears that you were right. Mr. Fields was seeing a local woman without his wife's knowledge. Sarah Fields would like you to identify her."

Nora looked up and saw Mrs. Owens and her dog coming through the front door. Putting her hand over the receiver, she whispered, "I have Julia Morgan on the line. She wants me to meet her at La Playa immediately."

"That's fine, dear. I'll handle things here."

Nora couldn't help but notice how terrible Dasher smelled. The dog avoided her and scurried under the desk.

Stepping out of the back room, Mr. Owens overheard the conversation. Covering his nose, he pointed at the door. "Go ahead, Honora, but don't do anything that could get you into trouble."

Nora's thoughts swirled as she hurried down Ocean Avenue on her way to La Playa. Had Mrs. Fields discovered a clue that would lead to her husband's killer?

CHAPTER FIFTEEN

La Playa was deserted, except for Miss Morgan, who was waiting for Nora in the alcove off the lobby. A large woman, presumably Sarah Fields, sat across from her. As she walked up to them, Nora remembered the disparaging remarks that the inn's manager, Paulette Villard, had made about Martin Fields' wife. She would attempt to assess the woman's character for herself. "Good afternoon, Miss Morgan," she said, "and how do you do, Mrs. Fields. I'm Nora Finnegan."

Up close, Nora noticed that the widow's hat brim concealed most of her auburn hair, but not her thinly penciled, shaved eyebrows. "I'm very sorry for your loss," she added. "It must be a difficult time for you, especially so far from home."

Dressed in black from head to toe, Sarah Fields looked up at Nora. "What I'm about to show you, Miss Finnegan, must be kept in confidence. I don't want a scandal."

Julia spoke up. "Mrs. Fields, as I told you on the telephone, Miss Finnegan knows many people in the community through her employment. Of course she will respect your wishes. Please take a seat, Nora."

Sarah Fields seemed dubious. "I need to be assured that she'll get to the bottom of this quickly. If not, I intend to call the sheriff."

"First I should know what you're asking of me," Nora said, as she sat down. She had expected the woman to show signs of bereavement. Instead, she was assertive.

Taking Nora's hand, the widow thrust a man's gold pocket watch into her palm. "What do you make of this?" she asked.

Nora looked at the timepiece and saw the initials, "M.F." engraved on its cover. "I assume this watch belonged to your late husband."

"Open it. It was my gift to Martin on our 25th wedding anniversary."

Pressing the stem winder, Nora popped open the cover. Tucked inside was a photograph. She recognized the young woman's face immediately.

Leaning forward, Sarah Fields lowered her voice. "Who is she, Miss Finnegan?"

Deflecting the question, Nora asked, "How did you come by this, Mrs. Fields?" She knew the watch hadn't been in the dead man's bedroom when she searched it.

"Why do you need to know that?"

"Let me explain, Nora," Julia interrupted. "A package was left by Mr. Fox, the fix-it shop owner, at the front desk for Mrs. Fields. It included a note with the watch that said her husband had dropped it off for cleaning and hadn't returned to pick it up. Fox delivered it here to the hotel. I suggested to Mrs. Fields that you might be able to identify the young woman in the picture."

The name was sitting on the tip of her tongue, but if Nora revealed it, Claudia Woodward's reputation would be sullied. She had to figure out what to say. She wouldn't tell a lie, not even a white one. *Not again.* She said, "I can help you, but I'll need to borrow this and check with my sources."

Sarah Fields shook her head. "That's unacceptable, young lady. I can't give you the picture. It could be evidence in my husband's murder case. I should call the sheriff."

"I don't think he will know her," Julia said. "He isn't from Carmel. Nora is. If she can't help you, and if you wish to pursue the matter, there will be time to contact the authorities."

The widow considered Julia's words. "All right then. I'll give her 24 hours."

Nora removed the photograph from the watch and slipped it into her purse. "I'll have an answer for you," she said, as she gave the watch back to the widow.

Leaving the hotel through the lobby, Nora headed uphill, turned onto San Carlos Street and entered the grounds of Sunset School. As she passed by the open doors to the classrooms, she heard the students' high-pitched voices reciting the day's lessons to their teachers. At the door marked "Grade 4," she peeked inside. Rob Jacklin stood at the blackboard, his back to the class.

Nora's eyes scanned the dozen desks. Sally, the Owens' daughter, was seated in the second row behind Freddie Woodward. The boy was engrossed in his book and hadn't looked up. Sally, however, saw her. She called out, "Hi, Miss Finnegan!"

Turning around, Jacklin put down his chalk and walked over to where Nora stood waiting. "Hello, Miss Finnegan," he said. Then, addressing the class, he added, "I want you to continue with your geography lesson on latitude and longitude. Answer the five questions I've put on the blackboard." Stepping out into the hall, he took Nora's arm and steered her away from the open door. "You look like something dreadful has happened."

Opening her purse, Nora took out the photograph and handed it to him. "I couldn't think of anyone else to confide in but you, Rob. You must have heard that Mr. Fields' widow is in town. I've just come from meeting her at La Playa. She asked me to identify Mrs. Woodward. She found this picture in her husband's pocket watch."

Holding it between his thumb and index finger, Rob said, "This looks bad for Claudia, I know, but I can assure you, there's a good explanation."

"There had better be, because when Mrs. Fields finds out who she is, she's going to notify Sheriff Terry. I intend to do the right thing, but I can't let Freddie get hurt."

"Freddie?"

"Yes, Freddie Woodward. He's caught up in this, and he's an innocent little boy."

"What about Claudia? Are you considering his mother?"

"Why should I? Why are you protecting her? Everyone expected to see you at Carlotta's last night. Someone said you were with Mrs. Woodward. Were you?"

"Hold on! That's a personal matter. Look, I do want to talk with you, Nora, but I can't leave my class. Come back after school lets out. Say, four o'clock?"

"I need answers now. Mrs. Woodward's photograph shows that she and Fields were intimately acquainted. How did they know one another?"

Rob handed the picture back to Nora. "She first met him when she was studying photography in New York. Last summer he came to one of her shows in San Francisco and bought a few of her pictures. They were friends. That's all."

Nora's mind flashed back to the postcard on the desk in Fields' bedroom. Had Mrs. Woodward taken that picture? "You still haven't explained why he would carry her likeness," she said. "Don't take me for a fool, Rob."

He sighed. "If you must know, they were involved, but only briefly, and after her husband died. Remember, Claudia has a son and that brings financial responsibilities. Fields offered to help them. But she became afraid of him, due to his temper. She broke off their affair and came to Carmel to get away from him. She swore to me that she didn't know the man was married."

"And you believed her?"

"Why don't you listen to me, instead of criticizing Claudia? Fields hired a private detective, who located her here. As soon as Fields showed up, he began hounding her again, threatening to harm Freddie if she didn't come back to him."

Nora was confused. "Where does Mrs. Woodward live? I'd better speak to her. Then I'll decide what to do."

Rob glared at her and started to enter his classroom.

She put out her hand to stop him. "I'm a reporter and I'm doing my job. She might know something that will help the sheriff solve Martin Fields' murder. If you don't cooperate with me, I'll telephone him and explain what I've learned."

"You're willful and stubborn. If you persist, you'll cause nothing but trouble."

"Let me be the judge of my actions. Shall I go back to the newspaper office and call the sheriff? Or will you tell me where I can find Mrs. Woodward?"

Angry now, Rob said, "I can see there's no reasoning with you. She lives in Hollyhock House on the north end of Monte Verde. You'll come to a wood sign on a picket fence. The Woodward cottage is a few doors down from your librarian friend's house." With that, Jacklin turned around and shut the classroom door behind him.

Nora left the school grounds. As she crossed to the other side of the street, she heard children shouting. Looking over her shoulder, she saw the 4th graders coming out to the playground. Rob was at the end of the line. Stopping to speak to another teacher, he pointed at his students. Then he ran over to a motorcar, jumped in the driver's seat, and drove off.

Nora continued walking. However, when she arrived

at the next corner, she suddenly realized that her emotions were clouding her judgment. What if Claudia Woodward had murdered Martin Fields? Would going alone to Hollyhock House to confront the woman put her in danger? She recalled Mr. Owens' admonishment: 'Don't do anything that could get you into trouble, Honora.'

Instead of continuing on to Hollyhock House, Nora headed straight for the Carmel library.

CHAPTER SIXTEEN

"All I'm asking is that you walk with me to the Woodward cottage," Nora said. She had just shown Keith Claudia's picture. "I'd rather not face Freddie's mother alone."

Keith frowned. "I don't like to meddle in other people's business and I don't like being away from the library for any length of time."

Nora looked around the empty reading room. "It should only take a few minutes, and there aren't any patrons clamoring for your attention."

Shaking his head as he picked up his jacket, Keith came around the reference desk. "You have an annoying way of wheedling things out of me."

"I do? Are you saying that because you saw me tacking a note on the front door saying that you'll return shortly?"

He groaned. "You're a manipulative woman. Now let's get this over with."

A few minutes later, they turned north onto Monte Verde Street. Midway down the block, Keith stopped in front of his house and said, "Did I ever tell you that my place was once rented by Robinson Jeffers and his wife, Una? It was when they first came to live here as young newlyweds."

Nora looked up at the small log cabin set high above the street. Though anxious to talk to Claudia Woodward, she felt obliged to humor Keith. "I hadn't known that."

"My landlord said that the Jeffers lived here before they bought a lot on Carmel Point, where they built Tor House a few years later."

"You being a librarian, you must enjoy living in a home that a famous poet once occupied," Nora suggested.

He nodded. "The cabin's builder used saddle notches to interlock those split cedar logs that you see. He chinked every one of them with cement."

"That's all well and good, but don't your neighbors take a dim view of your overgrown yard full of weeds?"

"Things look a mess, don't they? Between the library and the house painting jobs, I rarely have a free day for anything else."

"I don't blame you. Anyone would rather be outdoors, painting landscapes than doing gardening."

As she pulled him along, Nora had an idea. "Since you're doing me this favor, why don't I help you clean up the yard next weekend?"

"Now that's an offer I willingly accept."

Three doors down from Keith's cabin, they came to a wood sign on a picket fence. "That's Hollyhock House," he said, pointing to a rustic, one-story cottage set back from the road.

Someone had left the front gate open. As they approached it, Nora imagined what the place would look like when the hollyhocks were in bloom. Tall, slender columns of bell-shaped flowers waving in the breeze always reminded her of ballerinas. But her nostalgic vision faded when she noticed a police wagon and a black motorcar parked in the cottage's side yard. Two Monterey County lawmen were coming out the front door. Having met them at the Fields' crime scene, Nora recognized Deputies Connery and Jensen. Walking between them was Rob Jacklin.

"Why do they have Rob in handcuffs?" Keith asked, as he grabbed Nora's arm.

Nora called out, "Rob! What have you done?"

Jacklin looked up, and then quickly put his head down.

Jensen opened the police wagon's rear door. After making sure that Jacklin was secured, Connery walked over to Nora and Keith. "Hello again, Miss Finnegan," he said. "I need to speak with you alone."

Jensen shouted, "Time to go, Jimmy."

"Hold on," Connery said. "I want to ask her something."

"You never could avoid talking to an attractive lady," Jensen shouted. "Don't take long, Jimbo. Sheriff's waiting on us."

Connery ignored him, looked at Nora, and pointed to the

other side of the road.

"Will you excuse me?" Nora said to Keith. "I won't be long." She headed across the street to where Connery was waiting for her.

"Why were you coming to visit Mrs. Woodward?" Connery asked, as she came up.

"Is that important?"

"I'm the one asking the questions, Miss Finnegan, not you."

She disliked his officious attitude. "Why are you arresting Mr. Jacklin?"

"Why do you want to know?"

Nora bristled. "Can you at least tell me if Mrs. Woodward invited you here?"

"No, she didn't. The President of your Board of Trustees, Mr. Fox, telephoned Sheriff Terry and gave us information about Mrs. Woodward and Mr. Fields. Deputy Jensen and I came here to interview her."

Claudia's photograph was in the bottom of Nora's purse. *It must be that. The picture tied her to the dead man.* She said, "Has Mrs. Fields been told of her husband's involvement with Mrs. Woodward?"

"She knows all right. The sheriff just called her."

"Then why aren't you arresting Mrs. Woodward, instead of Rob Jacklin?"

"Mrs. Woodward refused to answer our questions. We were about to arrest her when Jacklin appeared. He voluntarily confessed to killing Fields and claimed she had nothing to do with it. He shot Fields with his service revolver, the one he brought back from the war."

The news shocked Nora. "What motive could Rob have for murdering Fields?"

"We're investigating that. I can't say anything more."

Nora recalled Rob's heated defense of Claudia at Sunset School, but she couldn't picture him as a killer. She said, "If you intend to prove that Mr. Jacklin murdered Fields, then you'd better have indisputable evidence. Everyone thinks of Rob as a dedicated teacher, a decorated veteran and an asset to our community. I plan to mention your name as the arresting officer when I write my article, Deputy."

Connery laughed. Glancing at the police wagon, he waved

his hand at the other deputy. "I have to go. Jensen and I are searching Jacklin's place next. Even if we don't find the murder weapon, we're taking him to jail, based on his confession."

Just then, Claudia walked out of her front door. She was in tears. Nora decided not to bother the poor woman with any questions.

Jensen yelled, "Come on, Jimmy. What's taking you so long?"

Connery placed his hand on Nora's forearm. "I suggest that you not interfere with police work."

Keith, who had been listening to their conversation, bolted forward. "The young lady doesn't want you touching her, Deputy. Don't think that she's impressed by your uniform and badge."

"Stop it, Keith! I can take care of myself," Nora said.

Connery signaled to the other deputy. "Go ahead, Al. I'll catch up with you at Jacklin's." Stepping around Keith, he smiled at Nora and headed to the second motorcar.

As they watched him drive off, Keith said, "Sorry about my outburst. You're like a little sister to me. I feel protective towards you."

"I'm glad you intervened. I find that deputy offensive."

"I do too, but I'd better get back to the library. From the sounds of it, you should have plenty of information for your news story without having to talk to Claudia."

As they made their way down the street, Keith asked, "Do you remember that Carlotta and some of our group are meeting this afternoon with Mr. Devendorf?"

Nora nodded. "They're making an offer to buy the beach property. In light of Rob's arrest, I wonder if their efforts will be weakened."

"All the more reason for you to come to the residents' meeting tomorrow night. You need to hear the results of their negotiations and report on it."

"What time does it start?" Nora asked.

"Eight o'clock. I'll stop by for you again."

"Promise me that you'll forego any more of your zany singing on the way home like the last time."

Keith grinned. "Marshal Englund won't arrest us for disturbing the peace with a verse or two of the Abalone Song."

A few minutes later, they spotted two patrons sitting on the library's front steps.

Keith said, "Thanks for your patience, gentlemen. The young lady had an emergency. You men understand that I had to help her out."

Waving goodbye, Nora headed back to the newspaper office. She was eager to tell Mr. Owens what had happened to Rob. At the same time, she felt sad about putting together a story naming him as the accused murderer. The only good thing that would come out of it was that Sheriff Terry would release an innocent man — Hotel La Playa's concierge. And since the sheriff had already told Mrs. Fields who Claudia Woodward was, Nora could return the woman's photograph without betraying Freddie's mother.

One thing bothered her, however. Would Carmel's elected officials vote to approve the beach hotel out of misplaced sympathy for Martin Fields' bereaved widow?

CHAPTER SEVENTEEN

Putting down the telephone receiver, Mary Lee Owens looked up as Nora hurried into the *Carmel Pine Cone*'s front office. "Hello, dear," the receptionist said. "You seem excited. Is anything wrong?"

"I need to speak to Mr. Owens. He'll want to know that Rob Jacklin has just been arrested for Martin Fields' murder."

"How can that be? I thought the concierge at Hotel La Playa was the culprit."

"I can't believe it myself, but apparently Rob confessed."

"I'm sure Mr. Owens will be very interested in your news, Nora, but he's meeting with Trustee Milliken."

"What brings the barber here this afternoon?"

"They're conferring in the back room, but the door isn't completely shut. Roland wants my husband to write a favorable editorial on the beach hotel before the Trustees take it up again next week."

"Did Mr. Owens agree?"

Mrs. Owens shook her head. "I overheard Roland say that he signed on to an option agreement to buy the property from the Carmel Development Company, but he didn't trust Mrs. Fields to keep him in the deal. That surprised me."

Nora frowned. "Do you mean to say that Mr. Milliken is an investor? Wouldn't that be a conflict of interest for him to vote on the hotel?"

"It seems so."

"I just met Mrs. Fields at La Playa," Nora said. "She's a

very forceful person. Did Mr. Milliken reveal any of the other hotel investors' names?"

"He mentioned that Doctor Taylor might want to invest also." Mrs. Owens looked at Nora. "I know that you're hoping the beach can be kept in its natural state. Sadly, it's beginning to look like that's impossible."

Not knowing how long Mr. Owens' meeting would take, Nora said, "I'd like to share the news about Rob with Carlotta Fleming before she and her group leave for Mr. Devendorf's office. Will you let Mr. Owens know that Rob has been arrested?"

"Of course. You go ahead. Who knows how long it will take that old wind bag in there to convince my husband to do something that he is already going to do."

"Thank you," Nora said, and headed out the *Pine Cone's* front door.

She had no difficulty finding Oak Bower. Taking the front steps two at a time, she pulled down on Carlotta's homemade door-knocker. The staccato motion of the red-headed woodpecker's beak as it hit the wall made cracking sounds. The noise set off a spate of barking by Maisie, Carlotta's spaniel. Stepping to the front window, Nora peered into the room. Everything looked as it had last night. The French doors leading out to Carlotta's rear patio were open. Nora could see the curtains flapping in the breeze. The woman must be in her garden, she thought. She went to the side gate and walked past some white camellia bushes, her mother's favorite flowers. The 'big white saucers with egg yolk centers,' as Alice Finnegan liked to call them, took up a large area next to Carlotta's fence.

"Hello," she called out. It's Nora Finnegan. I hope I'm not disturbing you."

Two stellar jays jabbered at her from the branches of the neighbor's oak tree. Nora's shouting had also attracted Maisie. The dog raced towards her from the rear yard. Kneeling down, she took hold of the spaniel's collar, hoping to calm her. That was when she noticed Maisie's coat. It was covered with brown splotches. The dog's fur felt stiff to her touch. "Did you hurt yourself, girl?" she said.

Suddenly the animal wriggled from her grip and ran back to the patio. Nora stood up and followed her. As she rounded the corner of the cottage, she stopped and stared.

Carlotta was lying on the flagstones, her left arm bent beneath her. Her eyes were wide open. Legs askew, her bathrobe and nightgown were torn and bloodstained. She was barefoot.

The outdoor table and chair where the artist had been having breakfast were overturned. Scattered in a wide arc were pieces of broken crockery and the remains of her meal. The only thing that seemed to be in place was Carlotta's long hair. At some point after rising, she had tied it back with a red ribbon.

Maisie nudged her nose into her mistress' shoulder.

Grabbing the dog by the scruff of the neck, Nora pulled her away, to keep the animal from disturbing the blood that had pooled under Carlotta's body. Then she sat down on a nearby stool. She warded off thoughts of running away. Instead, she focused her attention on what to do next.

Getting up, she carried Maisie inside through the open French doors. Stroking the dog's matted fur and soothing her with low, soft sounds, helped to clear Nora's mind. She recalled seeing a telephone in the front room when she had been here for the residents' meeting. Going over to it, she picked up the receiver and held it close to her mouth. "Operator, this is Nora Finnegan. I have an emergency. I'm at Oak Bower on Carmelo Avenue. Carlotta Fleming is dead. Tell Marshal Englund to hurry."

She replaced the receiver and sank down on the sofa to wait for Carmel's policeman. Lying on the braided rug next to her, Maisie had curled up into a ball.

CHAPTER EIGHTEEN

"You and the dog stay in my office, Miss Finnegan," Marshal Englund said. "I'm heading back to Oak Bower to keep an eye on the crime scene until Sheriff Terry and his deputies get there. One of us will return to take your statement." Sensing her anxiety, he added, "There's a tin of Mrs. Englund's gingersnaps in my desk drawer. Have some with your cup of tea. They always give me a boost." He grinned and left by the side door.

The panic Nora had initially experienced had subsided. When she and the marshal arrived at City Hall, she took Maisie into the bathroom and washed the dried blood off her fur. Now, sitting at Englund's desk with the dog stretched out at her feet, she began to wonder if she could remain dispassionate if she were assigned the Fleming murder story.

She had been grateful for the marshal's quick response to her call for help, not to mention being impressed by the way he took charge and secured the premises. However, she hadn't called Keith yet to let him know about Carlotta's death. The secretary at City Hall insisted that the telephone was not for Nora's personal use. Luckily, she had reached Mrs. Owens from Oak Bower before Marshal Englund showed up, and notified her and Mr. Owens of Carlotta's murder.

Nora stood up and stepped over Maisie to take a slow turn around the sparsely furnished office. The only decorative items she saw were a framed copy of the U. S. Constitution and a sepia-toned photograph of Gus and Billy that had been taken in their younger days. There were no pictures of Mrs. Englund, though

Nora had heard from Mrs. Owens that the marshal was happily married.

Apparently he wasn't much of a reader, but she did notice an issue of the *Farmer's Almanac* on the desk. She picked it up and glanced at a story making a point of planting seeds by the light of a full moon, in order to get the best results from a vegetable garden. Another article had the weather forecasts for the coming year. She wished it had been possible to forecast Carlotta's fate. Perhaps her death could have been prevented. Nora couldn't stop thinking about the woman and the way she had captured the crowd's affection at the last Trustees' meeting. Now she was lying lifeless on Oak Bower's patio.

Since her cottage was a few blocks away, Nora debated snatching up the spaniel and running home. She could telephone Keith from there. Then she considered Marshal Englund's order. She had promised to wait here.

A child's voice interrupted her thoughts. "Is that you, Miss Finnegan?"

Through the half open window, Nora spotted the dirt-streaked face of Freddie Woodward. He looked frightened. "Who allowed you to leave school, Freddie?" she asked.

"No one did," he mumbled. "Mr. Jacklin didn't come back to class after recess was over. I figured something bad happened, because the principal came in and took over for him. I slipped out when he wasn't looking. I'm worried cuz my mom isn't home. I don't know where she is. I came here to ask the marshal to help me find her."

Nora remembered watching the boy working on his geography lesson in Rob Jacklin's classroom. Since then, Freddie's teacher had been arrested and Sheriff Terry's deputies had subjected his mother to a series of unpleasant questions. Now she apparently had disappeared. Nora stepped out the office's side door to speak to the boy.

Their voices had awakened Maisie, who charged through the open door, wagging her tail and sniffing at Freddie's shoes. Nora couldn't grab her before she jumped up on him. Her exuberance gave him a scare, and he tried to push her away.

"You needn't be afraid," Nora said. "She's just trying to cheer you up." Bending down, she made the dog sit and encouraged the boy to pet her. Putting a hand on his arm, she said, "Don't worry. I'm sure everything will be fine. Your mother probably had something to attend to. She wasn't expecting you home from school yet, or I'm sure she would have been there."

He rubbed his eyes. "No, there's something wrong. Mama always works on her photography when I'm at school. This morning she was too upset to walk me there like she usually does. She called Mr. Jacklin and he drove me." He hesitated. "She's been sad for a lot of days."

"Has something bad happened to her lately?" Nora asked.

Twisting his cap, he blubbered, "I don't know why, but Mama's been acting funny. She asked Mr. Jacklin to take me on a hike with his Boys Club. I didn't want to leave her, but she made me go. She said it would be good for me." Looking up at Nora, he added, "And I did have fun after I met you."

An elderly man passed by them on the sidewalk. Nora thought he must have wondered why they were loitering outside the marshal's office. Smiling at her, he crossed the street and headed towards the library.

Not wanting to attract further attention, Nora motioned Freddie to follow her inside. She knew boys were usually hungry, so she took the cookie tin out of the desk drawer and popped it open. Freddie reached in, helped himself to a few gingersnaps, and flopped into the marshal's chair to eat them.

Nora said, "I want you to shut your eyes and think back to last Friday — the night before your mother wanted you to go on the hike. Do you remember anything unusual happening?"

Still munching a mouthful, Freddie leaned back and closed his eyes. "I'll try. After supper, Mama says it's time for my bath and then bed. I'm allowed to read for half an hour before going to sleep. I always do that." Opening his eyes, he squinted at Nora and gave her a little smile. "I remember a loud noise woke me up. I didn't know where it came from. I got up and went to Mama's room. She wasn't there. I looked all over for her, but she wasn't anywhere. She never leaves me alone at night. I got so scared that I telephoned Mr. Jacklin at his house. He came right over."

As she listened, Nora thought back to the Board of Trustees meeting last Friday evening. Rob was one of many who had spoken out against the beach hotel. The meeting had continued at City Hall until sometime after ten o'clock. She figured that Rob's late-night visit to the Woodward cottage at Freddie's request had occurred after that. She said, "It was thoughtful of your teacher to help. Did he stay with you until your mother came home?"

Shaking his head, Freddie said, "No, he said we should go out and look for her. It was raining hard. We got in his motorcar and went on a ride. I must have gotten tired, because I fell asleep in the front seat right away. When I woke up, I was still there, but Mama was in the back seat. She was crying. I didn't know what was wrong with her. Mr. Jacklin took us home and then he put me to bed. When I got up the next morning, Mama had stopped crying, but she was still acting kind of nervous."

Nora decided that the boy's need to find his mother was a sufficient reason to disobey Englund's order. Scratching a note and leaving it on the desk, she said, "Let's go. We'll take the cookie tin. I'm sure the marshal won't mind. I'm going to help you find your mother."

She grabbed a rope from a hook on the door, one that Englund probably used to tether his horse, and tied it around the spaniel's neck. "Dogs are good at finding lost people," she said. With Maisie straining on the end of her makeshift leash and Freddie in the lead, she closed the marshal's side door.

Inside his general store up the street from City Hall, Joe Levy was checking his camera stock in the shop's front display window. He was positive that he had the exact Kodak model that Deputy Connery wanted to buy. As he stretched his hand out to retrieve the camera, he happened to look up. Nora Finnegan, a boy, and a dog were walking along the sidewalk on the other side of Ocean Avenue.

Standing next to Levy and waiting for him to find the right camera, Deputy Sheriff Jimmy Connery also spotted the trio.

"There goes a smart young woman," Levy said. "She writes a good feature story for my money, and she's easy on the eyes too."

Jimmy Connery took in the reporter's fair skin and curly black hair slipping out from underneath her beret. She had the look of a proper Irish lassie, he thought. He said, "I like the way she controls that dog, while keeping a watchful eye on the child."

Connery wondered where Nora Finnegan was going. A short while ago, Gus Englund had told him that she was waiting in the marshal's office to give a statement about what she had seen at Carlotta Fleming's cottage. Connery had been planning to go there after making his purchase and bring Miss Finnegan to the sheriff to be interviewed. Paying for the camera with the department's cash, he exited the general store and walked across Ocean Avenue. He would see for himself where the pretty reporter and her two charges were headed.

CHAPTER NINETEEN

Spotting the plumes of smoke, Freddie took off running before Nora could stop him. By the time she and Maisie caught up with him in front of Hollyhock House, flames had burst through the roof. Its cedar shakes were curling up at the edges as the fire spread.

Freddie reacted to the sounds of shattering glass and falling timbers by covering his ears. Using his sleeve to wipe his eyes, he cried, "Mama's pictures are on fire! Is she burning up too?" He dropped to the ground and began sobbing. Maisie ran over and nuzzled against him.

Nora knelt down and tried to console him. "Don't cry. I'm sure your mother is safe. I only wish I could save her photographs, but it's much too dangerous to try."

Seeing them huddled in the middle of the road, a neighbor across the street opened his cottage's front door. "I called for help, young lady," he yelled to Nora. "They'll be here any minute now."

She could hear the piercing noise of the electric siren atop City Hall summoning Carmel's volunteer fire brigade.

"Bring the boy and his dog over here out of harm's way," the man shouted.

A garter snake seeking sanctuary from the fire's heat slithered across their path into some tall grass. Nora yanked on Maisie's leash as she barked and lunged at the elusive creature. With Freddie holding her hand, and the dog safely in tow, they began to climb the steps to the man's front porch.

"Miss Finnegan!" an out-of-breath Jimmy Connery yelled,

as he came running down Monte Verde Street towards them. "Are you and the boy all right?"

Nora turned when she heard his voice. She could see that Hollyhock House was engulfed. Her eyes filled with tears. "I was bringing Freddie home to his mother," she called out to Connery. Swiping tears away with her hand as the deputy came up the porch steps, she pointed at two large trees at the rear of the Woodward property. "I hope the recent rains protect those pines from going up too."

"The fire crew has auxiliary water sources if they need it to save them," Connery said. "The holding tank and the water trough on Ocean Avenue are available to the firemen. I'm afraid it's going to be too late for the house."

Just then, the village's 750-gallon Mack pumper and two other pieces of fire apparatus kicking up a dust cloud rolled down the street towards them. When they came to a stop, Nora recognized the local men of Carmel's Chemical and Hose Companies. Recently Mr. Owens had written an article about the village's volunteer fire crew and their equipment. Led by Chief Jess Nichols, the men included the Leidig brothers, Delos Curtis, and A. C. Stoney, among others. Immediately they jumped off the sides of the trucks and began laying and setting up hoses to the pumper. Some ran into the house to look for any trapped occupants.

A while later, Chief Nichols walked over to the neighbor's house and stopped at the bottom of the porch. Shaking Deputy Connery's hand, he said, "My men didn't find anyone inside the cottage."

"I'll let Sheriff Terry know the good news as soon as I report to him," Connery said. "Any idea what might have started the blaze?"

Nichols shook his head as he walked away. "Not yet, but you're free to look around, Jimmy. We're damping the embers."

Nora could see that all that remained of Hollyhock House were smoldering embers and the cottage's stone fireplace. To her relief, however, the trees at the back of the lot had been spared. Looking at the deputy, she said, "I'll make some arrangements for Freddie's care until his mother is found."

Connery nodded to her and went over to join the fire chief and his men.

Even though the Woodward's neighbor had told her that he

could watch the boy, Nora wanted to find a more permanent place for Freddie. At the moment, he was sitting on the porch swing with Maisie lying beside him. She said, "I'll keep looking for your mother, dear. I want you to stay here and keep a close eye on Maisie until I come back for the two of you. I promise it won't be long."

"All right, Miss Finnegan."

Bending over, she kissed his forehead and thanked the Woodwards' neighbor.

When Nora walked into the *Pine Cone's* reception area, Mrs. Owens looked up from her typing. "Thank heavens! I've been worried sick ever since you called me from Carlotta's house," she said. "Finding her body must have been horrible for you, Nora. I only wish that Mr. Owens were here, because he was also very concerned."

"I feel better now," Nora said, as she went around the front counter to her desk and sat down. "Where is Mr. Owens?"

"He just left to check on the fire. You must have heard the new siren. It was terribly loud. They probably heard it as far as Monterey."

Looking down at her trembling hands, Nora replied, "I was at the fire. I just came from there. It burned the Woodward cottage to the ground."

"Oh, my goodness!" Mrs. Owens stood up and came over to Nora. "You've had so much to deal with lately." Putting her arms around the younger woman, she went on, "What can I do to help make things better?"

Through her tears, Nora said, "Freddie's mother has gone missing. The boy needs her, Mrs. Owens. He's scared, and it's up to me to find a place for him to stay until Mrs. Woodward returns."

"Don't worry. I can fix Freddie's problem, dear. I want you to go home and leave everything to me."

After searching the village shops for Claudia Woodward and failing to find her, Nora picked up Freddie and brought him and the dog back to the newspaper office. On arriving home, she had wanted to speak to her friend, Keith. But when she telephoned the library, nobody answered. Finally, by three o'clock, she gave up trying. Now she was lying face down on her bed. However, each time she closed her eyes, her thoughts went back to seeing Carlotta's body, and picturing Hollyhock House on fire. She couldn't figure out where Mrs. Woodward had gone. For the first time since she had come to live in Carmel-By-The-Sea, she felt overwhelmed.

The telephone's ring jarred her. Forcing herself to get up, she went to the front room and picked up the receiver.

"Miss Finnegan, this is Deputy Connery. I'm sorry to bother you, but I pestered Mrs. Owens for your telephone number."

Hearing his voice, Nora perked up.

"I'm still in Carmel," he said. "We're finishing up our work at Carlotta Fleming's cottage."

His words sparked Nora to remember something. She should have been waiting in Marshal Englund's office. She said, "Were you supposed to take my statement?"

"Yes, but after seeing you at the fire and realizing how concerned you were over the little boy, I consulted with Sheriff Terry. He suggested that I call and see how you're coping. When a proper young lady like yourself comes across a dead body, you need some time to recover from the shock. However, the sheriff has to ask you some questions about what you observed when you found Miss Fleming. I'm calling to reschedule your interview for tomorrow, if that's convenient."

"That would help if we delayed it until then, Deputy. I'm finding it difficult to erase the memory of her murder. I should be feeling much better by tomorrow."

"I'm sure you will."

She was expecting him to set a time, but he said, "After you left the fire scene, I poked around and found something that might interest you. Someone left a pile of rags reeking of kerosene at the rear of the cottage. I'm going to look into that next. By the way, did you find a place for Mrs. Woodward's son?"

"He's with the family I work for. The Owens are going to care for him." As she spoke, Nora recalled her last vision of Freddie. He was sitting in the *Pine Cone's* back room, engrossed in a game of checkers with Mr. Owens, while Dasher and Maisie chased each other around the publisher's desk. She said, "They have a young daughter named Sally, who is the same age as Freddie."

"She'll be good company for him until his mother returns."

"By the way, Deputy, when you speak to Marshal Englund,

will you explain why I left his office this afternoon, and that Freddie is accounted for?"

"I will, as soon as we hang up, but I wanted to tell you that Hotel La Playa's concierge, Oresto Santoli, was released from jail, due to Rob Jacklin's confession. It turned out that the five hundred dollars Santoli deposited in his bank account wasn't stolen from Mr. Fields after all. It was a gift sent by wire from his uncle in New York."

"That's good news for Mr. Santoli," Nora said, and she meant it.

"Let's settle on the time for your interview tomorrow, shall we? Sheriff Terry plans to do it himself."

"How about eleven o'clock?" Nora suggested.

"That's fine. Why don't I come to the *Pine Cone* around ten and drive you to our office in Monterey."

"I'll meet you there."

Putting down the receiver, Nora headed back to bed. She pulled the blankets up to her shoulders and tried to sleep. Suddenly, she remembered another promise she hadn't kept. With all that had happened, she had forgotten to return Claudia Woodward's picture to Mrs. Fields. It was still at the bottom of her purse. Her talk with the deputy had revived her spirits. She climbed out of bed and began putting on her clothes.

As she dressed, she thought about Connery's mention of the possibility of arson at Hollyhock House. Could a jealous woman have caused the fire, she wondered? Julia Morgan had said that Sarah Fields was used to 'getting her own way.' *Revenge can be a powerful motive.* What if, after learning Claudia Woodward's identity from Sheriff Terry, Fields' widow had found someone to set fire to Hollyhock House, perhaps hoping to catch Claudia inside?

Closing her cottage's door behind her, Nora knew what she was going to do. She would go back to Hotel La Playa, and, under the guise of returning Claudia Woodward's photograph, she would ask Sarah Fields some questions. There was a chance that she might discover an arsonist in Carmel-By-The-Sea.

CHAPTER TWENTY

Walking along the beach, Nora watched the waves tumble ashore and disappear into the white sand. If only it were as simple to clear her mind of Carlotta's murder. Crossing the dunes, she came up the path leading to a row of potted palms at the hotel's front entrance. She could hear the voice of the Italian concierge, Oresto Santoli, who kept repeating the words, "*Si, Signora. Si, Signora.*"

Separating the palm fronds and peeking between them, Nora saw Sarah Fields sitting in the front seat of a black sedan parked at the entrance. The woman was ordering the concierge to do a variety of things for her.

"Deliver this note to Julia Morgan's room," the widow said. "Also, tell housekeeping that my dinner dress needs pressing and have the dining room hostess reserve a table for seven this evening." She pointed her finger at Santoli. "You'd better see to it that my sitting room's windows get washed. I'm paying good money and I shouldn't have to look out at the ocean through dirty glass."

A man who was standing next to the sedan stopped whistling the bars to a show tune and turned around. Nora was surprised to see that it was Davey Chatham!

Recalling his appearance the night before at Carlotta Fleming's cottage and earlier, at the Trustees' meeting, she was stunned by his transformation. Chatham's army coat had been replaced with a "jazz suit," its jacket tapered to fit tightly at the waist. His old denim pants were now cuffed wool trousers of the wide-legged type that Nora knew college men called "Oxford bags." She wouldn't put it past him to parade around Carmel in a raccoon-skin coat, in an attempt to impress people that he was a man of substance.

Adjusting the brim of his Windsor cap, Chatham took a few coins from a pocket and gave them to Santoli. Then he got into the sedan, started it, and drove away. Making a u-turn in the middle of the street, he and Mrs. Fields sped off in a northerly direction.

Since her purpose for getting out of bed was to return Claudia Woodward's photograph to the widow, Nora had to think of something. "Excuse me, Mr. Santoli," she said, as she stepped out from behind the palms. "Where is Davey Chatham going?"

"Why you wanna know, *signorina*?"

Nora could tell that he was paying more attention to her bosom than to her question as he pocketed his tip. "I have an item to return to Mrs. Fields," she said.

Santoli smiled. "I'm sorry for what I did to you last Sunday when the sheriff arrested me. He scared me. He was wrong."

Nora appreciated his apology for taking her hostage. "You scared me too."

"Listen, *signorina*, if you wait an hour, I take you myself to the Chatham house in my cousin's motorcar. It's a nice ride."

"That really won't be necessary, Mr. Santoli."

His face registered disappointment. "Too bad. I like to drive you through the iron gate by the cypress trees, like a *principessa*. You know, I used to work for *Signora* Chatham before she go to Europe. I can show you the whole place. My cousin Angie goes to clean and cook for the son. I no go there any more."

As he came closer, Nora feared that the short, swarthy man might grab her again.

However, he stopped short and tapped his forehead. "*Un momento*. I have an idea. If you no want to wait, I get Rudolfo to escort you to Bella Vista."

"Thank you, but now that I know Mrs. Fields' destination, I'm capable of going alone." Spotting her means of transportation, Nora hurried over to a bicycle that had been propped up against La Playa's fence. As she got on it, she said, "Please let Miss Villard know that I'll return this to her shortly."

Santoli laughed. "I tell my cousin, Angie. It's her *bicicletta*. *Arrevederci!*"

Settling onto the hard seat, Nora headed in the direction

that the sedan had taken down Camino Real. The wind picked up as she approached the village's business district. Fortunately, there were only gentle rises in the roadway, so that she could move along at a good pace. A flared skirt and a snug sweater under her jacket made a comfortable cycling outfit. Before long, she arrived at the street's intersection with Ocean Avenue where it dead ended at the beach. 17-Mile Drive lay straight ahead.

The clouds had disappeared and the sun was beginning to set over the water. Nora watched the seagulls rising and falling, gliding with the air currents, as they took advantage of the wind's changing direction. She slowed the bicycle as she came to a sharp curve in the Drive. Beyond the next bend, she spotted the stand of cypress trees that Santoli had mentioned. A pair of stone columns bracketed an open iron gate. Entering the driveway, she pedaled past a reflecting pool in the courtyard. Davey Chatham's black motorcar was parked under the *porte-cochere*.

As she parked the bicycle, she admired Bella Vista and its unobstructed ocean view. It was much larger than the wood-framed Craftsman cottages she was used to seeing throughout Carmel village. She knocked on the front door, unsure of what she would say to Mrs. Fields.

When Davey Chatham opened it, she could tell by the look on his face that he wasn't pleased to see her. Brushing his sandy-colored hair out of his eyes, he said, "No matter what you're selling, miss, I'm not buying."

"Mr. Chatham, I'm Nora Finnegan. I'd like to speak to Mrs. Fields. I have something that belongs to her."

"She isn't here." He put out his open hand. "I'll give what you have for the lady to her the next time I see her, but I want you to leave now."

Nora didn't back down. "That's your motorcar," she said, pointing at the black sedan. "I followed you here from La Playa, and Mrs. Fields was in the front seat when you left the hotel."

Chatham shrugged. "All right, she is here. But she doesn't care to be disturbed."

Nora thought the man seemed unsteady. Had he been drinking? She heard the rustling sound of a dress swishing along the parquet floor behind him. A woman's hand reached out and grasped his shoulder, pulling him back.

"I'll deal with her," Sarah Fields said. "What do you want, Miss Finnegan?"

"I respect your privacy, Mrs. Fields," Nora said, "but before you tell me to go, I want to return this to you." Opening her purse, she took out the photograph.

Like a rattlesnake striking its prey, the widow's left hand snatched it from her fingers. "You've no right to follow me here! I shouldn't have given this to you in the first place. You were no help, and you've deliberately held onto a piece of evidence."

Nora's temper got the best of her. "Didn't Sheriff Terry tell you that it's Mrs. Woodward's image on this photograph? And didn't that cause you to hire someone to burn down the woman's home?"

Sarah Fields' back stiffened. "That's ridiculous talk. I couldn't care less about that hussy, and I don't know anything about a fire. My only interest here is carrying out my late husband's dream. That's all."

"I haven't come here to talk to you about the beach hotel, Mrs. Fields. I'm very concerned about a boy's missing mother and I'm angry that the Woodward cottage was destroyed this afternoon. I want an honest answer. Did you have anything to do with it?"

Suddenly the widow leaned forward and shoved Nora backwards. "If you don't leave the premises, I'll have Mr. Chatham telephone Sheriff Terry and say that you're harassing me. Now get off this property!" With that, she slammed the front door.

Nora caught herself in time to keep from falling. Crossing the courtyard, she stopped when she came to Bella Vista's reflecting pool. Sitting down on the edge of its low wall, she tried to calm herself. Had she done the right thing by confronting Sarah Fields? Unfortunately, the woman hadn't revealed anything incriminating. Getting up, She retrieved the bicycle, got on, and headed down the driveway.

By five o'clock, Deputy Connery had returned to Monterey from Carmel and had shown the sheriff the remnants of the kerosene-smelling rags he had discovered at the fire.

It had been a difficult day for him. Feeling tired, he left the jail and took the path to the lot where he had parked his Model T. Getting in, he started it up. When he reached the road leading out of town, he pushed the accelerator to the floor board. The motorcar responded and picked up speed.

By the time he came to Lighthouse Avenue, Pacific Grove's main thoroughfare, he was cruising at twenty five miles an hour. Connery liked working in the same area where he and his brothers had gone to the public schools and his family attended Sunday mass at the parish church. He knew everybody in Pacific Grove and they all knew him.

Turning right onto Fountain Avenue, he was sure that she'd be waiting for him. He wondered what she would think of the pretty Carmel reporter that he had taken a liking to. Sometimes, when he needed to mull over problems, he headed for Lovers Point, the cove at the edge of town, where he could stare out at Monterey Bay, listen to the surf and the cries of the resident sea lions. The place helped him think more clearly. But it was late tonight, and their supper would be waiting.

Parking in front of his cottage, he saw her standing on the porch. She waved and ran towards him. He stepped out of the Model T and hurried up the path.

CHAPTER TWENTY ONE

"This may sound harsh, Honora, but a single girl like you needs to be extra careful about where she goes alone and what she says."

Nora and Mr. Owens were seated across from one another on the sofa in the publisher's living room. He looked more serious than she had ever seen him since she had started working at the *Carmel Pine Cone*.

"You went to the Chatham home uninvited," he continued. "You accused an influential woman of the crime of arson. What were you thinking? Your actions showed poor judgment. How would your father react to your reckless behavior?"

Nora hoped that he wouldn't tell him, but she couldn't worry about that now. She said, "From the moment I arrived at Bella Vista, Mrs. Fields behaved rudely towards me. I was merely trying to find out what the woman knew about the Woodwards' fire. I have to be able to question people's motives, don't I? How else can I sharpen my interviewing skills and become a better reporter?"

"I'm glad that you take your job seriously, but your actions could have opened up the newspaper to an expensive libel suit from a high-powered attorney that Mrs. Fields would hire. Did you stop to consider that?"

Nora had never imagined that a lawsuit might be the outcome of her talk with Mrs. Fields. She chose not to respond to his question.

He surprised her by smiling.

"On the other hand, you used good judgment by alerting the

principal at Sunset School that Mrs. Owens and I will be caring for Freddie until his mother returns."

"It occurred to me that if Claudia were going to tell anyone in Carmel about her whereabouts, it probably would be the head of Freddie's school," Nora said.

"And that's exactly what she did. The principal told me that Mrs. Woodward telephoned him from Monterey and that she sounded pretty frantic."

"What was she doing there?"

Owens scratched his head and leaned back on the sofa. "Apparently she went there to see Rob Jacklin at the jail. She told the school principal that she had lost track of time and missed the last autobus. She's been forced to stay there at a hotel overnight. The principal assured her that Freddie was safe here with us. She told him she would call us this evening and will return on the first autobus back to Carmel tomorrow morning."

"Do you know if the principal told her that her cottage burned to the ground after she left town yesterday?"

Owens shook his head. "I don't think so. He didn't seem to be aware of it, but I'll tell her when she calls tonight."

Nora sat up straight. "There's something else I must tell you, even though you may not want to hear it. I've discovered that Mrs. Fields has an excellent motive for setting fire to Claudia Woodward's home."

"Why are you continuing to pursue this? I don't think it's healthy for you."

Nora felt she had to defend herself. "The woman's terribly jealous of Freddie's mother, sir. Soon after she arrived in Carmel, Mrs. Fields confided in me that she found Claudia's photograph hidden in her husband's pocket watch."

The news took Owens aback. "I wasn't aware of it, but it doesn't prove that Sarah Fields arranged for someone to set fire to her cottage." He hesitated, and then continued, "Do you know what really bothers me? It's how Mrs. Woodward has behaved. Running off to Monterey to be with Rob was foolish of her. To my mind, she's neglecting her motherly duties."

Still thinking about the fire, Nora shook her head. "People might think of Mrs. Fields as a proper lady, but I beg to differ. She's ill-tempered and mean. Even Julia Morgan described her as a determined woman who usually gets her way."

"I want you to stop all this speculation, Honora. Do you

understand?"

Nora looked down at her hands. "I'm only trying to develop my intuitive skills. I have to, if I want to become a successful journalist like you and Father."

The sound of a burning log dropping to the bottom of the Owens' fireplace ended their argument.

It seemed Owens had heard enough about Sarah Fields. Leaning down, he patted Maisie's head. "Carlotta's dog is going to need a new home soon. You know that, don't you? Mrs. Owens and I can only handle one dog at a time."

"I realize that," Nora said. "You two have been wonderful to take Maisie in. But I believe I may have a solution to that problem."

"It doesn't surprise me. You're an enterprising reporter, despite your inexperience. Oh, before I forget, there's something I want you to look into. Marshal Englund needs our help with finding the culprit who burglarized Joe Levy's storage shed sometime today. I realize that the assignment doesn't sound as intriguing to you as murder or arson do."

Nora giggled. "Are you trying to turn me into a crime reporter, Mr. Owens?"

He laughed. "I should say not. Due to all the excitement over Carlotta's murder and then the Woodward fire, Englund hasn't had time to investigate the burglary. I said you would talk to Joe Levy in the morning and find out what was stolen. Then I want you to write up the details. The marshal figures that somebody may have noticed something and will come forward after reading about it in the paper."

Nora remembered her ten o'clock appointment with Deputy Connery. "I'll meet with Mr. Levy first thing before going to Monterey for my interview with Sheriff Terry," she said.

Owens raised his hand. "There's one more thing. Will you go in and say hello to Freddie before you leave for home? Mrs. Owens and I are doing our best to make him feel comfortable, but I think he would appreciate seeing you."

"I was just about to suggest it," Nora said, as she stood up and moved towards the hallway.

As she passed Sally's bedroom, she heard loud noises. Looking in, she saw the little girl. Her blonde pigtails flying, she was jumping up and down on the bed. Dasher, the Owens' corgi, was alongside her, doing the same. Nora waved at Sally and continued down the hallway to the rear bedroom. She knocked on the one with the partially opened door. "May I come in?"

Freddie lay on top of the bed, fully dressed. He was facing the wall, but he turned over when he heard Nora's voice. She spotted traces of moisture on his pale cheeks.

"Hello," he said, as he wiped his eyes on the sleeve of his sweater.

"I came to see how you are and if everything is all right."

"I'm O.K, Nora, but I'm feeling sad. Mama always tucks me in at night, and she won't be doing it this time. And another thing I'm worried about is where we're going to live when she comes to get me after school tomorrow."

Nora felt sorry that the boy had to feel anxious about such things at his young age. Sitting down on the edge of the bed, she stroked his cheek. "Your mother will work things out and you'll be safe here with Sally's family. They'll take good care of you."

"I know that, but is Mama in trouble? Is that why she had to leave today and go to Monterey?"

"No, of course she isn't. You remember Sheriff Terry, the lawman who was with us that day in the canyon? Well, he's working hard to straighten things out with your mother. They had some things to talk about at his office today. It got late and she couldn't get a ride home."

Freddie sniffled. "I miss her a lot."

Somehow Nora had to find a way to cheer him up. She remembered his interest in birds. "Before I go, would you like me to tell you a story?"

His face brightened. "Yes! You're a great storyteller."

Nora took his small hand in hers. "Once upon a time there lived a spotted owl named Oscar whose territory covered the entire one square mile that makes up Carmel. Oscar's nest was hidden deep in Pescadero Forest. With his best friend, Henry Hawk, he would fly to Carmel each night from the big pine tree where the two birds had made their nests, but on different branches, of course. Every evening the birds raced each other to see who could get to the village first."

"Mama takes pictures of hawks," Freddie interrupted, "but I don't remember any of an owl."

Nora went on, "One cold, moonlit evening, the two friends flew into Carmel and happened upon a saucy black crow named Calvin. He was hopping from tree to tree in back of the Carmel library and he was making lots of noise. What in the world was Calvin looking for, Oscar and Henry wondered? So they asked him. Do you know what Calvin said?"

Freddie shook his head.

"Calvin Crow said, 'I'm looking for bookworms!'"

Freddie laughed out loud.

Nora continued to spin her woodland tale about the goings-on of owls, hawks and crows cavorting in and around Carmel-By-The-Sea. When she finished, she bent down and kissed Freddie's cheek. She told herself that nothing would stop her from finding the perpetrator who had destroyed his home.

Ten minutes later, she walked back to the front room, intending to say goodbye to Mr. Owens. Only the embers of the fire glowed in the fireplace. Owens' head lolled back and rested on the sofa. His eyes were closed, and she could hear him snoring softly. A book lay open on his lap.

Just then, Mrs. Owens came out of the kitchen. "Supper's on the table, William."

Her voice awakened her husband. He stood up and stretched. Seeing Nora, he said, "Why don't you join us?"

"Thank you, but not tonight. I have some unfinished work to do at home."

Walking her to the front door, he helped her into her jacket.

Although she had been fixing supper in the kitchen, Mrs. Owens had overheard the discussion over Mrs. Fields. She said, "William and I are so fond of you, Nora. You're brave, smart, and good with children. Please be extra careful and don't attempt anything that could prove dangerous to you." She gave Nora a hug.

"Neither of you need worry about me," Nora said, as she opened the front door.

Mr. Owens' reaction was unexpected. Reaching over, he also hugged her and said, "If anything was to happen to you, I could never forgive myself, or for that matter, face your parents again."

Stepping off the porch, Nora turned around and waved at the couple. They were standing arm in arm in the doorway. She had been touched by their concern.

Angie Daneri's *bicicletta* waited for her at the base of one of the Owens' oak trees. It was too dark, even with the moon overhead, for Nora to ride it to Hotel La Playa. Most likely, Angie didn't need it tonight. Grabbing the handlebars, Nora walked the bicycle back to Pine Log.

On her way home, she listened to the sounds of the forest creatures moving about in the darkness, rustling in the bushes, and creeping around tree trunks. She would have another animal story to tell Freddie the next time they were together.

When she reached her cottage, she thought about Deputy Connery. He had been kind to her today. Perhaps she had misjudged him. She wished she could think of something that would help him with the investigation into Carlotta Fleming's murder.

Walking across the darkened front room, she switched on the light in the kitchen. It was time to fix supper. Leftovers again.

CHAPTER TWENTY TWO

Wednesday

With no answer to her repeated knocks, Nora assumed that Joe Levy must have overslept. Irked at having to wait in the cold outside the general store, she debated going back to the newspaper office and returning in half an hour. Looking towards Ocean Avenue, her attention was drawn to a middle-aged man in work clothes who was coming across the street. Nora recognized him immediately. "Good morning, Mr. Newberry," she said. "Cold weather for November, isn't it?"

"I couldn't agree more," Perry Newberry replied. "Do I know you, young lady?"

Although she had made a point of introducing herself to him at Carlotta's cottage, it didn't surprise her that he didn't remember their meeting. "I'm Nora Finnegan. I work for Mr. Owens as a reporter at the *Carmel Pine Cone*. May I ask you something, sir — that is, if you have an extra moment?"

Newberry's lop-sided grin seemed friendly. "That depends on the question, Miss Finnegan."

"I wondered if you have any thoughts about Carlotta Fleming's murder."

His smile faded. "I can't imagine why anyone would want to kill her. Her death has saddened me to the point that I almost feel numb."

"I assume tonight's residents' meeting will be postponed, then."

He nodded. "Everyone's shocked by the news. I'm going to

suggest that we regroup and arrange another time to speak with Mr. Devendorf. We'll try to delay his decision regarding the sale of the beach."

"Do you think Miss Fleming's death could be related to the fact that she was leading the fight against the proposed hotel?"

"I really don't know. If that were true, then I'd better watch out too." Tipping his cap to Nora, Newberry walked away.

The snap of a window shade rolling up caused her to turn around. Joe Levy waved through the store's plate glass window. A moment later, he opened his front door and said, "Morning, Miss Finnegan."

As Nora came inside, he reached up to pull on the string that turned on the ceiling light. "Sorry I was late," he said, "but Mrs. Levy is down sick with a fever."

"I'm sorry," Nora said. "If things are too hectic for you this morning, I can come back this afternoon. Mr. Owens has asked me to write a story about your burglary."

Levy went around the counter. "I have some time now if you'll join me in the stock room. I usually hear the bell when a customer walks in."

Nora followed him to the rear of the store, and as soon as they entered the room, she could see dozens of wood cartons that were stacked up on all sides.

"I've got to unpack all these boxes," the shopkeeper said. "Gumps delivered them yesterday, just in time for my Christmas trade. Each one contains some expensive items. I'm glad the robber burgled my shed out back and not in here."

His mention of San Francisco's premier store caught Nora's attention. "When I lived at home, my mother and I frequently shopped at Gumps," she said. "We always found such interesting gift items from around the world."

"I agree. On my last trip I chose some very special pieces for the holiday sale." Leading her to a table in the center of the windowless space, he said, "I'd like to show you a few things."

Nora thought Levy might be hinting that she ought to write an article on his Christmas gifts for a future issue of the *Pine Cone*. She knew the idea would appeal to Mr. Owens. Curious now, she waited as Mr. Levy opened a straw-filled carton and removed a foot-high alabaster statue.

"Here's a perfect little goddess that some European sculptor has carved," he said, as he handed it to her.

Nora took the statue and studied the figurine. Head tilted and arms raised, the young woman appeared to be fixing her long flowing hair. Suddenly Nora's cheeks became warm. The goddess' filmy dress had left her breasts exposed.

"The Greeks called her Aphrodite," Levy said. "She's the goddess of love."

The statue was exquisite, Nora thought. As she returned it to him, she pictured Aphrodite occupying a place of prominence on her fireplace mantel. "She's lovely, Mr. Levy, and quite an exceptional work of art. She'll make a perfect Christmas gift for a lucky someone."

The shopkeeper smiled as he put the statue on the counter. Taking another object out of a small box, he said, "Here's something unusual. Let's see how it looks on your wrist." He held out a silver bracelet.

Nora was taken aback when she saw that it was in the shape of a coiled snake. Its pointed head and bulging eyes repelled her. "I'd rather not try it on, sir," she said. "I have an aversion to reptiles of any sort."

"It takes a bit of daring to wear it, I'll grant you that," Levy said, as he returned it to its box. "Let's see now. What else can I show you?" Opening another carton, he went through some bead bracelets and necklaces. "I bought these because the salesman told me they're modeled on 5th century designs." Handing Nora a bracelet embedded with ruby-colored stones, he asked, "What's your opinion? Will they sell?"

This time, Nora tried it on. "I definitely think they will sell quickly." As she gave the bracelet back to the shopkeeper, she heard the sound of a tinkling bell.

A man's voice called out, "Hello, Mr. Levy."

"We're in the stock room," Levy shouted.

When Deputy Connery walked in, Nora was surprised. "Surely it can't be ten o'clock?" she said.

"I'm early, Miss Finnegan. I stopped by the newspaper office and Mrs. Owens said you had an appointment with Mr. Levy. It looks like I'm interrupting."

"We're evaluating Christmas gifts for the ladies," Levy replied, as he walked over to a supply closet, took out his white coat and put it on. Tucking a pencil behind his ear, he said, "Hope there was nothing wrong with that camera I sold you yesterday, Deputy."

"No, sir. It works just fine."

"Thank you for showing me your new stock, sir," Nora said. "What if I were to put together a feature article about these unusual pieces to come out in time for our Christmas issue?"

Levy chuckled. "I was thinking along the same lines."

Nora thought she had better draw his attention back to the reason why she was here. "But today, Mr. Owens would like me to write about your recent burglary. Exactly what did the thief take?"

"That's the funny thing," Levy replied, as he went ahead of her and Connery to the front of the store, pulling off draped sheets on his display counters along the way. "It wasn't much, but I reported it to the marshal just the same."

Nora was puzzled. "But it was a break-in and burglary, wasn't it?"

Levy stopped walking and turned around. "Well, a lock got broken, but what the robber took didn't amount to anything."

"What did he steal?" Deputy Connery asked.

"Why anybody would break in and run off with what they did is a mystery to me," Levy said. "I've got plenty of nice items here in the store that he could have taken."

"Like those cameras over there," Connery said, pointing at the front window.

"Yes, but that's not what he took. Out back's an old shed where I store fertilizers and flammable liquids. On my coffee break yesterday, I noticed that the door lock was missing. I went inside the shed and realized that someone had uncapped my kerosene container and siphoned off a couple of pints. That's the sum of it. The burglar got away with some kerosene."

Nora and Connery exchanged glances.

"Why don't we go out and take a look, sir," the deputy said.

Leading them to an outbuilding behind his store, Levy entered first and pointed to a five-gallon drum. Nora saw a piece of black hose and a discarded lock on the ground.

"Was it just like this when you saw this yesterday?" Connery asked.

Levy nodded. "I had to recap the kerosene, but everything else is the same way I found it. I wanted Marshal Englund to see this before I picked things up."

"That was a good decision," Connery said. "I'll have Deputy Jensen come here to check for fingerprints. It's the latest technique we use to catch criminals."

"Seems like an awful lot of fuss for what was stolen."

"It may help us solve an arson case," the deputy said.

Nora took her notepad out of her purse and began writing. "I'm afraid finding your intruder is more important than you might realize, Mr. Levy."

"Well that was a suspicious burglary," Deputy Connery said to Nora, as they left Levy's store and headed across Ocean Avenue.

"What do you make of it?" she asked.

"Under ordinary circumstances, what was taken wouldn't be a serious matter. But if the burglar used Levy's stolen kerosene to commit arson, well, that's different, and it needs following up."

"Could this be someone getting back at Mrs. Woodward?"

"We'll look into it. I'll let Marshal Englund know what we find. If the burglar didn't wear gloves, there will be fingerprints."

Connery had parked his motorcar near the library. Rounding the corner, Nora saw Keith coming out the door.

"Miss Finnegan," he shouted. "I need to speak with you."

Recalling that he had confronted Connery at the Woodward home yesterday, she noticed that the librarian didn't make eye contact with the sheriff's deputy. "I'll be back in just a minute," she said.

"We need to get going, Miss Finnegan," Connery complained.

When she returned, he couldn't hold back. "What's the connection between you two? Are you a couple?"

"It's no business of yours, but Mr. Preston invited me to play fan-tan with him this evening." She was fibbing, but she wouldn't give the deputy the satisfaction of knowing what her friend had actually told her. In light of Carlotta's death, Keith had explained that the residents' meeting would be rescheduled to a night to be determined. He promised to keep her informed.

Connery looked irritated. "Fan-tan's not a game for ladies to even watch. Players make bets on how many coins are in a hidden pile after a *croupier* removes all but a few of them. It's a silly pastime. I play poker, which is a thinking man's game that requires cleverness in assessing one's fellow players."

Nora had no idea whether his description of fan-tan was

accurate, since she had never played the game, and she knew nothing about poker. "You strike me as a man who enjoys taking a chance," she said. "Wouldn't poker be called gambling? Isn't gambling illegal, Deputy?"

He wondered how she had guessed his secret. Before becoming a policeman, he had struggled with a serious gambling problem. He opened the motorcar's passenger door and said, "Your interview with the sheriff is a priority, Miss Finnegan. That is, if you have no other personal business here. I don't plan to waste an entire day catering to your whims." As soon as the words left his lips, he wished that he could take them back.

"In my opinion, your attitude could stand improvement. Shall we go?" Nora said, and stepped into the passenger's seat.

Connery knew he had broken a public servant's cardinal rule. He had just insulted a member of the citizenry. Sheriff Terry expected his deputies to act courteously at all times. "Excuse my manners, Miss Finnegan," he said. "I've no intention to pick a fight with you." Shutting her door and coming around the front of the motorcar, he opened the driver's door and got in next to Nora.

"Let's be civil and respect each other's jobs," she said. "I will be writing an article for my paper about Miss Fleming's murder. Marshal Englund said that she was stabbed. Have you found the knife that killed her?"

"No, I'm afraid we haven't. After you discovered her body yesterday, we searched Miss Fleming's house and garden from top to bottom. Sheriff Terry and I concluded that the killer took the murder weapon with him and probably discarded it."

Nora was quiet for a moment, and then said, "I don't think so. I have an idea. There are two stops I want you to make before we head to Monterey. They won't take long." Folding her hands in her lap, she waited for his answer.

Connery curbed his impatience. "And where would these two stops be?"

Nora couldn't hold back a smile. "I'll be happy to direct you, Deputy," she said, as she made herself comfortable.

"Our first stop is to pick up a passenger." Seeing his reaction, she added, "She can sit in the back seat."

Connery shrugged. "I'm glad to hear that it's not going to be that librarian."

CHAPTER TWENTY THREE

"I see you found my missing reporter, Deputy," William Owens muttered, as Jimmy Connery accompanied Nora into the *Carmel Pine Cone*'s reception area.

"She was at the general store, sir, just as Mrs. Owens said," Connery replied.

Hands on his hips, the publisher stared at Nora. "I need your articles, Honora. I'm typesetting today."

Pulling a sheet of paper from her purse, she handed it to him. "I've finished the one on the fire, but there's a problem with Levy's burglary. The deputy and I think that the break-in might be connected to the Woodward fire."

Connery interrupted, "It would be more accurate to say that I'm looking into the possibility, Mr. Owens."

"But my story might help us come up with a witness," Nora said. "And another thing. As I was talking with Mr. Levy just now, I thought of a topic for our Christmas issue, sir. If you approve, I'll start working on it."

Scanning her article on the fire, Owens looked up. "I don't have time to discuss a Christmas assignment, but I suggest you take the initiative and go ahead." Walking back to his office, he quickly closed the door to keep the two dogs from following him.

Mrs. Owens had been listening to the conversation. "It may not appear that Mr. Owens appreciates your ideas, Nora," she said, "but he's been under a lot of pressure lately. The typesetter he hoped to hire called to say that he can't take the job. And these dogs are causing us so much trouble. We couldn't leave them at home. Dasher hates sharing his domain with Maisie and she hasn't adapted to her new surroundings."

"I understand," Nora said, "and I've come up with a solution. That's the reason the deputy and I came back. We're taking Maisie off your hands for a while."

On hearing Nora's words, Connery shook his head and stepped outside, to avoid saying something that he would later regret.

"Wonderful! Then I can get some work done without them underfoot," Mrs. Owens said. "Oh, there were two messages for you, dear. Miss Morgan called from La Playa to invite you to dinner tonight at seven, and your mother telephoned to ask when to expect you home for Thanksgiving."

Nora wasn't eager to tell her parents that she planned to stay in Carmel for the holiday. "I'll call Mother when I return from my interview with the sheriff," she said. "If it isn't too much trouble, will you let Miss Morgan know that I accept her invitation?"

"I'll be happy to. Oh, Mrs. Woodward did call us last night after you left. She was ever so grateful. She's made new living arrangements for her and Freddie. With Rob in jail, they'll be staying at his place on Torres Street in the Eighty Acres."

The news surprised Nora. "They aren't even married. Doesn't she know this will cause talk? She's exposing herself to gossip that will affect Freddie too."

"What choice does she have, Nora? The woman's house burned to the ground. It's my hope that people will be more tolerant, given her circumstances."

The telephone's ringing startled Maisie, who darted out from under Mrs. Owens' desk and ran over to stand next to Nora. Attaching a leash to the spaniel, and waving at Mrs. Owens, Nora and the dog left by the front door.

Outside on the sidewalk, Deputy Connery saw them coming towards his police sedan. "So this is your female passenger, Miss Finnegan."

"Yes, but before we go, there's something I've been meaning to ask you. Do you know when the Fleming autopsy will become available?"

"All in good time. I'll give you a copy when the coroner makes it public."

Coming up to him, Nora tapped his shoulder. "Are you

going to be irked with me all day?"

"I'm not irked. It's just that your actions continue to surprise me."

Can you at least tell me what time Carlotta was killed?" Pulling on the dog's leash, she added, "Don't pay any attention to his bad mood, Maisie."

The deputy grimaced. "The coroner will have an approximate time of death in his report. From my examination of Miss Fleming's body, rigor mortis had already set in, meaning that the murder had occurred sometime in the morning."

Nora shivered at the thought.

Connery opened the doors of the motorcar for his two passengers. What else could he do, but to "protect and serve?" Turning the sedan around, he headed west. At the next corner he stopped and waited while an elderly woman took her time crossing to the other side of Ocean Avenue. Unable to lie quietly in the back seat, Maisie paced, looked out the windows, and barked at the passersby. Her behavior was beginning to annoy him. "She's worse than any whining prisoner that's ever sat back there," he said.

"Why don't you admire the view of the ocean from here and forget about Maisie?" Nora said. "Or you could try watching the sun as it comes out from behind that gray cloud over your head."

Connery's response was to stare straight ahead and accelerate faster.

When they came to the road's intersection with Carmelo Avenue, Nora shouted, "Slow down, will you? Here's where I want you to turn left."

He glared at her. "When are you going to tell me where we're going? I need to get you to the sheriff's office. And why you insisted on bringing that mutt along is beyond me. Maisie's a real pest."

Hearing her name, the spaniel put her paws on top of the front seat and began panting on Connery's neck. Nora pushed her off. "Get down, girl. We're almost there."

"I can hardly wait," the deputy groused.

Ignoring his sarcasm, she said, "Will you do me a favor? After I speak with Sheriff Terry, I'd like to interview Mr. Jacklin. I think he'll be willing to tell me his side of the story. I want to report it to our readers. Can you arrange that?"

"You'll need the sheriff's permission, but in my opinion, you'd be wasting your time. We have Jacklin's signed confession. He's admitted to killing Fields."

Nora shook her head. "No one in Carmel believes that Rob is a murderer."

He turned to her. "Are you serious? Jacklin told us how he shot Fields in cold blood. You saw the gunshot wound after he was brought up from the ravine."

His words aggravated her. Folding her arms across her chest, she said, "I think the Fields and Fleming murders are somehow connected."

Connery snickered. "There's no logic in that line of thought."

Looking out the passenger's side window, Nora spotted her next door neighbor and waved at her. She realized that she would likely hear a few critical comments from Mrs. Newsom about riding alone with a young policeman.

Just then, Maisie let out a yelp.

Putting her hand on the deputy's forearm, Nora said, "Pull over here."

Connery jammed on the brake and steered the motorcar to the side of the road. He was astounded when he saw that he had stopped in front of Carlotta Fleming's cottage. "What are we doing back at Oak Bower? Can't you tell that the woman's own dog doesn't want to be here any more than I do? Just listen to her yowling."

"She wants to get out," Nora said. "When I release her, we'll need to keep a sharp eye on her."

Connery weighed the pros and cons of starting another argument, but decided to remain in policeman's mode: silent, decisive, but cooperative. He turned off the motor, got out, and came around the front of the sedan to open Nora's door.

Stepping out, she opened the rear door. The dog raced down the path to the side yard. Following closely behind, Nora unlatched the gate and she and Connery watched the animal head to the spot where Nora had found Carlotta's body yesterday.

Connery looked around. He could tell that nothing had changed since his previous visit. "Why are we here?" he asked.

Nora didn't answer. She was picturing Carlotta's body. The vision made her feel sick to her stomach. She turned her attention to Maisie. The dog was zigzagging back and forth between the rear patio and the bushes along Oak Bower's side yard.

"All she's doing is picking up her mistress' scent," Connery said.

Her nose low to the ground, Maisie disappeared into the dense shrubbery and began digging into a pile of leaves.

"What's she up to now?" Connery asked.

Nora called out, "Maisie, come here!"

When the dog didn't obey, Connery knelt down, leaned in, and pushed her away. "Good God!" he called out. Pulling a handkerchief from his pocket, he scooped up a thin, narrow object and examined it. "She's uncovered a boning knife," he said to Nora. "The handle is made out of abalone shell. The murderer must have thrown it in here as he ran out of the yard. It was buried under the foliage and we didn't spot it yesterday."

Nora looked at the knife and saw the dried blood on the blade. She said, "I began to wonder if Maisie was trying to tell me something yesterday. A short while after I entered the yard, she went into the bushes, came out, ran back to Carlotta's body, and began licking her face. Then she lay down next to her mistress and stared up at me. I didn't understand her then, but as I thought more about it, I wanted to bring her back here, to see what she would do."

"That was a smart idea. I want you to wait here with the dog. I'll be right back."

Hurrying out to the motorcar, Connery removed an evidence pouch and tucked the cloth-wrapped knife into it. When he returned to Nora, he said, "Hopefully, Deputy Jensen will be able to find an identifiable set of fingerprints on the handle."

"It's part of a cutlery set," Nora said, recalling her mother's collection of similar looking serving utensils. "It looks rather expensive."

"We searched Carlotta's kitchen from top to bottom and found nothing that matched it."

Slipping Maisie's leash around her neck, Nora said, "I'm going to give our heroine a drink." Heading to the patio to find the dog's water bowl, she looked back at Connery. "You may not like my continued interference, Deputy, but I'm determined more than ever to find the knife's owner."

Connery raised his eyebrows. "Don't do anything foolish, Miss Finnegan. Leave this up to us professionals. It won't be easy to locate the rest of the cutlery set. You can't scour every pantry in Carmel."

"We'll see. Now let's take Maisie back to the *Pine Cone* and go on to Monterey."

"Whatever you say," the deputy replied.

On the drive back to Carmel's business district, Connery stole a glance at Nora. He had to admire her pluck. With the dog's assistance, she had found the knife that had killed Carlotta Fleming. Still, he didn't think the reporter should be permitted to interview Rob Jacklin, let alone attempt to locate the owner of the abalone knife set. Glancing up at the blue sky, Connery saw that the gray cloud that had hovered over his head earlier had disappeared. He felt exhilarated at the thought of delivering the murder weapon to Sheriff Terry as soon as they arrived at the jail in Monterey.

CHAPTER TWENTY FOUR

Nora's nose was buried in a book when Julia Morgan walked downstairs to the hotel lobby that evening. "I'm sorry to have kept you waiting," she said, "but it simply couldn't be helped."

Closing her library book, Nora stood up. "I was early, Miss Morgan."

The architect studied the young woman in the gray gabardine suit as she came closer. "What a lovely strand of matching pearls you're wearing," Julia said.

"They were a birthday gift from my parents when I turned 21. Actually, this is the first time I've worn them since coming to live here. I rarely get a chance to dress up."

"You have a good sense of style, dear."

"Before I forget my manners, Miss Morgan, I want to thank you for inviting me tonight. I've been looking forward to having dinner with you all day. This is the first time that I've come to the hotel for pleasure rather than business."

"Now that we're better acquainted, Nora, it would please me if you'd call me by my first name."

"I'd like that, Julia."

The two women walked into the dining room and stood behind a man and a boy who were waiting to be seated.

Nora looked around. Her eyes were drawn to two vases filled with yellow and white chrysanthemums on the fireplace mantel. Candles and straw baskets of seasonal fruit had been placed on each of the linen-covered tables. She approved of the effect that had been created by the hotel's staff.

The hostess showed them to an ocean-view table. Seated

next to the oversized window, Nora watched the outdoor lanterns cast flickering shadows on the garden's native plants. A wide pea gravel path led to the sand dunes and eventually the beach.

Julia looked over her menu at Nora and said, "I want to apologize for not sending a thank you note for the special meal you prepared the other evening. It was delicious. I don't cook much myself, but I admire women who have culinary skills."

Nora smiled and let the compliment pass. She leaned back in her chair and said, "I hope your day was easier than mine."

Julia shook her head. "Truth is, I'm exhausted. I had a long meeting with a new client in Pacific Grove, and then spent the past hour on the telephone with my senior draftsman. To top it off, I missed my afternoon stroll on Carmel beach."

"Is it difficult to accomplish everything when you're so far away from your San Francisco office?"

"Not really. I always make sure that I'm available to my staff whenever I'm traveling."

"I'm glad that you made time to be with me, Julia. I've been eager to share what has happened in the past two days." Nora went on to describe finding Carlotta's body and how Maisie had discovered the knife that was used to kill her mistress.

"That was hard for you, but how clever of you to suspect the dog could do that."

"But not everything went well afterwards. During my interview with Sheriff Terry this morning, Deputy Connery did most of the talking. When I said I wanted to discuss the Fields murder investigation, the sheriff cut me off. He said, 'You're here to answer our questions, not bring up ones of your own.' It made me furious. Do all men in positions of authority behave this way?"

Julia nodded. "Naturally, you were disappointed by being shut out, but perhaps my experience will be of some help to you. During my meetings with clients, I often get similar reactions from the men, even though their wives are present. The husbands tend to dominate the conversations."

"I was also very disappointed that Sheriff Terry wouldn't allow me to talk to Mr. Jacklin. He's accused of killing Mr. Fields. I'd been counting on interviewing Rob and developing it into a feature story that people would be interested in reading."

"Perhaps the sheriff believes that murder is too gruesome a subject for you to delve into."

Recalling Mr. Owens' concerns, Nora said, "You're

probably right. My boss at the newspaper holds a similar view. But I'm doing all I can to change his mind."

Their waiter arrived to fill the water glasses and set rolls and butter on the table. In a monotone, he related the night's dinner special of corned beef with a variety of boiled vegetables. Neither woman seemed interested.

As Julia reached for her menu, she noticed the library book lying on the table next to Nora. She recognized the author's name. "I see that you've discovered Mary Austin," she said. "I met her once in San Francisco. She's a superb writer."

Nora's face lit up. "I'm one of her biggest admirers."

"Then you must have read her first book, *The Land of Little Rain*. Did you know that she created the plot for that novel while living here in Carmel?"

Nora nodded. "One of my college professors told us about her famous wick-i-up. He described it as an open-air platform that was built into the tree next to Miss Austin's cottage. Sadly, a winter storm destroyed it."

"That was such a loss. I first became interested in her wick-i-up because an architect friend of mine, Louis Christian Mullgardt, designed it for Miss Austin. He told me that she bragged that she did her best writing while sitting high in the treetops."

"I've heard that story too. While it lasted, the wick-i-up was Carmel's most photographed landmark."

"With the exception of the Carmel Mission, of course," Julia added.

"Talking about Miss Austin reminds me of when I first met her. Shall I tell you about it, Julia?"

"By all means, please do."

"As a present for my 13th birthday, my parents took me to see "Fire," Miss Austin's play at the Forest Theater. It was a box office success. During intermission, we went back stage. As you might imagine, I was terribly excited to meet her. She looked like a Grecian goddess, in her long, white tunic. I told her that I wanted to become a writer just like her."

"Did she give you some helpful advice?"

"Yes, she did. She encouraged me to attend college and concentrate on learning the craft of writing. She also said something that I've never forgotten. 'If you are truly serious, you must make sure that writing comes before anything else in your life.'"

Waving off their waiter, who was hovering over them, Julia said, "Her advice was sound. In my experience, it's difficult for a woman in these times to sustain a career unless she's dedicated and passionate about it. Society has other expectations of us. We're supposed to marry and bear children, not seek out a profession."

The waiter had been listening for a break in their conversation. Stepping forward, he said, "Did I hear you ladies mention Mary Austin's name? I too have a story about the famous playwright."

Julia looked up and smiled. "Tell us, and then we'll order our dinner."

Lowering his voice, he said, "I'm a struggling actor and currently I have the lead in the new Perry Newberry drama opening at the Forest Theater next summer. Yesterday during rehearsal, Perry explained that it was Mary Austin who first dreamed up the idea of creating a theater venue here in Carmel. Were you two aware of that?"

"I was," Nora said. "But her concept was made a reality by another playwright, Herbert Heron. That's how the Forest Theater came into being."

"That's interesting," he said. There's something else I want to share with you." Taking a pencil from his shirt pocket, he leaned closer. "Forget about the dinner special. Choose our standard roast beef with Yorkshire pudding and creamed spinach. It's our best meal overall."

When Julia and Nora nodded their agreement, the self-proclaimed thespian did a quick pirouette and disappeared into the kitchen. The two women looked at one another and burst out laughing. For the next hour, they enjoyed their meal and each other's company.

When the waiter returned to clear their table, they both heard a commotion near the dining room entrance. Looking over Julia's shoulder, Nora spotted Sarah Fields arguing with La Playa's hostess. Dressed in a long evening gown and a fur stole, the widow pointed at an empty window table and headed straight for it.

Nora heard the hostess say, "But it's not your reservation, madam."

Intimidated by her guest's obstinate attitude, the hostess

forced a smile and followed Mrs. Fields and Davey Chatham into the dining room. Leaning over, she removed the "Reserved" sign from the table directly behind Nora.

As Sarah Fields sat down, she said, "If it isn't Miss Annoying Finnegan. I haven't forgotten your rudeness to me yesterday at Bella Vista. To think that you accused me of starting a fire! Why, you're nothing but an impertinent mischief-maker."

All conversation throughout the dining room ceased.

"Excuse me?" a flustered Nora said.

Never one to tolerate abusive language, Julia spoke up. "I can see that you're upset, Mrs. Fields, but please lower your voice, calm down, and be civil to my young friend. We would like to enjoy our dessert and coffee."

The widow turned her attention to Chatham, who had taken refuge behind his menu. In a voice loud enough for everyone to hear, she said, "Aren't you surprised, David, by the company that some people keep?" Putting down her menu, Sarah Fields turned around in her chair. "Perhaps I won't pay my husband's debt to you, Miss Morgan. How would you like that?" Then she snapped her fingers to summon the hostess. "What must I do to get some service here?"

Julia's expression turned grim.

It was obvious to Nora that her presence had just cost the architect a commission. "I'm terribly sorry about this embarrassing incident," she said.

Reaching across the table, Julia patted Nora's hand. "It isn't your fault, and I don't want you to worry. My attorney will see that Mrs. Fields fulfills her late husband's contractual obligations. There is no doubt that I'll be paid for my work."

Just then, the door to the kitchen swung open. Apparently their waiter had also heard the exchange. Ignoring Sarah Fields' gesturing at him to draw his attention, he said, "Did I hear someone mention dessert?" He approached Nora and Julia's table, balancing a silver tray. "These treats are guaranteed to lighten the mood. Courtesy of Hotel La Playa, ladies."

Winking at Nora, he set a huge piece of apple pie a la mode in front of her and one at Julia's place. He leaned down and whispered in Nora's ear, "I for one hate that witch who's sitting in back of you."

CHAPTER TWENTY FIVE
Thursday

The following morning Nora arrived at the newspaper office feeling refreshed. After returning from Sheriff Terry's interview yesterday, she had been told by Mr. Owens to put together an eyewitness account of the Fleming crime scene.

Sitting at her desk, she decided to telephone several of Carmel's most prominent residents to ask for their opinions on the artist's death. It would give her article additional context.

"He has to be caught," said Ben Fox, owner of Carmel's fix-it shop and the President of the village's Board of Trustees. "Miss Fleming's killer is a dangerous man who threatens our city's peace and security. I've asked Marshal Englund and the sheriff to make inquiries into possible enemies that Miss Fleming might have had. Then again, it could be a random killing."

Next Nora spoke to Perry Newberry, who informed her that, due to Carlotta's death, he was taking over the leadership of the residents' group against the proposed hotel. "I know of no one who wanted Carlotta dead," he said. "She was respectful of everyone's opinions, even if they differed from hers. Her tragic loss is a blow to Carmel's cultural community. We will make sure that her vision is memorialized when the residents buy the beach and preserve it for future generations."

Shopkeeper Joe Levy explained to Nora that he didn't have time to discuss Miss Fleming's death at length. He had a bevy of customers at the store that required his immediate attention. "I'm confident that the sheriff will do what it takes to find this deranged killer and bring him to justice," he said. "We can't have our residents living in fear."

Next Nora contacted the principal of Sunset School who said, "I'm outraged. Miss Fleming's murderer is likely wandering Carmel's streets today. Innocent children need protection from this type of sick individual who wantonly murders. I ask every parent to be mindful of strangers who approach our youngsters."

No one had suggested that the Fleming murder might be linked to the Fields murder. When she had finished transcribing all their comments, Nora left her desk and went into the back room to help Mrs. Owens put away several boxes of paper products that had been delivered at closing time yesterday. Noticing the closed bathroom door as she passed it, she went to the closet and found an apron. "I'll start organizing these supplies," she said through the door.

"I'll be with you in just a moment," Mrs. Owens replied.

Nora heard the office's front door open and close. Then a male voice called out, "Where the devil is everyone? Mrs. Owens, are you in the back?"

Rapping on the closed door, Nora whispered, "Shall I see who that is?"

"Will you, dear? I'm trying to do something with my hair."

Funny, Nora thought. Since her arrival this morning, she had detected a subtle change in Mrs. Owens' demeanor. Normally cheerful, she seemed unusually quiet. Taking off her work apron, she dropped it on a chair, tucked her silk blouse into her skirt, and returned to the reception area.

In the bathroom, Mary Lee Owens finished drying her hands. After placing the damp towel on the rack, she looked in the mirror above the corner sink. She wasn't quite sure when the fine lines at the corners of her hazel eyes had first appeared. Also, her close-up vision wasn't what it used to be. Since she and her husband had started up the *Carmel Pine Cone* six years ago, her life had been busy, but in many ways, unrewarding.

For example, this morning she had sorted through a dozen boxes of dusty, outdated newspaper files. The hardest part of the job had been carrying the discarded records out to the trash bin in the alley behind the building. When she had finished, her hands were filthy and her face covered with newsprint. No one could say that the office receptionist's job was glamorous, she thought.

On the other hand, life at the newspaper had become far

more interesting once Nora had arrived. She enjoyed the young reporter's company, and had quietly taken her under her wing. She was eager to help Nora develop her career —something that no one had done for her. Nora's enthusiasm for her work sparked a new purpose in her life, and for that, she was grateful.

The telephone rang as Nora entered the reception area. She smiled at the distinguished looking man who was standing at the front counter. "Excuse me, sir. I'll be right with you, just as soon as I answer the telephone."

"Hold on!" he shot back. "I was here before that damned thing rang and I'm a paying customer." Waving a piece of paper in her face, he went on, "Here's a classified advertisement that I want printed in your next issue."

Nora recalled when she had last seen the silver-haired man standing at the counter. It was Friday night at the Trustees' meeting. Mr. Owens had introduced her to Doctor Arthur Taylor, one of the three Trustees present.

He raised his voice and said, "Must I repeat myself, miss?"

Just then, the telephone stopped ringing. Nora went behind the counter and took the slip of paper from the man's outstretched hand. Scanning what was written on it, she silently counted the words and calculated the cost. "This is going to take two column inches, sir. At fifty cents an inch of type, that comes to one dollar. I also need to tell you that advertisements are payable in advance."

He groaned and shook his head. "I don't intend to pay until I have a chance to look over your typed copy."

"I'm sorry, sir, but I'm following the publisher's policy. I'm required to collect payment before I type up the order."

He slammed his fist down on the counter. "I'm not paying until I read what you put together! Why don't you get whoever's in charge to handle this."

The man was trying to intimidate her. Determined to remain polite, Nora counted out loud the number of words scribbled on one of his blank prescription forms. "As I said, it comes to one dollar, and I must insist on the payment first."

"Listen, Miss Nobody, I want you to type this up and I'll see how it looks first."

Standing her ground, Nora put her arms across her chest. "No, I'm afraid I can't."

Mrs. Owens, who had come out of the back room, heard

Nora's words. She said, "Hello, Doctor." Turning to Nora, she smiled. "You're correct about Mr. Owens' policy, Miss Finnegan, but I think we can make an exception with the doctor."

Nora said nothing more. Going to her desk, she snatched the cover off her Remington. Slipping some typing paper into the carriage, she began pounding on the keys as hard as she could.

The telephone rang. Going to her desk, Mrs. Owens picked up the receiver.

When she had finished with the caller, Taylor said, "Why is this office so darned cold? I'd like a cup of hot coffee to warm me up, Mrs. Owens. I take three teaspoons of sugar."

"I'm afraid there isn't any coffee, Doctor, but I'll make you a cup of tea."

He frowned. "Fine, but I consider it a poor substitute."

Nora fought off the urge to get up and kick the man in the shins, but she continued typing.

No sooner had Mrs. Owens left to fix the tea, than the doctor came around the counter and sat in a chair near Nora. Putting his elbows on his knees and resting his chin on his hands, he leaned forward and watched her type.

The telephone rang again.

"Get that, will you, Miss Finnegan," Mrs. Owens shouted from the back room.

Nora went to Mrs. Owens' desk and picked up the receiver. "Hello. You've reached the *Carmel Pine Cone*. May I help you?"

"This is Deputy Connery, Miss Finnegan. I'm at the general store. Mr. Levy is letting me use his telephone. The coroner's report has been completed. We can discuss Miss Fleming's cause of death. How about meeting me for an early lunch?"

"I'm actually very busy here. Could you drop it off, Deputy?"

"I don't want to drop it off. It would be much better if I explained the results to you over lunch."

Nora wanted the report so that she could include details from it in her article about Carlotta's murder. "All right then. I can meet you, as long as it's somewhere close by. My time is limited."

"Is your time any more valuable than mine?" Connery sounded angry.

She hadn't meant her words to come out the way they had. Checking the wall clock, she said, "All right. The Blue Bird Tea

Room is a block down the street from Levy's. I'll meet you there in ten minutes."

"Suits me fine."

He hung up without saying goodbye.

Returning to her desk, Nora was mystified as to why the deputy had cut her off. Her musing was jolted by the doctor.

"Do you suppose my advertisement can be done before next month?" he said.

Ignoring him, she resumed typing.

Mrs. Owens came around the front counter with a mug of steaming tea. She handed it to the doctor who was getting up from the chair.

Pulling the order form out of her typewriter, Nora checked the copy for errors. Seeing none, she held it out. "Make sure the wording meets with your approval, sir," she said. "It can't be changed after you leave."

With the paper in one hand and the tea in the other, he headed around the counter and began reciting the text out loud: "Experienced nurse urgently needed by busy physician. Prefer unmarried white Protestant female, age 25 to 30, non-smoker, teetotaler. Must be available to assist with home deliveries. Room and board provided. Salary $25 a month. Address inquiries to Arthur Taylor, M. D. Post Office Box 12, Carmel-By-The-Sea."

As she listened, Nora saw that he was spilling hot liquid all over the floor.

When he finished reading, he pulled out a fountain pen, wrote something on the paper and pointed at Nora. "Add these words: References required." Putting his hand in his pocket, he took out a dollar bill and left it on the counter. "Run the ad for as long as it takes to get results. I'll call and tell you when to stop." Gulping the rest of his tea, he set the mug down, opened the front door, and left the office.

"How did that man ever get elected to our Board of Trustees?" Nora exclaimed.

Mrs. Owens shook her head. "I didn't vote for him. He's arrogant, abrasive, and condescending. And did I mention he's discourteous? He didn't even thank me for his Earl Grey. Let's hope we've seen the last of him."

Nora opened the door and stepped outside. She was surprised to see the doctor standing in front of the Blue Bird. He was tipping his hat to a young woman in a paisley shawl. It was

Claudia Woodward. Pulling open the door, he followed her into the tea room.

Her opinion of Freddie's mother plummeted further. Not only had she inveigled an invitation from Rob to stay in his cottage, but now that he was in jail, she had attached herself to another man. Poor dear Freddie, Nora thought, as she went back inside.

Just then Mr. Owens walked through the front door.

"How did the meeting go, dear?" Mrs. Owens asked. "Did you get a few more residents to help pay for our new fire equipment?"

"You'd think everyone would be more than willing to give after the Woodward blaze. But it looks like I'll have to work on some people." Looking down, he noticed the tea puddle staining the floor. "Did one of the dogs have an accident?"

"It's a long story," Mrs. Owens said. "I'll mop it up and tell you later."

Nora sat down at her desk and retyped the doctor's corrected copy. Then she reached for her purse and stood up. "This advertisement is ready for typesetting, sir."

The publisher frowned. "Where are you off to, Honora? It isn't lunchtime."

"She has a business meeting with that young Deputy Connery," Mrs. Owens said. "Let her go, dear. I'm still young enough to handle this job without Nora's help."

Owens reached across the counter and took his wife's hand. "You've used the word 'young' twice, Mary Lee. Is there a message there? Don't forget, you'll always be young in my eyes. Honestly, I don't know where you get all your energy."

Outside, Nora stared down at her feet. The wood sidewalk was covered with wet pine needles left over from the last rainstorm. Stepping lightly, she walked down Ocean Avenue towards the tea room. While she waited there for Deputy Connery, she thought about Mrs. Owens' easy manner of handling difficult customers like Doctor Taylor. She could learn from her the virtues of patience and diplomacy. She would try to practice on Deputy Connery.

A minute later, he arrived. "Hello, Miss Finnegan. I hope I haven't kept you waiting long."

Nora smiled. "It's no trouble at all. I want to thank you for rearranging your busy schedule in order to make time for me."

"It's my pleasure," he countered. Opening the Blue Bird's door, he gestured that she should precede him. As they were being shown to their table, Nora looked around for Claudia Woodward and Doctor Taylor.

They were nowhere to be seen.

CHAPTER TWENTY SIX

Finishing the last of her sandwich, Nora eyed the remaining food on the table. Her confrontation with Doctor Taylor had stimulated her appetite.

The deputy couldn't help but notice. Pushing a serving bowl towards her, he said, "Would you like to finish off the potato salad?"

Shaking her head, Nora blushed and looked away.

Connery folded his napkin and put it next to his empty plate. He hadn't come to the Blue Bird to eat. He had come to enjoy Nora's company.

The waitress stopped at the table. "Are you and the young lady finished with your lunches, Deputy?"

Connery smiled. "Yes, and it was nice of you not to rush us, miss. Since you aren't all that busy, could you bring us some more hot tea?"

"I'll be right back with some. Stay for as long as you like." Picking up their dishes, she returned to the kitchen.

Nora could see that Connery's uniform and badge had impressed their waitress. She said, "Now that we've finished eating, I'd like to look at the coroner's report, Deputy."

"It's Jimmy. And may I call you Nora?"

Folding her napkin, she said, "I suppose that would be all right."

He reached down for the envelope he had stashed next to his chair. "Before we get to this, why don't you tell me why you've been looking around the tea room ever since we got here?

Are you expecting someone, or am I boring company?"

Nora hadn't realized that she had been so obvious. He deserved an answer. "Before coming to meet you, I had a run-in with Doctor Taylor, one of our city Trustees. He was very demanding. After he left, I saw him and Mrs. Woodward enter the tea room. I don't see them now, which puzzles me."

"I'm sure there's a logical explanation, but shall we get to the autopsy?" Handing her the report, he went on, "Take a look at the third paragraph, where the coroner says that Miss Fleming died from a stab wound in the neck."

Nora skimmed the document. "I see where he describes the stabbing as 'a downward thrust that severed Carlotta's right carotid artery and penetrated her trachea.' Doesn't that mean that her killer was left-handed?"

"That's very observant of you. It says that the coroner also found that her bronchial tubes and lungs were filled with blood. He concluded that the cause of death was severe hemorrhage and suffocation. Time of death: that morning."

Nora sighed. "She drowned in her own blood. What kind of person would commit such a terrible act, Jimmy? Do you and Sheriff Terry have a suspect?"

"Not yet, but thanks to you, we now have the murder weapon. We don't know who the knife belongs to or where it came from, but we're hoping to find some fingerprints on it."

Their waitress had returned with a fresh pot of tea. She set it in front of Jimmy, who reached across the table and refilled Nora's cup.

Taking a sip of the strong Darjeeling, she said, "After we found the knife, Keith Preston and I did some research. We learned that fingerprints are unique to each one of us. They're an accurate method of identification. In this case, the dried blood on the boning knife's handle could identify the murderer."

Jimmy nodded. "After my comments yesterday, I promise not to say anything more about your librarian friend, only that you two obviously did your homework. Most killers have no idea that they're putting what amounts to their signatures on the weapons they use when committing crimes."

"What do you plan to do next?"

"Last night, I sent in an order for two fingerprint kits — one to check the burglary at Levy's store and the other for the knife."

"Where do they come from?" Nora asked.

"We get them from the city of Oakland's police department."

"Why is that?"

"They keep a stock for the smaller police departments. And their detectives hold fingerprint identification seminars periodically for other law enforcement agencies. Our junior deputy, Alvin Jensen, has attended several of them. He's become quite an expert."

"I remember him. Which reminds me. Did he find any prints on Mr. Fields' motorcar after you pulled it out of the ravine?"

Jimmy shook his head. "It would be a waste of time, since Jacklin has already confessed. Besides, there would be a lot of smudged prints, since the garage's owner hires his motorcars out on a regular basis."

Pouring more tea into their cups, Jimmy continued, "However, I did check the wrecked Buick for any clothing scraps or hair. All I found on the floor were cigar stubs and some used matches."

"I know that Mr. Fields was a cigar smoker. They probably belonged to him."

At that moment, an attractive blonde woman appeared at their table. As she placed the lunch check next to Jimmy's elbow, Nora saw her nudge the deputy's arm before returning to her station by the front door. According to Mrs. Owens, the Blue Bird's new hostess had just arrived in the country from Sweden. Was she flirting with Jimmy?

Opening her purse, Nora said, "I'd like to share the cost of our lunch."

"I won't hear of it. I was the one who invited you, remember?"

They stood up and walked to the cash register.

In halting English, the young hostess said, "Every thing is to your satisfaction, sir? You come back soon?"

Annoyed with the woman's obvious interest in Jimmy, Nora ignored her and stepped outside to wait for him to settle their bill. When he walked out a few minutes later, she said, "I'm sure Mr. Owens will want to read the coroner's report. May I take it with me, Deputy?"

He looked puzzled. "Of course, Nora, but why the formality again? I told you that I hoped you'd call me Jimmy."

"I guess my mind is still focused on Carlotta Fleming's

death."

"I know you're doing your job, but that shouldn't stop us from being friendly. Should it?"

She avoided looking at him. "Someone killed Martin Fields before he could get approval to build his hotel on the beach. A few days later, the woman who was leading the opposition was murdered. I can't help thinking there is a connection."

"I don't agree," Jimmy said, as they started walking up Ocean Avenue. "I know that both of us have to return to work, but in the spirit of friendly cooperation, I have some new information to share with you."

Nora slowed down. "And what is that, Deputy? Did you ask the friendly hostess for her telephone number?"

He grinned. "It's Jimmy, remember? That's not what I was going to say. While I was paying the lunch check, I took the opportunity to chat with her."

"Did she say what time she got off work?"

"If I didn't know any better, I'd say you have a jealous side. Can't you give me a little credit for sweet-talking the woman into revealing something that you told me earlier you were dying to find out?"

"I'm all ears."

"You're a tad more than 'all ears.' You said you had a spat with Doctor Taylor earlier. Well, according to the hostess, he and his female guest rushed out the back door soon after they were seated."

"Really? And did she say why they left so quickly?"

"It was because Mrs. Woodward developed a splitting headache. The doctor called it a migraine and said he could treat it. Being that his surgery is in the block behind the tea room and could be reached quickly via the rear courtyard, he asked the hostess if it was all right for them to leave by the kitchen door. Taylor said he had something he could prescribe for Mrs. Woodward that would stop her pain."

Nora was about to respond, when she spotted her next door neighbor making a bee line for them. As the woman drew closer, she said, "Hello, Mrs. Newsom. Is this the day your sewing circle meets at the Carmel Woman's Club?"

Lucinda Newsom ignored Nora's greeting and focused her attention on the deputy standing next to her. "Who might you be, young man?" she asked.

"I'm Deputy Sheriff James Connery, ma'am."

Jumping at the opportunity to engage a lawman in conversation, Mrs. Newsom said, "I hope you're going to catch the person who killed poor Carlotta Fleming."

"You can be sure of that, ma'am. It was very nice meeting you." Tipping his Stetson to the elderly woman, he said, "I need to be going, Miss Finnegan. I'll telephone you later. Good day to you, Mrs. Newsom."

Waiting until after the deputy had continued down the street, Mrs. Newsom turned to Nora. "I saw you with that young man in his police car yesterday. He isn't wearing a wedding ring. You really must protect your reputation."

"Deputy Connery is involved in two murder cases that I'm covering for my newspaper. I need to consult with him, so that I can be informed of the sheriff's ongoing investigation."

"That may be, but single women like you, living alone, can't be too careful."

"Deputy Connery and I are professionally acquainted. He treats me with respect."

Mrs. Newsom shrugged. "Well, I won't keep you, dear. I mustn't be late for my sewing club."

Moments later, Nora surprised the deputy, who was about to get into his motorcar. "I'm glad I caught up with you, Jimmy," she said. "I forgot to thank you for lunch."

He smiled at her. "We'll do it again. But stop following me, unless you know what's good for you," he teased.

"That's what my mother would call pure Irish blarney," Nora kidded back. Then she remembered Mrs. Newsom's admonition. "You know I only follow you because I need to be kept informed of any new developments."

He laughed. "Of course you do."

CHAPTER TWENTY SEVEN

An onshore wind moving up from the beach pushed Nora towards the Carmel library. As she opened the door, a blast of cold air chose that moment to propel her inside. The gust also scattered a pile of catalog cards that Keith was sorting at the reference desk.

"Oh, I'm terribly sorry, Mr. Preston," she said.

Two patrons, intent on their reading, didn't pay any attention.

Keith stood up and came around his desk. "That's all right, Miss Finnegan. Warm yourself while I retrieve them. I'll be with you shortly."

Nora removed her gloves and walked over to the Franklin stove where Mao, the library's resident feline, was stretched out. The formerly homeless creature earned his daily ration of milk and sardines by evicting trespassing mice that wandered nightly among the book stacks. Blinking his green eyes, Mao was studying Keith, who was crawling around on all fours. Looking bored, the cat got up, sauntered over to Nora, and rubbed against her ankles.

Having picked up the last of the cards, Keith motioned Nora into an alcove behind his desk where their conversation wouldn't disturb anyone. "I've been concerned about you, Nora," he said. "I called the newspaper, but Mrs. O. would only say that you were fine, but unavailable. She wouldn't say where you were. Are you feeling better after yesterday's ordeal?"

"Yes, and thanks for asking. I just need to keep busy, and not dwell on Carlotta's death."

He pointed to a nearby chair. "Sit down, and let me share some exciting news." Taking a breath, he continued, "I'm in love! It feels heavenly, but at the same time, my emotions are scaring me."

"Tell me all about the lucky woman. First, who is she?"

Pulling up another chair, he sat across from her. "I first noticed her at the residents' meeting that you and I attended at Carlotta's home. Since then, I've done nothing but think about her. Her name's Mayotta Brown. It's a pretty one, isn't it?"

Nora was surprised. "Where was she sitting? I must have seen her too."

"She was wedged between an older couple on the loveseat. When Carlotta was passing out the coffee, I heard her say, 'Would you like some, Catherine and George?'"

"Now I remember her. Those were the Seidenecks. George is an artist on the staff of the Carnegie Institute here in the village. On weekends, he paints landscapes. Catherine, his wife, is also an artist. She works in leather, hammered brass and copper."

"I'm serious about Mayotta. This morning she came into the library and asked if I had any books on doll-making. I said yes, and I helped her fill out a library card. You saw that flyer I posted by the door? Well, on her way out, she asked me to tell her about this Saturday's library benefit."

"Let me guess. She purchased a ticket to the fundraiser, didn't she?"

Keith nodded. "Yes. Then I acted on impulse. I asked if she would stay on for refreshments after our speaker finished his remarks. She said she would."

Nora giggled. "I bought a ticket too, but I didn't expect my 25 cents to include a personal escort to the social hour."

"Stop making fun of me. I told you, I'm crazy about her."

Nora could see that her friend didn't appreciate being teased. She said, "I'm sorry if I hurt your feelings. Do you think people are going to come this Saturday, given that Thanksgiving is the following week? Some are leaving town and others might not care to listen to an attorney expound on the benefits of another theater in Carmel."

"Despite your pessimism, we expect a large crowd. The fundraiser's sold out. Everyone's eager to hear Edward Kuster talk up a new theater."

Nora shook her head. "I, for one, have doubts that a village of 600 people can sustain another theater, in addition to the two that we already have. Only the other day, Mr. Owens joked that we're all so busy performing in the plays, that there isn't anyone left in town to see them. Why did you and the Library Board select Kuster as your speaker? I heard he's a practicing lawyer in Los Angeles."

"Mr. Kuster has a very distinguished background. He's traveled abroad and studied classical music and architecture. He's proving to be a big draw."

Nora remembered something Mrs. Owens had told her. "Local gossip has it that the reason he's thinking of building a theater in Carmel is that his former wife lives here."

"Do I know her?"

"Probably not, unless you're acquainted with Mrs. Robinson Jeffers."

Hearing the front door close, Keith stood up. "I'd better get back to work. By the way, why did you come in this afternoon, other than to make light of my love life and question my fundraising skills?"

"It appears I've ruffled your feathers. I came to ask if you knew where Rob Jacklin lives."

"Why do you want to know? The man's behind bars, Nora. Forget about Rob. From what I saw going on between him and Claudia Woodward at the tea room last Sunday, I'd say he's taken."

"What makes you think I'm interested in him? I'm only concerned about Freddie's welfare."

"What does he have to do with locating Jacklin's cottage?"

"I'm sure you've heard by now that the Woodward home was destroyed by fire. Freddie's mother told Mrs. Owens that she and the boy will be staying at Rob's place. I don't think that's a proper thing for a widow to do."

"Are you criticizing Claudia again?"

His tone irritated her. "I have good reason to question her motives. Maybe you don't know that Freddie had to fend for himself while she was gone overnight. The boy is only ten years old."

"Bosh! Claudia must have left an adult in charge of him."

"No, she didn't. No one knew where she was. I learned later that she'd taken the autobus to Monterey to visit Rob in jail. She made no provision for Freddie, who was at school when she left. Furthermore, she didn't come back until the next morning."

Keith frowned. "I can't believe that of her. She strikes me as a good mother." Searching for a pencil, he drew a quick sketch of Rob's cottage on a blank catalog card. Handing it to Nora, he said, "I don't know what Claudia has or hasn't done, but you'll do more harm than good if you get in the middle of her problems."

"That isn't my intention at all." But as the words came out, Nora had to wonder if he might be right. Changing the subject, she said, "When are the residents going to meet to discuss purchasing the beach property?"

"With Carlotta dead and Rob arrested, Perry Newberry is taking the lead. We're gathering at his place on Sunday night. He'll have all the details worked out by then." Keith's tone softened. "Are we still friends?"

"Of course we are."

"I'll come by Pine Log and we'll walk to Perry's house together."

Aside from their occasional tiffs, Nora valued Keith's friendship. He was like a brother. Touching his forearm as she got up to leave, she said, "Come early on Sunday and have supper with me."

"That sounds perfect to me. I'd enjoy a home-cooked meal for once. Canned pork and beans are getting tiresome."

Nora waved goodbye and closed the library door behind her. The wind had died down, and as she looked out towards Ocean Avenue, she could see the activity along the street. The main thoroughfare was bustling with residents drawn by the Thanksgiving decorations in all the shop windows. It would be a successful holiday for the merchants, she thought, if one could ignore the fact that two murders had occurred here this past week.

Crossing the road, she strolled past the general store and stopped to admire the items displayed in Levy's front window. Sandwiched between various-sized gourds and pumpkins, Mr. Levy had assembled a colorful display featuring the new jewelry he had shown her yesterday. She searched for the little statue of Aphrodite, but it wasn't there.

An idea popped into her head.

Heading back to the newspaper office, she walked into the reception area. Going around the counter, she went to Mrs. Owens' desk, sat down, and picked up the telephone receiver.

"Did you and Deputy Connery have a nice lunch, Nora?"

Mrs. Owens said, as she came out of the back room, her arms laden with office supplies.

"We did, and I'll give your desk back to you just as soon as I complete this call."

"There's no hurry, dear."

Nora asked the telephone operator for the San Francisco number.

A moment later, a woman's voice came on the other end of the line. "Good afternoon," she said. "You've reached Gump's. How may I direct your call?"

CHAPTER TWENTY EIGHT

Nora completed her article on Levy's Christmas gift items by four that afternoon. Getting up from her desk, she walked to the back room to deliver it to Mr. Owens. "If it's all right with you," she said, "I'd like to leave a little early, sir. I want to make sure that Mrs. Woodward picked up Freddie from school today."

"If there's any problem, bring him back here, Honora. Mrs. Owens and I will watch him. We're both fond of the boy."

What Nora didn't say was that she was going to Rob's cottage, to check on Claudia Woodward. She hoped Freddie's mother hadn't gone off somewhere with Doctor Taylor and forgotten about her son again.

Nora headed up Ocean Avenue. After several hours of working at her desk, it felt good to stretch her legs. She climbed the Carmel hill and within minutes, arrived at Rob's neighborhood. Its higher elevation afforded her with a view of the distant Santa Lucia Mountains. Her parents had told her that, following the 1906 earthquake's devastation, many creative people left San Francisco and relocated here in the part of town called the Eighty Acres. Artists and writers built their cottages among the pines and oak trees. The settlers became the nucleus of the Bohemians.

Pausing in the middle of the road, she took Keith's map out of her purse. He had sketched a small clearing with three houses arranged in a semi-circle. The drawing verified what she saw ahead. She remembered Mrs. Owens commenting: 'Rob is the youngest of three boys who all live near one another.' It was likely that two of the cottages in front of her belonged to Rob's older brothers.

An open gate with a vine-covered trellis welcomed her to the Jacklin compound. Each cottage had been separated off from the others by a low grapestake fence covered with ivy. Agave bushes, their trademark red and gold pokers in bloom, were planted next to the paths leading up to the cottages' front doors.

Coming up the center path, Nora spotted a vegetable garden off to the side. Wire mesh protected it from rabbits in the nearby woods. The ambiance seemed indicative of the self-sufficient person that she imagined Rob to be.

A few yards ahead, she spotted Freddie. Sitting alone on the steps of the middle cottage, he was cradling something in his hands. Feeling relieved that he was here and not waiting by himself at Sunset School, she shouted, "Freddie. It's Miss Finnegan."

When she came closer, he raised a cupped hand to show her a yellow bird with a black-feathered crown. Its head rose above the boy's loosely knit fingers.

"Do you know the species?" she asked, as she sat down beside him.

"It's a Wilson's warbler. I saw a picture of one just like this bird in my library book. Guess how much he weighs."

"I don't know, but he certainly doesn't look very heavy."

He grinned. "I asked Mr. Preston at the library that question. He put two quarters in the palm of my hand and said that would give me an idea."

"That's a good comparison. Your warbler seems tame, Freddie. I don't think he's afraid of you, nor does he look as if he wants to fly away."

He shook his head. "That's because he's hurt, or else he might try to. I found him in the woods and I named him Willie. He has to rest, so his wing heals. Then he can join up later with his friends."

Nora thought the bird was as homeless as the boy was. She said, "With you taking good care of him, I'm sure he'll mend quickly."

"My book says that warblers can fly over ninety miles on one gram of fat. I've been feeding Willie lots of worms and grubs so he gets stronger."

"That's the right thing to do. By the way, Freddie, is your

mother here? I'd like to talk with her."

"She's in Mr. Jacklin's studio," he said, pointing to an unpainted building behind Rob's cottage. "There's all sorts of smelly stuff in there."

Though she had been critical of the woman, Nora was glad that Mrs. Woodward was here with her son following her unscheduled visit to Doctor Taylor's surgery.

"Do you think she'd mind if I went over and spoke to her?"

He shook his head. "Uh, uh. She's lonely. Company will cheer her up."

Nora patted his shoulder and headed for the studio. From the outside, it was a smaller version of the main house. Beneath the pitched roof was an entry with windows on each side. Both were covered with pieces of burlap. Nora guessed that Freddie's mother had left the door ajar, in order to keep track of his whereabouts.

Stepping inside, her eyes found it difficult to adjust to the darkened interior. On a side wall she noticed a deep metal sink, and adjacent to it, several film hangers resting on wood shelves. Rows of chemicals lined most of the lower ones. Freddie was right. This was a smelly place. Her vision, still not completely focused, allowed her to make out a divan along the rear wall. It looked like someone was lying on it.

She moved towards the supine figure. Stepping over a discarded paisley shawl on the floor, she called out, "Mrs. Woodward? It's Nora Finnegan from the *Carmel Pine Cone*. I came to ask you a few questions about Mr. Fields, the deceased developer."

Except for the wind's swishing noise as it parted the makeshift window curtains, Nora got no response. She moved closer, to get a better look.

Lying on her back, her eyes shut, Claudia Woodward had tucked her right arm under her neck to prop up her head. An empty medicine bottle lay next to her. The dropper that should have been inside it was on the floor. Nora bent over and picked up the bottle.

The label read:

> *LAUDANUM. Tincture of Opium.*
> *Maximum use, 2 to 4 drops every 2-4 hours.*
> *Use for severe headaches.*

She recognized Doctor Taylor's penmanship. It was the

same as the words he'd written for his classified advertisement earlier that day. Putting her hand on Claudia's shoulder, she shook her gently. No reaction. Her eyes remained closed. Nora checked to see if she was breathing. She placed her ear near Claudia's nose and mouth, but all she could hear were shallow, infrequent breaths. She shook the woman again, this time, more forcibly. Had Doctor Taylor warned Claudia of the dangers of overdosing? Had she taken too much?

The thought frightened Nora. Just then a shuffling noise from somewhere behind her made her turn her head.

Freddie was standing inside the door, his thin arms at his sides. His voice wavered as he said, "What's wrong with Mama? Did she fall asleep?"

"Come here, dear," Nora said. "I need you to stay with your mother and talk to her, even though she isn't going to answer you. I'm going to the house and call the doctor. I'll be back as soon as I speak to him."

Freddie knelt down and held his mother's hand. He looked up at Nora and then began talking. "Mama, I want to tell you about my bird Willie," he said, "and what I'm doing to heal his broken wing."

As Nora ran out of the studio towards Rob's cottage, her mind focused on only one thing. Would Doctor Taylor arrive before it was too late?

CHAPTER TWENTY NINE

Julia Morgan was reading in her upstairs sitting room at Hotel La Playa when the telephone rang. She looked at the ship's clock on the desk and saw that it was a few minutes after 6:00 P.M. Since she had talked with her senior draftsman earlier, she didn't think it was a business call. Picking up the receiver, she said, "Miss Morgan speaking."

"It's Nora. I'm sorry to disturb you, Julia, but about an hour ago, I discovered Claudia Woodward lying unconscious in Rob Jacklin's studio."

"How upsetting for you. Is the poor woman going to be all right?"

"She's alive, but it was very unnerving. It would help if I could talk to you."

Closing her book, Julia said, "Of course, dear. Where are you now?"

"I'm at the newspaper office. I didn't want to go home."

"Why don't we meet for dinner at the Pine Inn in fifteen minutes?"

"I'd like that, but will you be walking? It's awfully dark at this hour."

"Don't worry. I'll get a lift from Rudolfo the bellman."

"I'll be waiting for you in the lobby," Nora said, as she felt a sense of relief.

Once they had been seated in the Inn's festively decorated dining room, the two women ordered the nightly special. Concerned about her young friend, Julia said, "Now tell me more about Mrs. Woodward."

"The doctor said that she didn't take enough Laudanum to kill herself, but he thought she might have tried to end her life. He wants her to remain under his care so that he can observe her."

"Did Mrs. Woodward say anything to you when you found her?"

"Claudia mumbled something that sounded like, 'an evil man,' but I really couldn't make sense of her words."

"I imagine she didn't improve while you were there with her."

Nora shook her head. "No, she didn't. I know that I shouldn't dwell on her problems, but I'm worried about what will happen to her son Freddie."

Julia noticed the tears in Nora's eyes. "Do the Woodwards have a relative or neighbor who could help out?"

"Not that I know of. Mr. and Mrs. Owens are taking care of the boy again, but it isn't a permanent solution. The doctor said that his mother needs counseling and supportive therapy. The best place for her to receive that is while she is staying at his sanitarium. I visited her after I brought Freddie over to the Owens' home, but Claudia was still non-responsive."

"What was your impression of the place?"

"The sanitarium seems adequate, if understaffed. I saw a few patients who were convalescing and just one nurse, but no one in Claudia's condition. I don't think that she has any other option."

Pursing her lips, Julia thought of something. "Didn't you tell me that the Woodwards had lived in San Francisco before moving here a few months ago? It's possible they might have relatives there. I might be able to locate them."

"Thank you for trying, Julia. That would be very helpful."

"I'll call my secretary tonight to begin making inquiries. By the way, do you know if there is a husband in the picture?"

Nora shrugged. "When I first met Freddie, he said that his father was dead. I thought he might have been killed in the war."

"Well, I'll do my best," Julia said, as she placed her napkin on her lap. "It would be helpful if there was an aunt or uncle to take care of the boy until his mother's mental health improves."

"If Rob wasn't in jail, I'm sure Freddie could stay with him. Oh, before I left the office and came to meet you, I telephoned the sheriff's office to see if I might talk with Rob tomorrow. I'm hoping that Sheriff Terry will reconsider. Deputy Jensen said he would have the sheriff call me at home later this evening."

"If he agrees to the interview, I'd be happy to provide you with a ride to the jail. This afternoon I hired the services of a chauffeur through Mr. Quinlan's garage. I'm to be picked up at my hotel early in the morning."

"That sounds ideal, but I didn't realize that you were leaving Carmel so soon."

Julia heard the disappointment in her friend's voice. Picking up her water glass, she took a sip. "I'll only be away for the weekend. I'm working with a client by the name of Hearst on a design for a residence he's building on a stretch of isolated land north of Santa Barbara. Every Friday I travel by train from San Francisco and hire a taxi to take me to the job site. Tomorrow I'll stick to my schedule, but I'll go by motorcar from here instead. I can drop you off in Monterey before heading south. However, you'll need to find a way back to Carmel, once your interview is over."

"That sounds wonderful. Will you be staying in Carmel for Thanksgiving?"

Julia nodded. "Are you spending the holiday with your parents?"

"No, I'm going to remain in Carmel this year."

When they had finished their meal, Julia caught the waiter's eye and signaled for the check.

Coming up to the table, he smiled and said, "There's no bill to pay, ladies."

"What do you mean, young man?" Julia asked.

"The manager has taken care of it. He says to tell you it's his way of thanking Miss Finnegan for writing the feature story on the Inn's Thanksgiving plans."

The gesture took Nora by surprise. As the waiter walked away, she called out, "Please tell him that I'm most appreciative." Looking at Julia, she said, "Guess who our waiter is?" On seeing the architect's puzzled look, she went on, "He's another part-time actor, just like the waiter who served us at La Playa last night."

"Do you know his name?"

"Yes, it's Randall King. He played a supporting role in 'Immortal Fame,' a play my parents took me to see at the Forest Theater five years ago. I remember it well, because it was my first exposure to dramatic comedy. I became infatuated with Mr.

King. His hair is gray now, but I still think he's handsome."

"It sounds as if you have a little crush on him," an amused Julia said. "I'm sorry, Nora, but I need to make this an early evening." Putting down a tip for the waiter, she went on, "I have some work to do before leaving for San Simeon in the morning. And I must thank you for dinner tonight."

Getting up, Nora kidded, "Don't tell anyone I was paid off."

The two women left the dining room and passed through the lobby on their way out the Pine Inn's front entrance.

"I wish you lived here," Nora said, as she took Julia's arm. "You're such a comfort, and, in many ways, like a mother to me."

Julia seemed pleased to have played a role in helping her friend recover from the sobering scene she had come upon in Jacklin's studio. "We'll get together frequently," she said.

On the darkened street outside, they were greeted by a medium-sized dog that had run up to them. Unleashed and collarless, it wagged its tail and jumped up on Nora.

"I hope this isn't another homeless creature," she said, as she leaned down to pet the mutt. "I'm not ready to take on any more responsibility."

Behind them, a voice yelled, "Down, Ginger. Don't bother those nice ladies." The dog stayed at Nora's feet until the man came up to them. After tipping his bowler, he bent down and tied a leash around the animal's neck. Ginger barked a few times as she and her owner moved on.

"Carmelites love their dogs, don't they?" Julia said. "It's only a short distance to La Playa and your cottage. Shall we walk?"

The pair strolled down Ocean Avenue, turned south, and walked for several blocks. When they arrived at Pine Log, Julia said, "I hope the sheriff allows you to interview Mr. Jacklin tomorrow. Telephone me tonight, dear, no matter how late."

Nora nodded as she opened the gate to her yard. "Thank you for listening. Your counsel was invaluable. Do you remember how to get to La Playa from here?"

"Like an old dog remembers its way home," Julia said with a chuckle.

CHAPTER THIRTY

Friday

At seven o'clock the next morning, a tall, good-looking man in a belted trench coat strode through the open door of the Shamrock Garage.

Pete Quinlan, who was working under the hood of a motorcar, looked up. "What can I do for you, mister?"

"I'm Randall King, Mr. Quinlan. On my way to the theater last night, I noticed the advertisement for a chauffeur on your garage door."

"Got any references?"

Reaching into his coat pocket, King pulled out a sheet of letter paper. Handing it to Quinlan, he said, "Straight from the pen of playwright Herbert Heron himself."

A working man who considered most theater people nothing but lazy ne'er-do-wells, Quinlan was unfamiliar with the name of Carmel's leading dramatist. Nonetheless, he perused the document, nodded, and motioned King outside to a second motorcar that looked identical to the one inside his shop, but showed no signs of damage.

"You're going to have to get your hands dirty," Quinlan said. "First, fill up the tank with gasoline from that pump over there. Then I want you to wash the wind-screen."

"Does this mean that I get the job?"

"Yes, but it's only for a few days." Having eaten a time or two at the Pine Inn, Quinlan had observed King waiting tables in the hotel's restaurant. He had no qualms about giving work to a local. He said, "I need you to drive a lady name of Julia Morgan to San Simeon and back. She's to be picked up at La Playa in half an hour. She'll pay you the fare we agreed on. Half of it's yours. Are you up to it, pretty boy?"

King grinned. "Of course I am. You know, I have a New Jersey driver's license."

Quinlan laughed. "That piece of paper ain't going to keep you from getting into an accident out here." Relieved that now he wouldn't have to close the shop and drive the woman to San Simeon himself, he smiled as he watched King fumble with the gasoline pump and clean the wind-screen.

King breathed a sigh of relief at getting weekend work so easily. It would help to supplement the meager pay from his waiter's job. Having borrowed a cap with a visor from the helpful wardrobe mistress at the Forest Theater last night, he put it on and got into the front seat of the Buick. On a practice run, he drove the length of Ocean Avenue twice and decided that he had the feel of the motorcar. This was going to be more fun than opening night, he thought. He turned south onto Camino Real. Luckily, Quinlan hadn't asked him if he had ever been a chauffeur-for-hire. He would have had to say, 'Only on the stage, I'm afraid.'

Julia Morgan was waiting outside the hotel's front entrance. She waved down the Buick when she saw it coming towards her. Greeting her driver with a nod, she pointed at her suitcase before climbing into the back seat.

King got out and went around the motorcar to pick up the petite woman's bag. Back again behind the steering wheel, he swung the Buick around, but made a clumsy hitch in the gears that jarred his passenger. Turning his head, he smiled congenially and said, "Sorry, Miss Morgan. The road will be much smoother as soon as we get to the highway."

"We all have a first time for everything," Julia replied.

Nora heard the motorcar approaching as she was closing her cottage's Dutch door. She ran down the path to meet it. Settling next to Julia in the back seat, she whispered, "By any chance did you recognize your driver?"

Trying in vain to make out the chauffeur's face in the rear

view mirror, Julia said, "No, I'm afraid I didn't."

Nora giggled. "It's the actor, Randall King, the man who waited on us at the Pine Inn last night."

Julia raised her eyebrows. "I have to admit, I didn't remember him. But don't say anything to get him more rattled than he is." Leaning back, she continued, "I believe we're his first fares ever."

"I assume he knows the way," Nora said, "but just in case, I have the sheriff's directions to the jail. He told me that his office is in the adobe directly behind the museum near the waterfront."

"Don't worry. I'm sure we'll find it."

"Speaking of the sheriff, when I interview Rob, either he or one of his deputies has to be present."

"Your persistence paid off. I'll be looking forward to reading your story in the *Pine Cone* when I get back."

Nora gazed out her window as the Buick lumbered through an older neighborhood situated at the edge of town. She knew it was where Carmel's working class people lived. Their modest homes and gardens looked well tended.

They reached the summit and started down the other side of Carmel hill until they caught up with the morning traffic into Monterey. The motorcar slowed to a crawl, as it followed others that were snaking their way into the city on the narrow, two-lane road.

Nora had time to study the houses lining both sides of the street. Curious about them, she turned to Julia and asked, "Did you design any of these buildings?"

"No, I didn't, but I do admire these early adobe structures. Have you heard of the growing movement in the state to preserve them from being demolished?"

Nora shook her head. "I didn't realize they were so valuable."

"Most were built close to a hundred years ago, prior to statehood, and during the Mexican settlement period. One of the best examples is that one over there." Pointing at a two-story structure, Julia continued, "Colton Hall was California's first capitol. And over there is the Thomas Larkin House. It's considered the prototype for the Monterey Colonial building style."

Nora was embarrassed about her lack of knowledge of architecture. "I didn't mean to imply that you were old enough to design these early adobes, Julia."

Her companion smiled. "You didn't insult me, dear. They inspire my work."

Their driver interrupted them. "We're approaching the main business district, Miss Morgan. The next street is Alvarado. Where to now?"

Julia leaned forward. "Head towards the water."

Exercising timidity, the chauffeur stopped often to allow crossing traffic the right of way, but then smoothly turned the motorcar off the main road onto an open plaza and an imposing two-story adobe fronting the town's fishing wharf.

Nora saw the painted sign with the word "Museum" on Monterey's former custom house. She tapped the driver on the shoulder. "Mr. King, this is where I leave you and Miss Morgan."

Someone had recognized him! Turning around in his seat, King smiled. "It's a pleasure to be acknowledged," he said, "especially by a pretty young lady."

Nora blushed. To think she'd been driven to her appointment by her former idol. Opening her door, she stepped out onto the plaza. "Thank you for the ride, Julia," she said. "I'm even a few minutes early. I hope you have a pleasant journey to San Simeon."

"I forgot to ask you. Did you find a way home?"

"I'm hoping to persuade Deputy Connery to take me back to Carmel."

"If anyone can do that, Nora, it's you."

They waved at one another as the driver turned the Buick around and slowly drove away.

Suddenly Nora felt cold. Was it due to nerves? Or could it be the chill in the air? That morning she had deliberately chosen her heaviest wool coat suit and matching leggings coming down to the tops of her shoes. She didn't think that her discomfort was a result of the weather. Then it dawned on her. She realized that the black motorcar that Miss Morgan had hired was identical to the Buick that had carried Martin Fields to his death in Pescadero Canyon.

Shrugging off her nervous jitters, Nora threw back her shoulders and walked quickly past the shuttered museum to her meeting with a self-confessed murderer.

CHAPTER THIRTY ONE

Sheriff's Deputy Alvin Jensen was sitting at the front desk. Through the adobe's window, he spotted Nora Finnegan walking towards the jail. Getting up, he came outside to greet her. "I'm Deputy Jensen, Miss Finnegan, in case you forgot my name."

Nora smiled. "I remember you from our first meeting in the canyon and I saw you again when you arrested Mr. Jacklin a few days ago."

He grinned. "That's right, you did. Well, everything's set up for your interview with him. However, Deputy Connery isn't in yet. He called to say he has a family emergency." Seeing Nora's frown, he added, "But Sheriff Terry's here. He just came back from a funeral mass."

Nora didn't want the deputy to get the wrong impression. "I wasn't expecting Deputy Connery to be here to meet me. The sheriff arranged my interview with your prisoner. I've come here this morning at his invitation."

Jensen appeared confused, but said nothing more. Opening the door, he ushered her into the jail's reception area. The room had whitewashed walls, a low, sloping roofline and small windows of wavy plate glass. It was furnished with a few chairs. Behind the waist high counter Nora could see a hall with three closed doors leading to adjoining rooms. The place looked old. She asked, "Do you know what this adobe was used for during Monterey's Mexican era?"

Jensen's face lit up. "If there's anything I know about, miss, it's local history. My grandpa says this was a rooming house for the rowdy sailors in the olden days. They came into port, bought a bottle of rum and bedded down in here. Some nights, we still use this place as a temporary jail to let the drunks sleep it off. He grinned. "Come to think of it, times haven't really changed much, have they?"

Nora found that she was enjoying their banter. She said, "History does repeat itself. I'm so glad the city leaders decided to keep this piece of the past."

Jensen was about to start off on another of his grandfather's tales, but before he could, one of the doors behind the counter opened.

Dressed in a dark suit, tie and white dress shirt, Frank Terry stepped into the corridor. "Hello there, Miss Finnegan," the sheriff said.

Nora thought that he looked less like a lawman and more like a banker or an attorney. Then she remembered that the sheriff had been to a funeral service.

"How was the ride from Carmel?" he said, sticking out his hand.

Nora recalled their last meeting at Hotel La Playa, but had forgotten his firm grip. She said, "It was fine, sir. And thank you for allowing me to interview Mr. Jacklin today. In no way do I intend to hinder your ongoing investigation."

Terry laughed. "If I thought you would, I wouldn't have agreed to your request." Walking over to the middle door, he pulled out a large key and inserted it into the lock. "Jacklin's inside," he said. "All we have is his unsolicited confession. You won't get anything more out of him than we have."

"I'd like to try," Nora replied. "As I said on the telephone, perhaps one of our *Pine Cone* readers might remember seeing something on 17-Mile Drive the night of Mr. Fields' death. By the way, Sheriff, have you found the murder weapon?"

Terry shook his head. "Jacklin won't tell us where he hid the gun. My deputies were all over his property and they couldn't locate it. I admit it isn't the best of cases, just relying on a man's confession."

"Are you saying that you don't have sufficient evidence to try Mr. Jacklin?"

"No, I'm not saying that, Miss Finnegan, and don't you print that in your paper. We do have his signed confession."

"But he could change his story before the trial and plead

innocent."

"Maybe so. Since Fields' widow arrived, she's been pressuring me to formally charge Jacklin. She wants to take her husband's body home for burial. I'm not ready to do that just yet. I want to make certain that we have the right killer."

Secretly, Nora would be delighted to see Sarah Fields leave town, but something else was nagging at her that she had to explore. She said, "At the last Carmel Board of Trustees meeting, Mr. Jacklin spoke out against Mr. Fields' hotel. He and Carlotta Fleming were leading the group that was working to stop it. Then Mr. Fields and Miss Fleming were murdered. Could their deaths be connected to the hotel project?"

Terry groaned. "I don't think so, but thanks to you, we have the knife that killed Miss Fleming. However, that murder is far from being solved. What bothers me is why Jacklin won't give us any details about his confrontation with Fields. All he says is that he killed him. Period."

"I know how to get Rob to talk, Sheriff."

"I doubt it."

Nora saw Deputy Connery walk through the jail's front door. Taking off his jacket and dropping it on a chair, he came over to them. "Sorry I'm late, Sheriff," he said. "It couldn't be helped."

"Everything under control at home?" Terry asked.

Nora didn't want to hear about Connery's domestic problems. She said, "I want to be alone with Mr. Jacklin during our interview, Sheriff. He has refused to say anything to you, but I think our private talk will offer him a chance to be candid."

"Absolutely not, Miss Finnegan! I told you last night that isn't protocol. Either I or a deputy I assign is to be present at all times. We never leave a prisoner alone with a citizen, especially a young lady like yourself. Only his lawyer will have that privilege."

Before Nora could object, a telephone rang. Connery walked over to the counter, picked up the receiver, spoke a few words, and then hung up. Coming back to them, he said, "That was the coroner, Sheriff. He wants to see us at his office. It's about that dead body Jensen discovered last night under the wharf."

"Our business with the coroner shouldn't take long, Miss Finnegan," Terry said. "Since Jacklin won't tell you anything anyway, there's no reason why you can't start without me.

Connery and I will be back shortly."

Nora frowned when he turned to Jensen and added, "I'm leaving you in charge, Alvin. Make darned sure that nothing bad happens to her."

"I'll take care of her like she was my baby sister." the junior deputy said.

Terry headed for the front door and said, "Let's go, Jimmy."

Nora felt disappointed that she wouldn't be permitted to be alone with Rob. She followed Deputy Jensen into the holding cell. The first thing she noticed was its narrow window with thick outside bars. The place was gloomy. Looking around at the meager furnishings, she saw a cot covered with an Indian blanket, a square table with a single chair, and a covered bucket in the far corner.

Hunched over the table, Rob was in the same sweater and slacks that he'd worn when she last saw him outside Claudia Woodward's cottage. Dark circles under his eyes told her that he wasn't getting much sleep. He was unshaven, but he had tried to make himself look presentable by combing his hair.

Apparently thinking ahead, Jensen had carried in two chairs. Coming to the center of the cell, he set them both down opposite the prisoner. Nora walked over, pulled one out and sat down, expecting the deputy to do the same.

Instead, he returned to the door, where he remained standing. Leaning up against the wall, he folded his arms across his chest and rocked back and forth on his toes. His demeanor communicated that whoever planned to leave the holding cell would have to go through him.

"How are you feeling, Rob?" Nora asked in a low voice.

He didn't answer.

"You're disappointing a lot of good people with your false confession."

Slumped down in his chair, Rob didn't bother to look up.

Although he was haggard and spent, she had to press him. "No one can understand why you would confess to a murder that you didn't commit."

When he still didn't respond, Nora knew the time was now or never. She had to do something extreme to jar the man out of his uncooperative mood. Turning her head, she stole a quick glance at Deputy Jensen, standing guard at the door. Then, leaning as far back in her chair as she possibly could, she deliberately caused it to topple over, taking her down to the floor with a loud crash.

The noise startled Jensen, who lunged forward. He was at her side in seconds and knelt down on one knee beside her. "Miss Finnegan, are you all right? Did he hit you?"

Lying on her back, Nora forced a whimper, but remained still, her eyes closed.

Turning to his prisoner, Jensen shouted, "Stay where you are. One move and I'll handcuff you."

Rob remained seated, a bewildered look on his face.

Nora opened her eyes and squinted at the lawman leaning over her. Reaching up and touching the back of her head, she felt a bump forming. "Ouch!" she cried. "What happened? Did I faint?"

"I want you to try to move your limbs," Jensen ordered, "but stop right away if it hurts your neck or your back."

Nora squirmed and moved her legs slightly. "Do you think I could have a glass of water, Deputy? I feel a little dizzy."

"You look awful pale," Jensen said, as he stood up. "Stay put, and I'll go get you a drink. Our well's behind the jail, so it's gonna take me several minutes."

"Oh, thank you," Nora said weakly. "I'll lie here and wait for you to come back."

As soon as she heard Jensen lock the cell door, Nora jumped up, righted her chair and sat down. Her head ached where it had hit the hard floor, and in fact, she actually felt a bit woozy.

"You purposely wanted that man out of the room," Rob said.

"I don't deny it. I had to fake a fall because I need to give you some disquieting news concerning two special people for whom you care deeply."

Rob frowned. "If you're still play-acting, Nora, I'm not interested in listening."

"No, I'm not." Leaning forward, she continued, "Yesterday afternoon, Claudia tried to take her life in your studio. She nearly succeeded, but I arrived in time to call the doctor. She's recuperating in his sanitarium for the next few days, but from what Doctor Taylor said, it was touch and go."

Rob's face paled. "Why did she do such a thing? Claudia and I agreed . . . ." His voice trailed off. His shoulders dropped, as he paused and hid his face in his hands. Nora could see that her news had upset him. Yet she had to push him harder.

"What did you and Claudia agree to? You haven't told the sheriff the truth, have you? Freddie has confided in me. After he telephoned you the night of the Trustees' meeting and told you that his mother was missing, he said that you drove to his home, picked him up and the two of you went looking for her. You had an idea where Claudia had gone."

"I don't know what you're driving at. Leave me alone!"

Impatient with his stalling, Nora's voice rose. "That was the night that Martin Fields was shot somewhere on 17-Mile Drive. After listening to Freddie's story, I asked myself, 'Where was the boy's mother?' If she wasn't with you, where had Claudia gone and who was she with? I think you know, Rob. You'd better tell me the truth."

"Give me a minute, Nora. I never imagined Claudia would want to take her life over this. The last thing I need is for something bad to happen to her or to Freddie." He began to sob.

Nora feared he wouldn't confide in her before the deputy came back with the water. She said, "Won't you explain what occurred that Friday night?"

He looked up and wiped the tears from his eyes. "You're right. I suspected who Claudia was with, but I wasn't sure where he'd taken her. I guess this is the time to tell everyone the truth."

Nora heard the click of the door-lock. Jensen entered and paused, as he realized that Nora wasn't lying on the floor, but sitting across from his prisoner. He hurried over. "Thank God, you're O.K., Miss Finnegan. I was really worried about you. Here's that water you asked for."

"Thank you," Nora said. Taking a few sips, she set the glass down on the table. "Deputy Jensen, will you get Sheriff Terry right now? Tell him there's been a break in the Fields case. Mr. Jacklin has decided to talk."

CHAPTER THIRTY TWO

Her notepad on her lap, Nora was sitting in the hall by the open door to Jacklin's holding cell. In view of the fact that she had been able to get Rob to talk, Sheriff Terry had agreed to let her listen to the interrogation as long as she didn't ask any questions. She had positioned her chair so that she could hear everything that was being said. Her article would be a very important one, for it would explain Rob's involvement in Fields' murder.

While she waited for the interview to start, her eyes scanned the cell's interior. The sheriff and Deputy Jensen were sitting across from the prisoner. Deputy Connery was on Rob's right. Jimmy was looking at a writing pad on the table in front of him, all set to record Rob's responses.

"All right, son," Terry said. "Let's hear the truth this time."

Nora lifted her pencil and noticed that Jimmy had done the same.

Rob spoke softly, "Claudia was widowed in San Francisco two years ago. Her husband was killed in a streetcar accident. As a single parent, she had to support herself and her son with her photography. That was when Martin Fields appeared. One weekend he came into her studio, admired her pictures, and said that he wanted to help her promote her work. Soon after, they became involved romantically, but Claudia broke it off when she found out that he was married. She tried to get away from him by moving to Carmel. Fields hired the Pinkerton detective agency to locate her. Once he learned where she was, he tried to force her to resume their affair."

Looking up from her notepad, Nora saw Rob begin to choke up.

"Would you like to take a short break?" Sheriff Terry asked.

"No, I just want to get this over with," Rob said, as he pulled himself together. "Fields came down to Carmel several times to pursue his hotel project. Each time, he pestered Claudia mercilessly. It came to a head after the Trustees' meeting last Friday evening. He arrived at her cottage unannounced and insisted that she go out with him to celebrate the positive response he'd received on his development proposal."

"Just a minute," the sheriff interrupted. "When did you come into the picture?"

"I met Claudia this past September. She brought Freddie to my classroom on the first day of school."

"That's not what I meant. Did you go to see her last Friday night?"

"Yes, but let me explain how that happened. I went home after the meeting ended around ten o'clock. I read for a while and then went to bed. Freddie telephoned me and said he was frightened. It was after eleven by then. He'd been awakened by a noise and went into his mother's bedroom. She wasn't there. That's why he called me."

Listening and jotting down his responses, Nora thought of poor Freddie and how terrified he must have been.

"Where was Mrs. Woodward if she wasn't at home?" the sheriff asked.

"I guessed that Fields had forced her to go for a drive."

Terry looked dubious. "We'll need some corroboration from her as to how much force the man used. If she was a willing partner, then her behavior certainly constituted child endangerment."

Nora could tell by the look on Rob's face that the sheriff's remark had upset him.

"Claudia told me he dragged her out of her house and into his motorcar. He said, 'Nothing bad will happen to your kid if you come with me.' That's what I call 'force', Sheriff. The man was threatening her."

"Tell me what happened when you got to the Woodward cottage."

"Freddie was bawling because his mother was gone. I had

no choice, but to go after Claudia. I knew that she must be in trouble because she would never leave her son alone voluntarily. I bundled Freddie up and off the two of us went."

"How did you know where to look for her?" Terry asked.

"I remembered Claudia saying that Fields kept complaining about having to do business with that 'worthless Davey Chatham.' I knew Chatham lived in his mother's mansion on the beach near the entrance to 17-Mile Drive. I assumed Fields probably took her to Bella Vista. Anyway, that's the first place I looked."

"Will Freddie be able to verify all of this?"

"I'm afraid not. He fell asleep a few minutes after we left his cottage. It was a school night and I could tell that he was exhausted and scared."

Nora saw the sheriff look in Jimmy's direction. "Are you getting all of this down, Deputy Connery?"

Jimmy looked up. "Yes, sir."

"Do you need a few minutes to rest your hand?"

"No, I don't need a break, Sheriff."

Terry turned around and looked at Nora. "What about you, Miss Finnegan?"

"Thank you, sir. I'm doing fine."

"O.K. then. Go on, Rob. What did you do next?"

"I checked Bella Vista first, but there was nobody there, not even Chatham. I figured Fields might have taken Claudia to a secluded spot that's popular with lovers — the old Pebble Beach Lodge. I went there next and pulled into the turnaround where another motorcar was parked. Light was flickering through the lodge's windows."

"What made you think that Fields and Mrs. Woodward were inside?"

"I recognized the parked Buick as one of two that Pete Quinlan owns. I figured Fields had rented it. I left Freddie sleeping on the front seat and went to check. When I opened the front door, I found Claudia curled up on the floor. She was hysterical."

"Was Martin Fields with her?"

"Yes. He was lying on his side next to the fireplace. There was blood all over the front of his shirt. I checked his pulse. He was dead."

Nora's pencil flew across the paper, as she took down Rob's words. When he paused, she looked up to see that the sheriff had gotten to his feet. Removing his suit jacket, he put it on the back of his chair and sat down again. He asked, "How do I know you're telling us the truth this time?"

"Go to the lodge and you'll find the evidence that supports what I've said."

Nora shivered, as she pictured the grisly scene that she and the Boys Club might have come upon the following day, had they hiked up to and looked inside the old lodge. She felt sure that Rob had intentionally steered them away from it. But what he hadn't counted on was Freddie's discovery of Fields' overturned motorcar in the ravine.

Sheriff Terry's face looked stern. "Did Mrs. Woodward shoot Martin Fields?"

Rob nodded. "On the way to the lodge, Claudia said that Fields complained that Freddie was a 'real bother.' He told her he was going to ship him off to some boarding school in upstate New York, whether she liked it or not."

"The man sounds heartless," Connery interjected.

Rob took another deep breath. "Claudia wouldn't go along with his plan. She told him that, under no circumstances, would she agree to it. That's when he lost his temper. He slapped her face, saying, 'You'll do what I tell you!' Then he grabbed her and began choking her, trying to force her to change her mind."

Connery put down his pencil. "There's something to what Jacklin's saying, Sheriff. Jensen and I went to Mrs. Woodward's cottage after learning that it was her picture in Fields' pocket watch. Both of us saw bruises on her neck and face."

Deputy Jensen nodded in agreement.

"Maybe Fields did attack her," the sheriff said. "If he did, what she did to him was self-defense. His actions constituted physical assault with intent to harm."

Rob nodded. "There's more. Fields dragged Claudia out of the Buick and against her will, carried her kicking and screaming into the lodge. He'd been there earlier to bring candles and leave some champagne. Once inside, he pinned her against the wall and forced himself on her."

"Did she try to get away?"

"Yes, she was able to squirm out of his grasp. But he slapped her again and began groping her. She couldn't take any more of his abuse. She shot him."

"Now we're getting somewhere. Where did she get the gun?" Terry asked.

"It was in her purse. I gave it to her."

"Your gun?"

"Yes, mine, Sheriff. It was my weapon that killed Fields."

"Why was it in her possession?"

"I felt that she needed protection after Fields kept showing up in Carmel. I showed her how to use it, and I'm glad I did. The man had evil intentions."

Terry's voice rose. "Why didn't you tell us this in the first place, Rob? Instead, you moved a dead body, disturbed a crime scene and destroyed valuable evidence. Why in God's name didn't you report Fields' death immediately? You and Mrs. Woodward could have explained what happened, just like you're doing now."

"I know I did the wrong thing, but Claudia was completely distraught. I could see that she was in no condition to be questioned."

"How did Fields' body end up in the ravine?"

"I got him out to Quinlan's motorcar and drove it to a clearing. After putting it in neutral, I went back and got my sedan and pushed Fields' motorcar over the edge. Then I took Claudia and Freddie home. I stayed with them the rest of the night."

"Are you denying now that you shot Martin Fields?"

"Yes. I wanted to take the blame for Claudia. We agreed to do that. I didn't want her involved. But Nora told me this morning that Claudia was so upset that she attempted suicide yesterday. She's under Doctor Taylor's care at his sanitarium in Carmel."

Nora noticed the surprised looks on Sheriff Terry's and his deputies' faces.

Jensen spoke up. "Then again, maybe Mrs. Woodward made the whole thing up."

Rob shot out of his chair and reached across the table. Pushing Jensen in the chest, he yelled, "Claudia's not a liar!"

The junior deputy reared backwards, but didn't retaliate.

Connery also jumped up. Grabbing Rob's forearm, he shoved him back in his chair. "Hold on!" he yelled. "There's no need to get physical."

Rob's voice became sullen. "You asked for the truth, Sheriff, and I told it to you. It was important to me that Claudia and her son be together. That's why I confessed."

Nora sympathized with his dilemma, but would the sheriff be swayed?

Terry stroked his chin. "From what you've said, Mrs. Woodward appears to have acted in self-defense. But before I can come to that conclusion, we'll have to check the lodge for any remaining evidence that Fields died there, and also question Mrs. Woodward at the sanitarium. In the meantime, you will remain in my custody. And another thing. Tell me where you hid your gun."

For the first time since his arrest, Rob smiled. "That's an easy one. I hid it in my studio when I got home the next morning. It's at the bottom of a vat of photographic developing fluid. I guess your two deputies didn't want to get their hands wet and smelly."

Neither Jensen nor Connery said a word.

Nora smiled and closed her notebook.

CHAPTER THIRTY THREE

Nora put on her coat and waited in the hallway outside Rob's cell.

"I'll take Miss Finnegan back to Carmel, Sheriff," Deputy Connery said.

Terry nodded his approval. "I want you to stop by Doctor Taylor's sanitarium afterwards. See if you can get a statement from Mrs. Woodward confirming Jacklin's story. I'm taking Jensen to search the old Pebble Beach Lodge. I want to close this case today."

As she followed Jimmy out of the jail, Nora said, "I appreciate your offer of a ride."

"I was counting on it." Helping her into his Model T, he went on, "How about getting something to eat before we head back over the hill? I know a place in Pacific Grove that has a nice view of the bay. I think you'll find the food to your liking."

"That sounds good," Nora said. "I skipped breakfast this morning and perhaps we can talk about Rob's interview as we eat."

They made the short trip to the Lighthouse Café in less than ten minutes. After they were seated at a window table, the waitress took their orders and brought coffee.

Nora said, "I could see how annoyed you were when Rob mentioned Fields' lack of concern for Freddie's welfare."

Jimmy took a sip of hot coffee. "That's true. I was sympathetic to the boy." He looked around the café and then added, "Could you delay the trip back to the *Pine Cone*? There are a couple of people I'd like you to meet before we return to

Carmel."

Nora knew she had a breaking news story to write. On the other hand, she had the exclusive details about Rob's retraction of his confession. She said, "Mr. Owens is a hard taskmaster at times, but I'm sure that will be all right."

Smiling, Jimmy said, "It's settled then. I'm taking a detour after we finish eating."

As they drove into an area of small houses, Nora read the sign at the corner: "The Retreat, Pacific Grove's Oldest Neighborhood." She had never been here before. They turned at Fountain Avenue and stopped in front of a cottage that was set close to the road. He parked, jumped out, and came around the Model T to help Nora out.

"As you can see, I don't have a garage," Jimmy said, "but what I like most about my place is its close proximity to Monterey Bay."

Walking up the porch steps, Nora spotted a tall, gray-haired woman at the front door. Her eyes focused on Nora, but she said to Jimmy, "She's been asking for you."

"Ma, I brought someone I'd like you to meet," he answered. "This is Miss Finnegan. Nora, this is my mother, Kathleen Connery."

"Hello, Mrs. Connery. I'm very pleased to meet you," Nora said.

The older woman smiled at Nora. "Before we go inside, I have to ask you something. Did you have chicken pox, Miss Finnegan? My granddaughter woke up today with bright red spots all over her body."

"That's why I was late for Mr. Jacklin's interview," Jimmy interjected.

"I did have a case as a child, Mrs. Connery," Nora replied.

Taking her hand, Jimmy said, "My mother thinks that I should have told you about my marital situation when we first became acquainted."

Nora stammered, "And just what is that situation?"

"I'm a widower. My wife and I got married right after we graduated from high school. Emma died in childbirth about a year later. Molly, our daughter, is five now. With the help of my parents who live next door, she's growing into a fine little girl."

Nora didn't know what to say, except, "I'm truly sorry

about your wife."

Kathleen Connery said, "Won't you come in, Nora? I'll fix us a nice cup of tea."

"We just had some coffee, Ma," Jimmy said. "And we're in kind of a hurry, but I would like Nora to meet Molly."

Nora told herself that her news article could wait a little longer. A more personal story was in the making.

CHAPTER THIRTY FOUR

At three o'clock that afternoon, William Owens came out of the *Pine Cone's* back room with the intention of speaking to his reporter. He found Nora at the receptionist's desk, where she had been answering the telephone in Mrs. Owens' absence.

Sitting down in the chair opposite her, he said, "I came out to tell you that I won't be making my usual Saturday rounds tomorrow, Honora. I have too much work to do. I also had a long talk with your father." Seeing the concerned look on her face, he added, "I thought he ought to know about your improved writing skills. The story you put together on Rob's role in Fields' murder was riveting. It's your best work to date."

Nora breathed a sigh of relief. "I appreciate your praise, sir, but did you feel the same way about my other article on Carlotta Fleming's murder?"

"No, I wasn't happy with it. You used too many graphic details."

Closing her eyes, Nora pictured the stab wounds on Carlotta's body. She said, "But they were all in the coroner's report."

"That might be appropriate for a big city newspaper like the *San Francisco Call*, but not for the *Pine Cone*. I'm going to edit your piece before going home tonight."

"I understand, Mr. Owens, but I hope you'll keep my written description of the kind of knife the killer used."

He nodded. "I'm going to run it as a sidebar. It's a very unusual knife and it will spark our readers' curiosity." Getting up from his chair, he went on, "As you know, Mrs. Owens left early to be home when Sally and Freddie returned from school. I'd like you to continue answering the telephone until closing time today. In addition to the editing work I have ahead of me, I'm expecting to hear back from a prospective typesetter whom I'm considering hiring. Let me know as soon as he calls, will you?"

"Of course, sir. Mrs. Owens told me about him before she left. Is he the same man who came in earlier today, looking for part-time work?"

Owens walked around the front counter on his way to the back room. "Yes, and if he agrees to all of my terms, his first assignment tomorrow morning will be to typeset your two articles."

For the rest of the afternoon, Nora's mood remained cheery, mainly due to Mr. Owens' unexpected praise. Even a complaint from an irate caller about a misspelled name in her wedding announcement didn't dampen Nora's spirits. Between calls, she mused about her morning meeting with Jimmy Connery's family. His daughter Molly had been polite and sweet. And Mrs. Connery reminded her of her own mother.

She didn't realize that it was after 5:00 until Mr. Owens walked out to the front again. He told her that the typesetter had taken the job, and that she should go home. Putting on her coat, she turned off the light, opened the front door, and left.

The evening temperature felt crisp. Moonlight lit the street. She would enjoy the short walk to her cottage, especially after sitting at Mrs. Owens' desk most of the afternoon. Crossing Ocean Avenue, she darted between the row of young trees that separated the dirt road into two lanes. As she did so, her shoulders brushed up against the pine needles on the trees' lower branches, causing the release of the fresh pine scent that she always associated with Carmel.

Tonight she was looking forward to a hot bath and a relaxing evening after supper. Her late-morning breakfast with Jimmy had carried her through the rest of the day, so that she only wanted a bowl of soup. Not having to prepare a hot meal would give her time to finish reading her Mary Austin novel before heading to bed.

As she closed Pine Log's Dutch door, she heard the telephone ring. She didn't have to turn on the table lamp, since moonlight streamed in the two front windows. She picked up the receiver, hoping that Mr. Owens hadn't changed his mind about her coming into work tomorrow morning. Slipping off her shoes, she said, "Finnegan residence."

"It's Jimmy, Nora. I wanted to see how you were feeling. You put in a long day."

"I'm well, but how is Molly? I hope her fever came down."

"No, it hasn't yet, but she's sleeping. My mother is spoiling her rotten. I'll have to be strict with her when she gets over her illness."

"Aren't policemen always telling others what to do?" Nora teased. "From what I observed today, Molly has you wrapped around her little finger. She'll have her way, no matter what you try to do to change that."

"Think so? Well, I wasn't asking for a friendly lecture," he teased back.

Nora held her breath, unsure of what she would hear next.

"I called to congratulate you. I don't know how you did it, but you were able to get Jacklin to retract his confession. Sheriff Terry was very impressed. We couldn't get the man to say anything, no matter how hard we tried."

Nora's confidence soared. His compliment made what she was about to ask him easier. "I know you have things to do," she said, "but can you spare me another minute?"

"I don't have to hang up yet. Ma's in Molly's bedroom with her."

"I'd like your advice about something that concerns the Fleming murder case."

"What is it?"

"I've been mulling over what to do with a vital piece of information I've received. It could help you find the owner of the boning knife that was used to kill Carlotta."

Jimmy remained quiet for a few seconds and then said, "You shouldn't be interfering with police business."

Bristling, Nora responded, "Then I won't tell you what I know."

"I'm sorry to be blunt, but we're working hard to identify the fingerprints on the knife and then we'll go from there."

"I understand, but what I've learned could be very helpful to you. You see, I've been thinking about my article on Mr. Levy's specialty Christmas gifts. It occurred to me that abalone-handled knives might be something that an exotic import shop like

Gump's would carry. So I telephoned the store in San Francisco and asked the salesman to check their records to see if they had sold such a set to someone in this area. He agreed to help, and when he returned my call late this afternoon, he said that a set that matched the description I'd given him was ordered for one of Mr. Levy's customers."

"Let me guess. You've already contacted Joe Levy."

"Yes, I have. The set was sent from Gumps to Carmel a year ago last December. And you'll be surprised to learn who purchased it."

"For heaven's sake, Nora, don't keep me in suspense!"

"It was Davey Chatham's mother. Mr. Levy clearly remembers the sale because the knives were so unique. I think that you and I need to make a visit to the Chatham residence tomorrow morning, to see if the rest of the knives are still there."

"Are you serious? A search requires a warrant from a county judge. And even if I agreed to accompany you without one, and we got our hands on the knife set, it isn't admissible as evidence in a court of law." He paused for a moment, and then went on, "However, I have a better idea. Why don't I let Sheriff Terry know what you've found out? Then he and I will take it from there."

"I don't agree with that. Any delay, even a short one, is going to give Carlotta's killer time to dispose of the rest of the set."

"Why do you think that?"

"Because the murderer will read about the discovery of the boning knife in the *Pine Cone's* special issue on Monday morning. I just wrote a full description of it for Mr. Owens. Whoever killed Carlotta will realize that we've found it."

"That may be, but there's a right way and a wrong way to do this. Only a judge's approval will allow us to search the Chatham home. What you're suggesting isn't legal. I'll call the sheriff at home as soon as you and I hang up. I'm willing to bet that we can get a subpoena by Monday."

"I asked for your opinion, Jimmy, and I'm glad you gave it," Nora said, but with less enthusiasm in her voice. "Do what you think is right, and thank you for calling tonight to see how I was."

Putting down the receiver, Nora went across the front room and turned on the lamp. The telephone rang again.

Her hopes rose. She said, "I knew you would change your mind."

"Is this Miss Finnegan from the newspaper?"

It was a male voice, but this time, it wasn't Jimmy Connery's. "This is Nora Finnegan," she said, as she sat down on the sofa. "And you are?"

CHAPTER THIRTY FIVE

"I'm the neighbor across the street from the Woodward cottage," the caller said. "I apologize for disturbing you at home, Miss Finnegan, but I found your number in the directory. You brought the little boy and his dog over to my place as the firemen arrived. The name's Donald Sharp. Do you remember me?"

"Of course I do, Mr. Sharp. You were kind to watch Freddie until I made other arrangements for him."

"I like helping people. Living alone makes for a long, dull day unless I do things for others. Young Freddie's company cheered me up and made me feel useful. I'm just sorry that his and his mother's home was destroyed."

"Do you know who owns it? Someone told me that Mrs. Woodward was renting the cottage."

"Yes, they only lived there since school started. The owner lives in San Jose. He's a friend of mine. He was very upset because Hollyhock House is a total loss. But let me get to the reason I called you. I overheard something in Levy's store today. Joe Levy was telling some customers that the blaze was deliberately set."

"If you know something, you should contact Sheriff Frank Terry, Mr. Sharp." As she listened to her words, Nora realized that they sounded exactly like Jimmy's advice to her only a few minutes ago.

"I know what you're saying, Miss Finnegan, but I'm not entirely sure of what I saw before the fire started. It's just that

my eyes are none too good these days. That's why I decided
to telephone you. I could use some advice and you seem an
understanding person. The last thing I want is to implicate an
innocent man."

Curious now, Nora said, "Why don't you tell me what you
saw, and I'll try to help you evaluate it."

"That sounds good. On the day of the fire, I remember
coming out on my front porch to get some air. I sat in my rocker,
which, you might recall, is directly behind my camellia bushes.
They're in bloom now. They have those nice pink flowers with
the yellow centers. The wife planted them when we bought the
cottage for our retirement. They're the reason why we named the
place Camellia Cottage."

Nora didn't dare rush the elderly man, but she had to redirect
his thoughts. "What happened next, while you were sitting there,
enjoying your flowers?"

"I was just getting to that. Well, before the fire started, I
noticed a black Pierce-Arrow coming down the street. In case you
aren't familiar with that type of motorcar, it's one that's pretty
hard to miss. You don't see them much around Carmel village."

Suddenly Nora remembered the unusual looking black
motorcar that she had seen parked under Bella Vista's *porte-
cochere*. It had also been waiting in front of Hotel La Playa when
she had visited there. That time, Davey Chatham had been behind
the wheel, with Fields' widow in the front seat next to him.

Mr. Sharp interrupted her thoughts. "Did you know that
Pierce-Arrows have a right-hand drive? Oh, I'm digressing again,
aren't I? Well, this one stopped directly across the street from my
cottage in front of Hollyhock House."

"What did you observe next?" Nora asked.

"I watched the driver get out and go up to Mrs. Woodward's
front door. He knocked on it a few times and then went around
back. I thought he was delivering a package to the lady. I didn't
see what he was carrying at first, but when he returned, I noticed
that it was a small container of some sort."

"Could you describe the man for me?"

"He was on the thin side and well-dressed."

"What happened next, Mr. Sharp?"

"A second motorcar came down the street and the driver of
the Pierce-Arrow bent over, like he was hiding. Then he got back
in his motorcar and drove off. It wasn't more than ten minutes

later that I saw smoke rising from the back of the Woodward cottage."

"I think you'd better give this information to the sheriff," Nora said. "You saw the arsonist, even if it's hard for you to describe him."

"You think so? As I said, my eyesight's not what it used to be."

"No matter. If you contact Sheriff Terry, he'll want to come out and talk with you. You might remember something else."

"Well, I'd enjoy having a cup of coffee with the county's top lawman. Do you know where I can reach him?" Pausing, he added, "Oh, there's no need, Miss Finnegan. I have the sheriff's telephone number right here in my directory."

Putting down the receiver, Nora's thoughts raced. Had Davey Chatham gone to the Woodward cottage, bringing with him a container of kerosene stolen from Levy's storage shed? If so, he was responsible for setting the fire. She felt sure that Chatham had been hired by Sarah Fields to get revenge for Claudia Woodward's attempt to break up her marriage.

Getting up from the sofa, Nora went to heat up a bowl of leftover soup, when a rustling noise startled her. She looked out the window over the kitchen sink. The moon was casting its light on the big Norfolk Island pine in the side yard.

Just then her next door neighbor, Lucinda Newsom, stepped out from under the tree branches. Wearing a bulky sweater over her long nightgown, she was heading for the back stairs.

Nora opened the door and called out, "Good evening, Mrs. Newsom. Will you come in for a while and keep me company?"

Shaking her head, the older woman said, "I can't stay, dear. I have a nice fire going and I don't want my kitty cat messing about when I'm not there." Holding out the tray, she pulled off the napkin to reveal a steaming bowl of something that smelled delicious. "I brought you some of my special lamb stew. I made enough for both of us this afternoon. I figure somebody has to see to it that you're eating properly, Nora, since you're never home to cook for yourself."

Nora took the tray and said, "Thank you, Mrs. Newsom. You're so good to me."

Reaching into her sweater pocket, Mrs. Newsom produced a pint of milk. "This is yours," she said, as she gave her the bottle. "You left extra early this morning. I saw you go off to work from my bedroom window. First I heard a motorcar stop in front, and then I watched you get in and sit next to that nice-looking, older lady. I knew you probably wouldn't be driving past our milk shrine for your order."

Nora decided she had better retract her impressions about her Carmel neighbors. From now on, she would make an effort to overlook Mrs. Newsom's nosy habits. "You're spoiling me," she said. "I'm lucky to have you as a friend."

Standing on the back porch, she watched her neighbor head home along the path between their cottages. Then she came inside and put the bowl of stew on the kitchen table. The morsels of tender lamb and roasted vegetables were comforting. After finishing her supper, she got up from the table and went over to the sink to wash Mrs. Newsom's bowl.

For the rest of the evening, Nora couldn't seem to relax. After hearing Jimmy's reluctance to move swiftly on finding the abalone cutlery set, she had felt disappointed. Then there was the matter of what she'd learned from Mr. Sharp's telephone call. The news about Davey Chatham's visit to the Woodward cottage had added another dilemma. What should she do with this new information pointing to the identity of the arsonist?

She wished she could seek out her friend Julia's counsel, but the architect was far away from Carmel, working with Mr. Hearst at the job site in San Simeon.

Then Nora remembered her mother's advice: 'when a woman faces a difficult decision, she should rely on her feminine intuition.' If the rule was good enough for Alice Finnegan, it certainly was good enough for her daughter. As she headed for her bath, she formulated her course of action for tomorrow.

CHAPTER THIRTY SIX

Saturday

After a restless night filled with frustrating dreams, Nora awakened to the chimes of the Grandfather clock in the front room. She slipped out of bed, parted the curtains, and was pleased to see sunshine for a change. Dressing quickly, she fixed breakfast and placed a very important telephone call. The concierge at Hotel La Playa answered on the third ring. Swallowing the last bite of toast, Nora identified herself.

"*Ciao, signorina,*" Oresto Santoli said. "I hope you're well on this fine morning."

"Thank you, I am, but is your cousin Angela working today?"

"*Si*, but why you wanna know?"

"Her brother Rudolfo told me a few days ago that she works for the Chatham family. Is that true?"

"Si, Angie goes to Bella Vista on the weekends. She cooks dinners for *Signor* Davey and his friends."

"Is she going to be there this afternoon, *per favore*?"

"For you saying please, I'll tell you that Angie goes to the Chatham house to fix the food at two o'clock."

"Will you tell her that I'd like to accompany her today?"

"Better you come here to the hotel first."

"No, I prefer to handle the matter now on the telephone."

"Well, I don't know, *signorina*."

"Don't you think you owe me a favor, Mr. Santoli? I'm sure

that you remember that I didn't press charges against you when you used me to get away from the police."

After a momentary silence, he said, "O.K. You help me. Now I help you, and please, call me Oresto."

"All right, Oresto. Tell your cousin Angie that I'll go with her this afternoon."

"What's so important at Bella Vista?"

"I want to learn how she cooks Italian food."

He laughed. "*Si, signorina*. That's good. I'll tell Angie. Rudolfo will drive you both. You meet them at the hotel's back door at two. But next time I see you, we talk together. Maybe you invite me to your house and cook me pasta that you learn from my cousin."

Nora put down the receiver without responding to his idea.

At two o'clock, a black Model T pulled up to La Playa's service entrance. Nora and Angie Daneri were waiting inside. When the driver sounded the horn, they ran out and got in.

Rudolfo insisted that Nora pay him a dollar for the ride to Bella Vista. "Is only half price," he said.

She thought it odd that the bellman would charge her, but she agreed.

For the next two hours, Nora smarted in silence because she had to obey all of Angie's instructions, none of them really divulging any secrets of Italian cooking. The young woman kept explaining how she had learned to cook from her mother — a tedious tale. Then she assigned her the task of setting the dining room table with Mrs. Chatham's Spode china, sterling silver and Waterford crystal. Angie's watchful eyes and constant demands didn't allow Nora any opportunity to investigate the pantry where she suspected the abalone cutlery set might be stored.

Angie kept her busy by saying: 'wash and peel the vegetables,' and 'fix the flowers Rudolfo picked for the table,' and do this and do that. The closest Nora got to the actual cooking was when she removed a steaming large copper pot from the top of the Chatham's oversized stove and set it on a nearby counter. It was getting late. She had to conjure up some diversion soon, so that her time here wouldn't be wasted.

"Damn! How can they be late? They'll miss my opening

remarks," Keith complained. He and Pete Quinlan had already taken their seats in the Forest Theater's front row.

Closing his program, Pete asked, "Why are you getting upset?"

"Because they know that the benefit starts at five o'clock."

Pete gazed around him at the people milling about. "Both of them better show," he said. "I didn't close the garage early to bathe and get dressed up for nothing."

Keith paced back and forth in front of the stage. "I'm confident that Mayotta is coming, but Nora should have been here by now. I hope she makes it before it gets dark." His eyes roamed the natural amphitheatre as the light began to fade. Pine trees surrounded the theater on all sides and blocked the last rays of the setting sun. The temperature was dropping. Carmelites opened their blankets and spread them out on the wooden benches.

"It's going to be cold without some female bodies to keep us warm," Pete joked.

"I told you, these are nice women, not street-walkers," Keith replied.

A man who was standing near an immense pile of logs to one side of the open-air stage leaned over and put a match to tinder in the fire pit. Pointing at him, Pete grumbled, "If they don't come soon, at least that bonfire will help us out."

Someone in the audience yelled, "Light the pit on the other side too, mister!"

Just then, the young lady whom Keith had persuaded to buy a ticket to his benefit strolled in, surrounded by a group of people. Waving his bowler in the air, he called out, "Miss Brown, it's Keith Preston. I'm over here."

Mayotta Brown waved and attempted to turn around, but was swept up the stairs by the crowd into one of the upper rows.

"I'll go say hello to her before I have to introduce our speaker," Keith said. "I want to make sure she joins us for the social hour after Mr. Kuster's talk." As he was about to leave, he noticed that Pete had pulled a flask out of his jacket pocket.

Keith's face turned red with anger. Reaching out, he grabbed it out of Quinlan's hand. "Hell's Bells, Pete! This is a cultural event. I told you not to bring that. What kind of a dumb ape are you? You can't drink out in the open. It's illegal. Now behave yourself, and keep an eye out for Nora."

Lifting the lid off the copper pot, Nora peered into the tomato gravy. "Goodness, Angie, what are those tender-looking pieces of meat floating in your sauce?" she asked. "Are they chicken breasts?"

Angie used her spoon to coat each of the pieces with the bubbling gravy. "This dish is one of my family's favorites. We call it *conigli alla cacciatora* — what you call rabbits. But now I want you to take the cooked vegetables out and put them in those big white serving dishes over there."

Nora sensed that Angie was getting impatient, and yet she still hadn't figured out how to sneak into the pantry to search it. "Should I find some carving knives to cut up this rabbit?" she asked.

"No. The meat will fall off the bones."

"There's so much food. How many people are you planning to feed with this meal? I only set three places at the table."

Angie smiled. "We Italians fix a lot of food because we have big families. *Signor* Davey say tonight he have two guests at five o'clock. He don't tell me their names, only to make plenty of food. After my brother and me serve it, we can go home and leave him to take care of the rest." Brushing her hair away from her face, Angie giggled.

"What's so funny?"

The young woman rolled her eyes. "*Signor* Davey he never cleans up the mess. Tomorrow when I come back to Bella Vista, the big mess still here. If his mama sees the trouble he makes, she wouldn't let him live here no more."

Both women stopped talking when they heard the front door open and shut. A man's voice called out, "Angelina, my guests are here. Tell Rudolfo he should bring out the champagne. I hope he put it on ice like I told him to."

"*Dio!* Where's that brother of mine?" Angie whispered to Nora. "He has to open the bottles for Mister Davey. Rudy is never around when I need him." Running to the window, Angie looked out at the beach below the house.

Nora joined her and saw Rudolfo sitting on the sand. He was watching the incoming waves.

"*Lazarone!* I better go get that lazy bum," Angie said, grabbing her sweater. "Nora, you get the champagne glasses. They're in the pantry over there."

"I'll bring them right out while you get Rudolfo."

Angie opened the back door and ran down the steps to summon her brother.

Nora knew that she had only a few minutes before they returned. Entering the pantry, she noticed counters on both sides, with drawers and open shelves below and cabinets above. In the center of the room sat a marble-topped counter holding the silver tray with the champagne flutes. She began opening the closed cabinets as fast as she could. Inside the first one she found neat rows of homemade canned goods. Other cabinets contained sets of china, glassware, and an assortment of large serving pieces. There were no utensils in any of them. What she was searching for had to be in one of the drawers. She opened one after another, but all she found were sets of matching silverware that needed polishing.

Looking around, she spied a single large drawer underneath the marble-topped counter in the center of the room. She pulled it open and found several rectangular boxes. One had the word "Gumps" embossed in gold on its leather cover.

Nora lifted the lid to reveal a set of five carving knives. Each was in its own niche and sported a handle of polished abalone shell. There was one empty space about the size of the boning knife that Jimmy and she had found in Carlotta's garden. Her heart pounded, as her fingers touched the purple felt where the missing knife should have been.

A guttural utterance startled her. She pushed the drawer shut and spun around.

Davey Chatham stood in the middle of the doorway, his body blocking her only means of escape. "Not you again," he shouted.

Moving towards him, Nora said, "I know you were the one who burnt down Freddie Woodward's home."

Shoving her back against the center counter, he slapped her hard. Nora started to raise her arms to protect herself, but not in time to deflect the blow from a fist on her cheek. Falling sideways, she tried to grab the marble counter, but her head grazed its edge as she fell to the floor.

The last thing she remembered was Chatham leaning over her and grinning.

CHAPTER THIRTY SEVEN

Angie carried the silver tray with the champagne flutes into Bella Vista's living room. Coming up to the guests and *Signor* Davey, she could see that he was sweating. "Where is *Signorina* Finnegan?" she whispered in his ear.

He looked at Sarah Fields and then at Doctor Taylor before answering. As he took the last flute from her tray, he said, "Miss Finnegan had to leave, Angie. Her boyfriend came for her. Now go back to the kitchen and get the dinner on the table."

Shrugging her shoulders, Angie retreated to the kitchen. She would tell Rudolfo that he wouldn't get another dollar from Nora on the return trip to La Playa.

"Who could that be at this time of night, William?" Mary Lee said, as she heard a knock on the Owens' front door. Checking the clock on the mantel, she saw that it was eight o'clock. Had the noise been a raccoon jumping up on the door, she wondered? Putting down her mending, she nudged her husband, whose eyes were closed. They were sitting next to one another on the front room sofa, listening to music on the Victrola. Then she heard two sharp raps.

Sally, with her dog Dasher close behind, came running out of her bedroom. "I'll get it, Mama," she shouted. It wasn't a school night, so the little girl had been allowed to read in bed. Anxious to join in, Carlotta's spaniel, Maisie, followed Sally and the corgi. Both dogs barked and lunged at the front door.

The hubbub awakened Owens. "Stop right there, young lady," he said. "I don't want you answering at this hour." Getting up from the sofa, he walked down the hall and switched on the front porch light.

Sally parted the window curtains. "It's the librarian, Daddy." After he opened the door, she said, "You can't pick up my library book, Mr. Preston. I haven't read it yet."

Knowing that his younger patrons often were surprised when they met him in situations other than at the library, Keith laughed. "Of course not, Sally. Take your time to finish it. You don't have to return it before the due date I stamped on the card."

Mrs. Owens joined them at the doorway. "Dasher and Maisie, quit your barking!" she said. "Freddie's asleep. What brings you here so late, Keith? Come inside and get warm. I'll put on a pot of coffee."

"Thanks, but none for me, Mrs. Owens. This isn't really a social call."

As the two dogs sniffed at Keith's shoes, Mary Lee sensed that something was troubling him. She turned to William and said, "You two men go in the front room and talk. Sally and I will read her book of fairy tales in the bedroom." Taking her squirming daughter's arm, she guided her down the hallway, a pair of frisky dogs running ahead.

"Tell me what's bothering you, Keith," Owens said. "You look tired."

"I'm worried. Has Nora come by or telephoned you any time this evening?"

Not wanting his wife to overhear any bad news about Nora, Owens grabbed his overcoat from the hall closet, stepped out onto the porch, and closed the front door behind him. "Let's sit over there on those wood chairs," he suggested.

"I may be imagining things, sir," Keith said, as he took a seat. "I know Nora's independent and can take care of herself, but something has happened to her. We'd arranged to meet at the Forest Theater for the library fundraiser earlier. It's unlike her, not to let me know if she wasn't going to come, and what bothers me more is that nobody I've talked to has seen her tonight."

William Owens felt a knot forming in his stomach. He was reacting as a surrogate parent would. It was a role he'd assumed from the time his best friend's daughter had arrived in Carmel to work for him at the *Pine Cone*. "Did you speak with her neighbors?" he asked. "One of them must know where she is."

Keith shook his head. "I checked, sir. Nora called me around noon. She said she had errands to do, but that she'd be finished in time and would meet me at the theater. She never showed up. The reception afterwards ended at seven and still, there was no sign of her. I escorted a lady friend home and then walked past Nora's cottage. Everything was dark. The curtains hadn't been drawn. It looked like she never returned."

Owens shook his head. "That's odd. Before she left the newspaper last night, Honora said that she intended to spend a quiet weekend at home. I can't think of where she could have gone without leaving word with someone."

Keith continued twisting the brim of his bowler until he realized that it had lost its shape. Staring down at it, he said, "I'm a bundle of nerves. I don't know what else to do. I thought Julia Morgan might have invited Nora to dinner at the hotel this evening. I even called La Playa and asked the concierge if anyone had seen them. He said that the architect was out of town on business, but he claimed to know something about Nora."

"What did he tell you?"

"He wouldn't talk on the telephone, so I went over there and spoke with him."

"Why was he being so secretive?"

"I wasn't sure, so I paid him a dollar to get him to tell me what he knew. I'm not sure how useful his information is, but he claims that Nora hitched a ride to the Chatham mansion earlier this afternoon with his two cousins. He said that she wanted to learn how to cook. He could have been lying, sir, because that doesn't sound a bit like Nora."

"You have to wonder what would make her go there with a couple of working people that she hardly knew."

"It puzzled me too." Keith said, as he got up. "I'm going to call my friend Pete at the garage and borrow his Buick. I'll drive out there and check on the concierge's story."

Owens stood up. "I'll go with you. We'll take my sedan since it has a full tank of gasoline. Let me tell Mrs. Owens that we're checking on something. I don't want to worry her unnecessarily. After all, this could prove to be a wild-goose chase."

Nora awoke. She was in a moving motorcar, her body wrapped mummy-like in a coarse blanket. She was unable to move her arms and legs, and the only parts of her body she could wiggle were her toes. She couldn't see out, her face and head hurt, and one of her eyelids felt swollen. Using her tongue, she explored the lump that had formed inside her right cheek.

She remembered being carried through the dining room, past the table filled with flowers, china and glassware. Everything shimmered in the light of the crystal chandelier. Then her image shifted to a clothes closet, a flight of stairs, a blast of cold air, and another man helping Davey roll her into a blanket. At some point, she passed out.

Now she heard two voices coming from the front seat, but the engine's noise and the motorcar's rattles made it impossible for her to comprehend what they were saying.

Suddenly the motorcar swerved and came to an abrupt stop. She heard doors open. One of her captors grabbed her shoulders and the other took hold of her legs. They pulled and dragged her across some hard ground. Stones — or they could be pine cones, she thought — were scraping into her back. She tried twisting, but she couldn't do anything to help herself. She heard a splashing, lapping sound in the background. Waves!

"Dump her in here." It was Davey's voice.

She was lifted to clear some sort of barrier and dropped onto a ribbed, hard surface that rocked from side to side. It felt like the bottom of a boat.

A deeper voice said, "She'll drown before long. We don't want her found with any restraints. I agree with Mrs. Fields, Davey. It has to look like an accident. Roll her out of that blanket."

Freed, Nora lifted her head and could make out two shadowy figures standing on what she presumed was a dock. One of them knelt down and grabbed her right arm. She tried to pull it back, but he pinned it and extended it. Instantly she felt the needle prick, followed by a burning sensation in her upper arm.

"That will take care of her for a while," a voice said. "She'll fall asleep and by the time she wakes up, she'll be in the water. It will appear to be a drowning."

Tears filled Nora's eyes as she recognized the man's voice. It was Doctor Taylor.

"Now give the boat a push," he said to Davey.

CHAPTER THIRTY EIGHT

"I'm sure I can find Bella Vista," Owens said to Keith. They had turned onto Ocean Avenue and were heading towards Carmel beach and 17-Mile Drive. "I was invited there for a fundraising benefit that Mrs. Chatham hosted last year. As I recall, the place has an iron gate with the letter C welded into it."

"What was the occasion?" Keith asked. He was feeling a little better, now that they were doing something to locate Nora.

"Major Chatham, her husband, had died in the war. Mrs. Chatham asked me to publicize the event and write a story in the *Pine Cone* about the major's sacrifice, along with those of the other Carmel men who went overseas to serve our country. I thought it would be an excellent way to commemorate Armistice Day."

Keith nodded and looked out the wind-screen at the patches of fog on all sides of the motorcar.

"It turned into a successful fundraiser," Owens continued. "We raised a thousand dollars for the local veterans who required medical care when they returned home."

Listening halfheartedly, Keith's thoughts kept returning to Nora. At the next bend, the headlamps illuminated the gate that Mr. Owens had mentioned. "We're here," he said.

The sedan crunched along the gravel drive and entered the deserted courtyard. Owens drove up to the *porte-cochere* and parked behind an expensive-looking black motorcar. Getting out, they walked up the front steps. Keith pounded on the door.

Both were surprised when it was opened by a middle-aged woman in a long evening dress. Neither man recognized her. Owens knew she wasn't Mrs. Chatham and she was too old to be keeping company with young Davey. Taking off his hat, he said,

"Good evening, madam. May we please speak to Mr. Chatham?"

"He isn't here," the woman said, as she waved her champagne glass in the air.

"And you are?" Owens asked.

"I'm Sarah Fields, Mr. Chatham's dinner guest," she said, slurring her words. "My late husband was in the process of buying Bella Vista. Who are you?"

"That's unimportant," Keith interrupted. "We're looking for Miss Finnegan."

"Then you've come to the wrong place. I don't know anyone by that name."

"I'm Mr. Owens, her guardian. We'd like to come in." Without waiting for permission, he pushed past the woman and entered the foyer. Glancing at a room filled with bookshelves along the walls, he moved to enter it. "Let's talk in here," he said.

Sarah Fields followed him and pointed to a small table next to the fireplace. "Care for a bit of bubbly, Mr. Owens? I hate to drink alone." Looking at Keith, who had just come into the library, she added, "What about you, young man?"

"If you won't tell us where Miss Finnegan is, let us speak to Angela Daneri," Keith said. "Her cousin at the hotel told me that she and her brother work at Bella Vista. He also said that Miss Finnegan came here with the two of them this afternoon."

Sarah Fields refilled her empty glass from an open bottle. As she turned back to Owens, she said, "I insist you try the champagne. It's French. My husband brought a case of it with him the last time he came here on business."

Suddenly Owens grabbed the woman's arm as she brought the flute to her lips. "No more games, Mrs. Fields," he said. "My friend and I demand answers."

Sarah Fields tried to move away from him, but Owens held on tightly, causing the glass to drop to the floor and shatter into pieces.

"You're hurting me," she cried out. "Let go, or I'll call the sheriff!"

Once Owens released his grip, she backed away and selected a fresh flute from the tray. "I've already told you," she said. "There's no one here but me." Her voice sounded faint and unsteady.

Grim-faced, Keith said, "We aren't leaving until you tell us where Miss Finnegan is."

The headlights of an arriving motorcar drew Owens to the window. "Someone's coming up the drive," he said.

Turning around, the two men headed back to the foyer. Keith opened the door. A black Packard that Owens recognized rolled to a stop and parked next to his motorcar.

Davey Chatham got out of the passenger's side and waved as he came up the front steps. "Evening, gentlemen." He strolled inside and made a beeline for the library as Sarah Fields walked out. "I see you two have met my business partner," Chatham said. "Did you come here to interview us about our joint hotel venture, Mr. Owens?"

"Don't think you can fool us with smooth talk," Keith interjected, as he came up to Davey. "You'd better tell us where Nora Finnegan is or there will be hell to pay."

Standing at the entry, Owens watched Doctor Taylor take the stairs two at a time.

The brass buttons on his double-breasted navy jacket glittered in the porch light.

Taylor greeted him. "Good evening, William. Is there a problem?"

Owens stared down at the doctor's rumpled trousers. They were wet with sand that clung to his pant legs. "Have you been beachcombing?" he asked.

Taylor laughed. "Davey and I went out for some fresh air. We did stroll along the beach, after what I would call a superb dinner. The exercise helped our digestion." Entering the library, Taylor walked up to Davey and said, "Where are your manners, young man? Offer these men some champagne before they take their leave."

Keith could barely contain himself. "Answer us!" he shouted. "Was Miss Finnegan with the two of you?"

Taylor shook his head and smiled.

Chatham, already filling a flute with champagne, turned around. "We never saw her," he said. Then he raised his glass and took a swallow.

"Let's go," Owens said to Keith. "We're wasting our time here."

Keith kept both hands in his pockets as he pushed past the doctor on his way out. He needed to control his emotions and focus his energy on finding Nora. Had he stayed a minute longer, he would have punched someone in the nose.

CHAPTER THIRTY NINE

Sunday

Nora opened her eyes. It was pitch dark. She turned her head slowly from side to side, trying to shake off her confusion. Flat on her back, her body rocking up and down, as if she were riding a carousel at a county fair, she felt sick to her stomach. She could tell she was in a rowboat, floating in the ocean. She wasn't sure how long she would be conscious, knowing that Doctor Taylor had injected a drug into her arm. She was frightened that its effect would be recurring.

Rolling over on one side, she felt around the boat's bottom. Someone had removed the oars. She lifted her head, but in the darkness, she couldn't tell where she was. Even though her mind was muddled, she thought it best to wait until sun-up. She was too groggy to reason. She closed her eyes and drifted off.

Bright sunshine roused her. Although the air was chilly, there was no wind and the sky was cloudless. Sitting up in the small boat, she saw the shoreline off in the distance. It was difficult to gauge how far she was from shore, but she judged it to be close to a mile. Luckily, she was not too far out in the ocean, as her captors had hoped the current would take her. Checking her clothing, she saw that her sweater and skirt were torn, but dry. She clung to the thought that Keith must have realized that something had happened to her when she didn't meet him at the library benefit. He would certainly alert Mr. Owens, who in turn, would contact Marshal Englund and Sheriff Terry. By now, they would have organized a search party. They would be combing the area for her. But would they look out at the water?

As the morning wore on, no one had spotted her. She tried off and on for what seemed hours to propel the boat towards shore, using her hands as paddles. She only succeeded in drifting farther out. She was getting nowhere. She imagined herself as a tiny speck with no means of drawing any attention to herself. She was becoming discouraged.

Already the sun had begun its descent on the horizon. Soon it would be dark and colder. Her anxiety seemed to make her more alert, but it also triggered scary thoughts. When night fell, no one could see her to rescue her. Also, the boat might be farther out to sea. Her hopes fading, she fantasized the obituary that Mr. Owens would write and publish in the next *Carmel Pine Cone*.

REPORTER DROWNS AT SEA

The battered body of Nora Finnegan was found in Abalone Cove last Tuesday. Apparently she drowned in the high surf and was washed ashore. Marshal Gus Englund spotted the body in the kelp. He waded in, tied a rope around her waist, and with his horse Billy's help, dragged her body out.

Miss Finnegan, 21, daughter of Mr. and Mrs. John Finnegan of San Francisco, relocated to Carmel 3 months ago to begin her career as a reporter at the *Carmel Pine Cone*. "My wife and I are simply devastated by her tragic loss," publisher William Owens said. "Miss Finnegan had great promise." Services are pending. In lieu of flowers, the family will plant a pine tree in Miss Finnegan's memory.

Nora's musing was interrupted by a breaking wave. She knew her situation was becoming desperate. What remaining physical strength she had would be ebbing soon. If she did nothing and simply waited to be found, she might not survive.

Craning her head, she was able to see the shoreline. *I can do this. I was the best swimmer in my college class.* The water was still calm, but she knew it would be cold. She would keep her sweater on, but decided she should rip her torn skirt to shorten it and free up her legs. Kicking off her shoes, she edged to the rowboat's stern and climbed onto the narrow seat. Taking several deep breaths, she grasped the side of the boat, and slipped into the water.

The cold temperature energized her. She swam, treaded water, and even surfed the incoming waves when she could. Every so often she rested by floating on her back. The sun had set and daylight was fading. But luck was on her side as she didn't have to cope with an undercurrent. Weary and cold, her only remaining hurdle was would she have enough endurance to reach the beach.

CHAPTER FORTY

Monday

Curled up behind a dune, Nora brushed away particles of sand that clung to her face. Day was breaking and the tide was out. She was wet and cold, but alive. Her spirits brightened when she heard a soft whinnying sound, followed by a familiar voice.

"Easy now, Billy."

Was she hallucinating? She pushed herself into a crouch and called out, "Marshal, I'm over here. It's Nora Finnegan!" It was all she could do to roll herself into a sitting position.

"And a pretty sight you are," Gus Englund shouted back, as he spurred his horse forward.

Nora knew with absolute certainty that she was anything but 'a pretty sight.' Nevertheless, she felt ecstatic. She had been found!

Stopping Billy a few feet from her, Englund dismounted and opened his saddle bag. Reaching in, he pulled out an army blanket and a water canteen. Kneeling down, he draped the blanket around her. He steadied her head with his hand and put the canteen to her lips. "I want you to take only small sips to begin with," he said. "If you don't, it will come right back up."

Nora drank slowly. Her lips felt parched. Between sips, she managed a crooked grin, given her swollen cheek. "You don't know how happy I am to see you, Marshal."

"Me too," Englund said, as he helped her stand up. "Let's get you on your feet and then I'll lift you onto the horse."

Nora's arms went around his waist like a vise. Billy carried them both across the sandy beach to the 17-Mile Drive turnout where Sheriff Terry and his deputies had established a base. They were greeted enthusiastically with waves and cheers by the dozen or so members of the sheriff's search party. Nora didn't know all of them, but wished she could thank each man personally. For now, she could only acknowledge them with a wave.

She spotted Mr. Owens, who cried out, "Thank God, it's Honora! She's safe." Both he and Keith came running towards her.

As she looked down at them, Nora could see the worry in their eyes.

"Are you all right?" Owens asked. Embarrassed by his emotions, he said, "I'm sure Keith and the others are eager to speak to you, but before they do, I want you to know that we wouldn't have stopped looking for you until we found you."

Tears streamed down Nora's cheeks. "I'm so grateful that you persevered."

Keith looked visibly affected by her disheveled appearance. He tried to say something reassuring. "You'll bounce back in no time, Nora." Putting his hand in his pocket, he brought out an apple and offered it to her. "You must be starved. Take this."

Thinking he was being rewarded for his efforts, Billy turned his head to feast on Keith's gift until Englund yanked on the reins. Everyone laughed. Nora knew that her aching jaw was no match for the apple. She pointed to her puffy cheek and offered it to the horse.

When they spotted her, Sheriff Terry and Deputy Connery broke away from the other searchers and hurried over to Nora's side. "It goes without saying that the marshal deserves a special citation for finding you, Miss Finnegan," Terry said.

Englund interrupted, "She swam from a boat to shore and came up in Abalone Cove, Sheriff. She's the one who deserves a medal for bravery, not me."

Deputy Connery raised his arms and helped Nora dismount. "I can't tell you how relieved I am that you've been found," Jimmy said. "We've been searching the entire area around Bella Vista since Mr. Owens called us last night."

Sheriff Terry leaned forward and touched Nora's cheek. "How did you injure your face?"

Nora cringed, remembering the scene yesterday in Bella Vista's pantry. "It was Davey Chatham, sir. He assaulted me. He tried to get rid of me, but it didn't work out the way he planned."

CHAPTER FORTY ONE

Nora collapsed in the back seat of Mr. Owens' sedan, while Keith took his place in the passenger seat. The curves on 17-Mile Drive demanded all of Owens' attention as they made their way back to Carmel. Rounding the next turn, Keith looked down at the churning surf. "Someone at the library told me there were two serious accidents this month along this particular stretch."

"One was due to excessive imbibing," Owens said, "which makes me think of Mrs. Fields. She was inebriated and was of no help to us in finding Honora."

"She lied, sir. She should have told us that Nora had been there."

On hearing her name, Nora stirred and sat up. "I didn't see her, but when I was at the boat dock, I recognized Doctor Taylor's voice along with Davey's."

Keith turned around in his seat to look at her. "They told us they'd been walking on the beach. We didn't know then that they were your kidnappers."

Owens added, "The doctor's involvement could be difficult to pin down. You didn't actually see him, did you, Honora?"

She remembered Taylor's recent visit to the newspaper office. "I spoke to him at the *Pine Cone* a few days ago," she said. "I definitely recognized his voice."

"Still, it might be hard to prove," Owens repeated.

"What I don't understand is why they wanted to get rid of you," Keith said.

Leaning back in her seat, Nora closed her eyes. "I accused Davey of burning down Claudia Woodward's home. When I left

Sheriff Terry, I told him to be sure and search Davey's pantry when he goes to arrest him. I think he'll find the proof that he murdered Carlotta Fleming."

"What kind of proof?" Keith asked.

Nora explained how she had found the abalone cutlery set with one knife missing.

"I wish you hadn't gone to Bella Vista without telling someone," Owens said. "You acted impulsively, Honora, and you put yourself in grave danger."

Keith rose to her defense. "She did a brave thing. My only wish is that Doctor Taylor could be arrested as Chatham's accomplice."

There was a pause in their conversation, as the motorcar slowed and came to a stop at the 17-Mile Drive toll booth. A uniformed guard came out and Owens handed him 50 cents. The guard lifted the gate and waved them through.

"I'll take you back to my house and Mrs. Owens will care for you until you recover," Owens said.

"That won't be necessary, sir. I'm going to be fine. All I need is a bath and some hot soup."

They had arrived at Nora's cottage. Keith jumped out and opened the rear door.

Nora pulled Marshal Englund's blanket around her and got out. "Thank you both for all you did to rescue me," she said. "I'll see you at the office tomorrow morning, sir. I plan to put together an article about the outcome of tonight's residents' meeting."

"Honora, I'm ordering you to stay home this evening," Owens said. "I'm giving you the day off tomorrow. You need time to recuperate."

"Mr. Owens is right," Keith said. Before she could voice her objection, he took her elbow to steady her and walked her to Pine Log's front door. "You're in no condition to go to the meeting," he said. "I'll telephone you afterwards and give you the details."

"I guess you're right, but promise to call me tonight," Nora said. "I hope the residents vote to buy the beach. Otherwise, we're going to see a hotel built there."

Keith grinned at her. "Don't worry. Perry Newberry delivered our offer to the Carmel Development Company and he all but guarantees they'll accept it. On a personal note, Nora, I think your swimming to shore was a fantastic achievement. Who knows? You might be the next Olympic champion to rival those Australian ladies I always read about in the newspapers."

Nora laughed as she pushed him away.

Waiting by the motorcar for Keith, Owens shouted, "The Board of Trustees meets at City Hall tomorrow night, Honora. If you feel up to it, I'd like you to join me. From what I hear, they're ready to make their decision on the hotel development."

"I'll be there," Nora yelled back. Giving Keith a quick hug, she closed her front door and walked to her bedroom. Throwing off the blanket the marshal had given her, she slipped out of her grimy clothing. In the bathroom, she opened the metal doors of the heater and lit the two kerosene burners under the water coils. Then she opened the tub's faucets.

A few minutes before noon, Deputy Connery pulled the patrol wagon up in front of the Monterey jail. Turning to Sheriff Terry, he said, "It's lucky we released Rob Jacklin after I corroborated his story with Mrs. Woodward. We'll have room to hold Chatham here until he's charged."

Stepping out, Terry motioned at their prisoner, who was sitting in the back seat with Deputy Jensen. "Keep the cuffs on him, Alvin, until you get Chatham inside. And be sure to take away his shoes, belt, and cane."

"Should I hold off on the fingerprints until tomorrow, Sheriff?" Jensen asked.

"Yes. We've been up all night. Do it first thing in the morning before we begin Chatham's interrogation. All of us could use some sleep now."

CHAPTER FORTY TWO

Tuesday

At eight o'clock the next morning, Deputy Alvin Jensen walked into the jail's holding cell. He went over to the narrow cot and shook the sleeping prisoner's shoulder. "Get up Chatham," he ordered. "I want to take your fingerprints before the sheriff comes in and you have to answer his questions."

"When's breakfast?" Chatham muttered as he rolled over on his back.

"After Sheriff Terry's finished talking to you."

Chatham sat up and yawned. "And when will that be?"

"Whenever he decides it will be. Now get up."

After his prints had been taken, Chatham remained seated at the table. "Where's the sheriff?" he groused. "Tell him I'm hungry!"

Jensen ignored his request.

Sitting in his office next door to the holding cell, the sheriff also heard Chatham. The prisoner could wait. He didn't care to be interrupted while he was writing a report on yesterday's rescue of Nora Finnegan. After another half hour went by, Terry got up, summoned Jensen, and the two men went into the holding cell. As he sat down across from Chatham, Terry said, "After you answer all my questions, we'll feed you."

"I'm a war veteran," Chatham countered, "and an injured one." He pointed at Jensen, who was standing by the door. "I demand the return of my cane, Sheriff. That man took it away and

I need it to get around."

Terry didn't like Chatham's attitude. "You can't have it. It could be used as a lethal weapon."

"Do you know who my mother is?" Chatham asked. "Send her a telegram in Florence, Italy, and she'll write you a check for your policemen's fund. I'll drop all thoughts of suing you and your men for false arrest."

"These aren't petty accusations against you, Davey," Terry said. "We're talking physical assault, kidnapping and Miss Finnegan's attempted murder. If you don't cooperate with us, my deputy will have to use stronger persuasion."

Chatham shrugged. "I don't know a Miss Finnegan. If she's making charges against me, then I deny them."

Terry looked over at Jensen. "Deputy, show this uncooperative man what I'm talking about."

Jensen left his post at the door and came up to the prisoner at the table. "The sheriff's a polite man, Davey," he said, "but don't expect no coddling from me. You better give him the answers he wants. If not, I'll go to work on you till we get the truth."

Chatham leaned back in his chair. "I know some powerful people who will get me out of here in no time if you so much as mess up my hair."

Without warning, Jensen shoved Chatham backwards, sending him and his chair to the floor. When he tried to get up, the deputy shoved him down again.

Chatham squirmed on the floor and cried out, "Stop, will you?"

"The next blows will be at your face," Jensen shouted. "You didn't mind doing that to Miss Finnegan, did you? That's what scums like you understand."

"O.K.!" Chatham shouted. "Listen, I didn't touch that stupid girl."

Gesturing to Jensen to pick Chatham up, Sheriff Terry said, "All right, Davey. I'm going to ask you about Miss Finnegan again. Did you kidnap her at Mrs. Fields' request?"

Chatham groaned as Jensen pushed him down into the chair. He looked around and then rested his arms on the table. "I told you, Sheriff, I didn't kidnap her. As far as that old broad Fields is concerned, we have a legitimate business deal. There's no law against that."

Frustrated, Terry decided to take a different approach.

"You're in a heap of trouble, son. We have more evidence against you. A neighbor saw you right before the fire broke out at the Woodward cottage last Tuesday. I've talked to him. He described your fancy motorcar to a T."

"Wait a minute," Chatham said. "You can't pin that fire on me, Sheriff. I wasn't near the place. If somebody says he saw me, he's a bald-faced liar or he's blind."

Terry grimaced. "Also, there are some items at Levy's store that point to you. Our new technique of identifying the fingerprints of perpetrators of crimes is going to tell us whether or not you were there to pick up the kerosene."

"You can't prove anything."

Terry bolted out of his seat, his body looming over the table. "Did Mrs. Fields pay you to start the fire? Was it her idea to punish Mrs. Woodward for her affair with her husband? If you're convicted of felony charges, you're going to rot in jail, not her."

Chatham looked confused. "Not that I'm admitting to it, but what if I did set the blaze? Nobody got hurt, and my mother's good for any damages. That should take care of everything. As for that reporter, well, she had no business trespassing in my home. I told her once before to get off my property and she weaseled her way back in by using a couple of ignorant foreigners who work for me. Anyway, it was Mrs. Fields who wanted her out of the house. Now, can I have my breakfast?"

Terry sat down again. "I thought you said you didn't know Miss Finnegan. You want me to drop the kidnapping and attempted murder charges? You must be thinking that she wasn't seriously hurt. After all, you only put her in a rowboat and sent her out to sea to drown. And all because she was trespassing? Is that your story?"

"I want a lawyer, Sheriff."

Drumming his fingers on the table, Terry said, "If you admit to working for Mrs. Fields and say that she gave you orders that you simply followed, it would help you."

Looking smug, Chatham replied, "No deal."

Suddenly a door slammed in the jail's outer office. Deputy Connery entered Chatham's cell. He was carrying a burlap sack.

"Find what you were looking for, Jimmy?" the sheriff asked.

Connery nodded. "I got the judge out of bed and he approved the subpoena." Dropping the bulky looking sack on the table, he continued, "It was right where Nora said it would be, sir." Reaching into the sack, he took out a rectangular-shaped wooden box with the word "Gumps" printed on its cover. He set it down in front of the sheriff. Raising the lid, Terry stared at the abalone cutlery set.

Connery looked at Chatham. "The only knife that's missing, Davey, is the one you used to stab Carlotta Fleming to death. We found that knife, and it has somebody's bloody fingerprints on it."

Chatham's face paled. "I had nothing to do with that."

"I'm about to process Davey's prints," Jensen interjected, "and I'll bet I find a match to those I lifted from Joe Levy's shed and from the knife in our evidence room."

Terry smiled. "I think you'll win that bet, Alvin. If we get a match, we'll have ourselves a killer, as well as an arsonist. You can go ahead and give Chatham his breakfast now."

CHAPTER FORTY THREE

A little before one o'clock, Nora awoke to a deep rumbling sound, the thunder of an approaching storm. Easing herself out of bed, she ignored the aches in her legs and shoulders and went to the window. Parting the curtains, she looked past the sand dunes at the ocean's wind-driven waves. She was thankful that the storm hadn't arrived yesterday.

Though it hurt her to do it, she reached up and stretched her arms several times over her head until she felt more awake. On the way to the bathroom, she realized that she must have slept through Keith's call last night about the outcome of the residents' meeting. She was anxious to know what they had decided. At this time of day, he would be working at the library, his regulars seated at the reading table with their books and newspapers. But before she could get to the front room, the telephone rang. She picked up the receiver and said, "You'd better have a very good reason for not calling me sooner."

"This is Deputy Connery, Nora. Were you expecting me to telephone you?"

"No, I wasn't, Jimmy. I thought it was someone else. Where are you?"

"I'm at the newspaper office. Mrs. Owens said it would be all right for me to telephone you at home."

"Of course it is."

"Sheriff Terry and I need your help — that is, if you feel up to it. May I stop by Pine Log and tell you what's involved? We're due in Monterey at . . . . Hold on a minute. What did you say, Mrs. Owens?"

Nora could hear garbled words and dogs barking in the background.

Then Jimmy came back on. "Mrs. Owens thinks that if I show up at your cottage, it might appear improper to your neighbors. Could you meet me here instead?"

Not knowing what he had in mind for her, Nora said, "It's going to take me about thirty minutes. Can it wait that long?"

"That's fine. Get here as soon as you can. I'll be waiting for you."

Nora rummaged in her closet and settled on a pleated skirt and heavy sweater to keep her warm under her raincoat. In the bathroom, she heard raindrops on the roof. As she washed her face, she looked in the mirror. Her right eye was still tender to the touch, but the swelling had gone down. If she applied a little face powder on her cheek, the discoloration would be less noticeable. Brushing her hair, she remembered something that had been puzzling her. She would follow up on it right now. She went to the front room, picked up the telephone, and called Hotel La Playa.

Her red umbrella pulled low to fend off wind gusts, Nora dodged the puddles accumulating along the length of Monte Verde Street. She was going to arrive at the newspaper office earlier than she was expected. Passing the milk shrine, she noticed two pints of milk sitting side by side on her designated shelf. One had been delivered yesterday and one early this morning. They would have to wait to be picked up until after her meeting with Jimmy. The cold weather would keep the milk from spoiling.

At the next corner, she glanced towards the beach and spotted Marshal Englund riding up Seventh Avenue. He had on a yellow rain slicker and matching head gear. Although she was in a hurry, she wanted to say hello. She waved at him.

"I thought it was you under that bright umbrella, Miss Finnegan," Englund said, as he pulled up on the horse's reins. "You look sprightly, considering what you looked like when Billy and I found you 24 hours ago."

"I'm so grateful to both of you," Nora said, as she stroked the horse's wet flank. "Thankfully, it didn't rain like this yesterday."

He dismounted and said, "It wouldn't have mattered, because we would have kept looking, no matter what the weather was like. But why aren't you taking today off?"

Nora smiled and shook her head. "I'm not really working, Marshal. I'm heading to meet one of Sheriff Terry's deputies at the newspaper office. From what he told me on the telephone, they need my help with something."

Pulling a sheet of letter paper out of his pocket and shielding it from the rain, Englund gave it to her. "Well, I'm glad I ran into you then. Saves me a trip. Will you see that Mr. Owens gets this? What I put down isn't all that interesting, but he seems to think that the residents might be curious to know what I do for them on a daily basis. This is supposed to be a sample of my policeman's log."

"I think that's a wonderful idea. Would you mind if I read what you put together before turning it over to Mr. Owens?"

Englund grinned. "It's not anywhere as good as your writing, but I'd be pleased if you did. Maybe you can give me a few tips? I'm only trying this writing idea out for a few weeks, to see what your boss and your readers think of it."

Tucking the paper in her purse, Nora said, "They'll probably love it."

Sloshing along the muddy street, she balanced her umbrella against the gusting wind with one hand and protected her purse from getting drenched with the other. When she reached the front door of the *Pine Cone*, she paused under the overhang and took out the marshal's paper. Scanning his report, she couldn't help smiling. Only four items were listed. Each one was an event that he had described in simple terms. She thought the overall result was charming.

7 P.M.	A cold evening. Arrested responsible party for domestic on San Carlos Street. Looks like his wife won the argument.
8:15 P.M.	Adult male resident again drunk in public on Ocean Avenue. Seems like prohibition isn't stopping people from drinking.
9:00 P.M.	Motorcar stopped. Out of gas. Gave him a ride home on Billy.
10:00 P.M.	Responded to Mrs. Mortimer's hen house on Dolores Street. Two chickens D.O.A. Raccoons got away.

Closing her umbrella and stepping inside the newspaper's reception area, Nora was immediately subjected to a cacophony of raucous barking. Dasher raced out of the back room in pursuit of Maisie. The two dogs circled Nora twice and then scurried around the front counter and back again.

Mary Lee Owens, her hairdo in disarray, chased after them. When she saw Nora, she smiled and said, "I'm so glad you feel better, Nora. You just missed Keith's call."

"Was it about the residents' meeting last night?"

Yes. They voted to take their offer to buy the beach to the Trustees tonight."

"Thanks, Mrs. Owens. I'll be there to hear the response."

"These dogs are driving me crazy, dear. I can't get any typing done. Will you do something with Maisie? You're so good with her and she minds you."

"I'll be happy to," Nora said, as she stashed her wet umbrella by the door. Grabbing the dog's collar, she pushed her rump into a sitting position. "Stay!" she said, as she took a leash off the counter and fastened it to Maisie's collar.

Jimmy was seated in the chair next to Nora's desk, his Stetson resting on top of it. He was reading the *Pine Cone's* front page story that Nora had written for the special issue that had come out yesterday. Looking up at her, he said, "You got here much faster than I thought you would. I've been enjoying your article. You write very well."

"Thanks for the compliment," she said, as she saw Mr. Owens walk out of the back room. Pulling Gus Englund's daily log out of her purse, she laid it on the counter and said, "The marshal asked me to deliver this to you, Mr. Owens."

He scanned the paper. "This is a special feature I'd like to try. Our readers might like it. But as I told the deputy a few minutes ago, I think you should stay home today."

"I feel fine, sir, and I want to help the sheriff and Deputy Connery. I know you have my best interests at heart, but I would like to assist them."

"You need rest, not more excitement." Studying Nora's face, Owens continued, "At least your eye looks better, but you must be sore all over. You've had quite enough stress for one young lady, Honora."

Jimmy stood up and walked around the counter. "The sheriff and I realize that Nora isn't fully recovered, Mr. Owens, but it's important that she comes with me. This won't be physically strenuous for her. I'm about to confront a person whom we believe has first hand knowledge of her assault. I'll get her home just as soon as we're done."

Turning to Nora, he went on, "I think we should leave now or we might be too late."

Mrs. Owens had been listening in. "Let her and Maisie go, William. I know the deputy's dependable. He'll make sure that she's not over-taxed."

Owens could see that he was outnumbered. "All right, but I'm relying on you, Deputy, to watch over her." As he held the door for the two young people, he grinned when he heard Connery mutter, "I can't believe it, Nora. Mrs. Owens passed this dog off onto us again!"

Nora had her hands full, pulling the dog through the rain to the patrol wagon.

Jimmy opened the rear door, while she lifted Maisie into the back. Exhausted from carousing with the Owens' dog all morning, the spaniel jumped up on one of the side benches and lay quietly. As Jimmy slammed the door, he said to Nora, "At least she won't be licking the back of my neck this time."

Already soaking wet, Nora decided not to tell him to go back for her umbrella. She climbed into the front seat.

He got in and started the engine. "You'll be interested to know that Davey Chatham admitted that he set fire to the Woodward cottage, but he's blaming Sarah Fields for it. He claims that she told him to 'get rid of that woman.' That's what we want to confirm when you confront her."

"I thought so. The blaze was her way of getting revenge. But what about Doctor Taylor's role in my kidnapping? Have you arrested him?"

Shaking his head, Jimmy looked both ways as they headed down San Carlos Street.

"We're still investigating his activities on Saturday night," he said. "His nurse at the sanitarium is providing Taylor with an alibi."

"I heard his voice, Jimmy. It was Doctor Taylor. He helped Davey drag me down to the boat dock below Bella Vista. He must have promised Davey money not to involve him and also intimidated his nurse. Don't you remember that he tried to do that to me a few days ago with a classified advertisement?"

"You didn't actually see him though, did you? Identifying a man by his voice alone isn't sufficient evidence, Nora. I can sympathize with your argument, but you were incapacitated at the time."

"I'm positive about this. Who else could have injected me with a drug and left me to die? And don't forget that he gave Claudia Woodward a large amount of Laudanum without adequate instructions on how much she should take. He didn't seem to care whether or not she overdosed. He's a terrible doctor, and if anything, he should at least lose his license to practice medicine."

Jimmy had turned onto Ocean Avenue. He shifted into a lower gear as they began to climb the Carmel hill. On reaching the crest, he moderated the engine speed on the down slope into Monterey.

Checking on Maisie through the back window, Nora was happy to see that the dog was asleep.

It was after two o'clock when they pulled into the lot next to the railroad station. Fortunately, the rain had turned to drizzle. They noticed several porters milling about, loading suitcases and trunks into the train's baggage car. A coal-burning locomotive spewed smoke into the air. The first passengers were beginning to board.

Turning off the engine, Jimmy reached for his Stetson on the seat between them. He said, "Early this morning Sheriff Terry received a telephone call from the local funeral parlor. The mortician said he thought we should know that Mrs. Fields had arranged to take her husband's body back to New York on this afternoon's train. We have Chatham's story of the woman's role in the fire, and possibly she may have been involved in your kidnapping. We're eager to charge her as an accessory to both crimes, but we aren't positive that Davey is telling the truth. Sheriff Terry thinks your presence might provoke Mrs. Fields into saying something incriminating. Then we'll arrest her."

Nora grinned. "I do have a way of getting under her skin. If her reaction to seeing me in Hotel La Playa's dining room the other evening was an indication of what she thinks of me, your idea is definitely worth trying."

"We're counting on her animosity towards you to work in our favor. Now let me explain what I want you to do. I'll be at your side the entire time."

Nora looked over at him. "Before we go, Jimmy, I have information to share with you. I learned it during a telephone call that I made before coming to meet you."

Their conversation lasted several minutes. When it was over, Maisie started yapping. Nora and Jimmy got out of the wagon. He walked around to open the rear door. The dog jumped out and ran over to stand next to Nora. It was almost as if the dog knew that she too was an important member of the Connery/Finnegan detecting team, Nora thought. Maisie was ready to assist them in subduing a dangerous adversary.

CHAPTER FORTY FOUR

As she and Jimmy walked with the dog along the wood platform next to the train tracks, Nora thought the depot had to be the plainest of all the stations in the Southern Pacific line between San Francisco and Monterey. But in all fairness, it suited the rural county's top priority of hauling wheat and other agricultural products to market.

Jimmy nudged her arm. "Look who's coming out of the baggage shed."

Nora recognized the two young men as Rudolfo and Oresto from Hotel La Playa. The bellman was pulling a four-wheel cart, while his cousin, the concierge, was pushing it. A polished mahogany casket sat on top of the cart. Trailing behind them trudged Sarah Fields, her face hidden under a wide-brimmed black hat. Her long black coat sported three silver fox furs at the neck. Even in mourning, she flaunted her wealth, Nora thought. The group passed between the assembled passengers and the baggage car. Its sliding door was open to receive Fields' casket.

The slow-moving convoy also attracted Maisie's attention. Head up, ears back, the dog growled and pulled on the leash.

"No, Maisie!" Nora said firmly.

"What's the matter with her?" Jimmy asked.

Tightening her grip on the leash, Nora said, "She's excited by the crowd."

A railroad employee ran out of the train shed and yelled at Mrs. Fields, "You've got to show your ticket and papers to the conductor first."

Abruptly changing course, the widow turned, just as a sudden burst of steam from the locomotive caught the hem of her long coat and swirled it out like a sail. The upward movement startled Maisie, who lunged forward. Before Nora could react, the leash slipped out of her hand and Maisie raced towards the woman.

Intent on opening her purse, Sarah Fields didn't notice the dog until it leaped up on her and tried to bite her. "Help!" she screamed.

The conductor tried to pick up the leash, but Maisie was too quick for him. Barking and snarling, she circled and clawed at the woman's coat. The widow tripped on a loose board, lost her balance and fell.

"Call her off," Jimmy yelled, as he and Nora ran down the platform.

When they reached Mrs. Fields, Nora bent down, grabbed hold of the dog's leash, and pulled her away. Panting heavily, Maisie dropped down at her feet.

With the animal finally under control, Sarah Fields rolled over on one side, sat up, and rubbed her ankles through her torn stockings. "You'll pay for this," she shouted. "I demand that your dog be tested for rabies and then shot."

Nora didn't say anything. Part of her wished that Maisie's bites could deliver the disease.

Seeing the widow in distress, Rudolfo and Oresto left the casket and ran over. Rudolfo helped her to her feet, while Oresto scurried along the platform, retrieving her ticket, hat, and purse.

The worried conductor looked at Nora. "Miss, will you help this poor woman into the ladies' room? I'll telephone one of our local doctors. She needs medical attention."

"No doctor!" Sarah Fields cried out. "I'm getting on that train before it leaves."

Jimmy assessed the situation. "You help Mrs. Fields, Nora. I'll put Maisie in the patrol wagon." Taking the leash, he led the subdued animal away.

"Come with me, Mrs. Fields," Nora said, and reached over to take her arm.

Sarah Fields pulled away from her. "Don't you dare touch me! I'll manage to get there without your help."

Shrugging, Nora walked along with her to a room that was set aside for female passengers. As they passed the ticket window, the station agent held out a cloth to Mrs. Fields. "Here's something to tidy up with," the man said.

Grabbing it without a word of thanks, the widow brushed past Nora, who had opened the door. As soon as they were inside, she said, "I'll make sure that you lose your job for the trouble you've caused me, Miss Finnegan. You'll regret ever having met me."

Nora frowned. "From all appearances, the dog didn't cause you serious injury. I think your fox stole may have invited her behavior."

"Are you saying it's all my fault?"

A knock at the door interrupted them. Nora went over to open it.

"I have some questions that I want to ask Mrs. Fields," Jimmy said.

Stepping to one side, Nora said, "Please come in. Mrs. Fields, this is Deputy Sheriff Connery. She's ready to talk to you now."

"How do you know?" the widow snapped. "You have no idea what I'm thinking, you impertinent person. But if cooperating with a policeman gets me on the train sooner, then I'm willing to speak to the deputy."

Jimmy closed the door and said, "Please take that seat by the window, Mrs. Fields." Once she was settled, he went on, "When did you first arrive in Carmel, and who met you at the train station?"

"I came a week ago yesterday. David Chatham, my late husband's business associate, met me here. He drove me to the mortuary, where I made the arrangements for my husband's body. Then he took me to Hotel La Playa in Carmel."

"Had you known Mr. Chatham previously?"

"Yes, I made his acquaintance last summer when my husband and I were visiting Carmel. Mr. Chatham was very helpful to us."

"Did you remain at Hotel La Playa that Monday evening?"

The widow shook her head. "After I checked in, Mr. Chatham kindly invited me to have dinner with him at his home. He could see that I needed consolation due to my husband's shocking death. I unpacked, freshened up, and then we left for Bella Vista."

"Did anyone else join you at Chatham's home that evening?"

"No, Mr. Chatham and I had many things to discuss. Among them, we reviewed the project that my husband planned to build. I told Mr. Chatham that I intended to go forward with the hotel. We agreed to work together to make it a reality. He's going to represent me tonight at the Board of Trustees' meeting."

Jimmy stole a glance at Nora. Neither said anything about Chatham's arrest.

"That leads to my next question," Connery continued. "It concerns the next day. Would you tell me what you did on that Tuesday?"

"For one thing, I needed my rest. I spent the entire day at my hotel."

"Did you meet with anyone else, or were you alone the entire time?"

"What a silly question, Deputy. I was grieving. I was struggling to recover from the shock of my dear husband's unexpected passing."

"Mrs. Fields," Nora interrupted, "Don't you recall that you asked Julia Morgan to telephone me at the newspaper office? You wanted to meet with me at La Playa on that Tuesday afternoon."

Sarah Fields kept her eyes on the deputy. "I'm talking to him. I didn't think that meeting with you was important enough to mention."

"You thought it was very important at the time," Nora said. "You showed me a picture of Claudia Woodward that was concealed in your husband's pocket watch. You asked me to help you identify her."

Sarah Fields glared at Nora. "You're lying. I found out who she was from the sheriff."

Trying to get a rise out of the woman, Nora decided to be blunt. "At your suggestion, didn't Mr. Chatham pay an afternoon visit to Claudia Woodward's cottage?"

"How should I know? All I'll say is, that woman got what she deserved."

"What do you mean?" Jimmy asked.

"I'm referring to a conversation I had last Saturday evening with a local physician who's a friend of Mr. Chatham. He told me that Mrs. Woodward tried to commit suicide soon after her house burned. It would have been no great loss if she had succeeded."

The widow's spitefulness infuriated Nora.

"Let's put aside your strong dislike of Mrs. Woodward,"

Connery said. "Is it fair to say that your husband was lobbying some of Carmel's elected officials to make sure that his beach hotel would be approved?"

Sarah Fields threw her head back and snickered. "What's wrong with that? My husband was doing everything possible to get his hotel project passed. I support his tactics and I'll do the same when the time comes."

"Are you aware that Mr. Fields paid David Chatham a fee to do what he could to eliminate all local opposition to your husband's hotel?" Jimmy asked.

"What are you driving at, young man? Martin's business with Mr. Chatham was completely above board. I don't understand what you're implying."

"Then I'll make it clear. We have Chatham's signed confession that details his schemes. His statement names you as the instigator and accessory to the fire that destroyed the Woodward cottage. I'm detaining you as we continue our investigation of the arson charge, Mrs. Fields. I'm afraid you'll have to miss your train."

"I'll do no such thing! You call your superior and tell him who I am. You're stopping me from burying my husband and you have no evidence to keep me here. The word of Davey Chatham, a man who drinks and talks too much, is worthless."

"There's far more to this," Nora said. "We'll telephone Sheriff Terry and ask him to come here and join us. Someone is waiting outside to provide vital information that implicates you, Mrs. Fields, in a murder case."

Sarah Fields looked apoplectic. "This ignorant reporter doesn't know what she's talking about, Deputy. I'm not answering any more of your questions. I want to call my attorney in New York."

"That's your right," Jimmy said, "but only after we contact Sheriff Terry."

"I'll go find a telephone," Nora said. She headed for the waiting room door.

CHAPTER FORTY FIVE

"I hope this is over quickly, Sheriff," an impatient Sarah Fields said. "My train is scheduled to leave any minute."

Ignoring her comment, the sheriff continued talking with his senior deputy until Nora entered the ladies' waiting room. The two lawmen then came over to greet her and the young man standing beside her.

"Sheriff, this is Rudolfo Daneri," Nora said. He's employed as the bellman at Hotel La Playa in Carmel."

Looking nervous, Daneri removed his cap, smoothed his dark hair, and bowed.

"I remember you now," Terry said, as he shook the bellman's hand. "Now what is this all about, Miss Finnegan?"

"Pure foolishness, that's what it's about," Sarah Fields interrupted. "I don't have time to waste, Sheriff. As you no doubt noticed when you walked in, my poor husband's body is sitting unattended outside. This unnecessary delay is highly insulting to me."

Deputy Connery stepped forward. "Miss Finnegan will explain why we asked you here, sir."

Nora nodded. "I think you'll find what Mr. Daneri has to say revealing, Sheriff. Would you mind if I ask him a few questions?"

Raising his eyebrows, Terry looked dubious. "All right, go ahead, Miss Finnegan, but make sure they're relevant to our detaining Mrs. Fields."

Deputy Connery pulled out a pencil and paper and prepared to take notes.

Nora began, "Mr. Daneri, do you recognize Mrs. Fields, the

woman sitting over there by the window?"

Rudolfo looked at the widow and muttered, "*Si*."

"Well, that's no surprise," Sarah Fields called out. "I've been tipping that man ever since I arrived in Carmel. Or was it his cousin? I get these foreigners mixed up." Annoyed by the woman's insensitive remark, Nora went on, "Did you take Mrs. Fields for a morning ride in your motorcar a week ago last Tuesday, Mr. Daneri?"

"*Si*, she ask me to drive her to a *casetta* not so far from La Playa."

"Did you charge her for the ride?"

"*Si*. It is like a taxi. Two dollars."

"Did you know whose house it was?" Nora continued.

"She say it was a friend's house."

"I never went anywhere, Sheriff," Sarah Fields interjected. "I told that to your deputy. I had an early breakfast that morning. Afterwards, I remained in my room and prayed for my husband's soul."

Nora ignored her comment. "After you drove Mrs. Fields to this cottage, Mr. Daneri, did you wait for her and take her back with you to La Playa?"

The bellman shook his head vigorously. "No, she tell me she wanna walk. It's a short distance, only five blocks. So I leave her there and drive back to the hotel."

"What happened after you returned to La Playa?"

"An hour, maybe a little later, Angie, my sister, she come down to the front desk from upstairs. She was upset. She say, 'Rudy, I did something for *Signora* Fields that worries me a lot.'"

"What did your sister do?"

Shifting his weight from one foot to the other, Daneri looked down at his clasped hands. "*Signora* Fields ask Angie to clean blood offa her dress." He hesitated and made a face. "She tell my sister she cut herself with sewing scissors."

"That's untrue," Sarah Fields said, as she started across the room towards the bellman. Deputy Connery grabbed her arm, and escorted her back to her chair.

"What did Angie do then?" Nora asked.

"She say, blood is all over sleeves. Is too much to wash off, she tell the *signora*. S*ignora* say, 'Throw dress away, Angie. You do it, please.' She give Angie one dollar."

"That's preposterous!" the widow shouted. "You and your

sister are lying, young man. I'll tell Miss Villard to fire the two of you immediately."

"Quiet, ma'am," Terry said. "Please continue, Miss Finnegan."

"Sheriff, I believe Mr. Daneri drove Mrs. Fields to Carlotta Fleming's house. Davey Chatham must have told her where she lived. She knew Miss Fleming was leading the opposition to Mr. Fields' hotel. She went to see her last Tuesday morning."

"That's the time the coroner says that Miss Fleming was murdered," Terry said.

Shaking her fist, Sarah Fields yelled, "Lies, all lies. You have no proof, Sheriff."

"I don't agree," Terry said. "We have a credible witness in Mr. Daneri. We'll take him back to Miss Fleming's home to either confirm or deny that's where he drove you on the day of the murder, Mrs. Fields."

"It seems that she not only had a motive, but also the means, Sheriff," Deputy Connery added. "Mrs. Fields had an opportunity to pick up the murder weapon in Chatham's kitchen when they had dinner together the night before."

The train's whistle stopped everyone's conversation.

Sarah Fields glared at the deputy as she stood up. "All of this is absurd and untrue. That's my train, and I'm leaving on it."

"I'm afraid you aren't," Terry said. "I'm arresting you on suspicion of the murder of Miss Fleming. As our prime suspect, you will remain here in Monterey County, but you can telephone your lawyer when we get back to the jail."

"You won't stop me!" the widow screamed, as she ran for the door.

Reaching out and grabbing her arm, Terry said, "Handcuff her, Jimmy. Then call the mortuary and have them take Mrs. Fields' husband back there. I'll take her to jail myself. Then I'll drive Mr. Daneri back to Carmel to visit Miss Fleming's cottage. I want you to take Miss Finnegan home and then go to Hotel La Playa. See if you can find what's left of Mrs. Fields' bloodstained dress, and speak to Mr. Daneri's sister to confirm her brother's story."

On the way back to Carmel, Nora looked down at Maisie and petted the dog. She lay sleeping between her and Jimmy on the patrol wagon's front seat.

"You did a fine job, questioning the hotel bellman," Jimmy said. "But you still haven't fully explained to me how you found out that Daneri drove Mrs. Fields to Miss Fleming's house on the morning of her murder."

Nora grinned. "Last Saturday, I asked Angie Daneri if I could ride with her and her brother to Bella Vista. Rudolfo agreed, but said that it would cost me a dollar."

Jimmy shook his head. "I don't understand. If they were going to Chatham's place anyway, why did you have to pay?"

"I thought it a bit odd, but I was eager to go, so I paid him the dollar."

"How did you make the connection that he took Mrs. Fields to Oak Bower?"

"For several days, I've been wondering why Rudolfo charged me. It was as if I was missing something. Today, before joining you at the newspaper office, I telephoned the hotel to ask Rudolfo about it, but he wasn't there. However, Angie was aware of her brother's taxi trip with Mrs. Fields. She said that Rudolfo bragged about making an easy two dollars last Tuesday. When I pressed for details, Angie explained that he took Sarah Fields to a very unusual Carmel house that was entirely covered with pieces of tree bark. I knew then that it was Oak Bower, Carlotta's cottage."

"But how did you know that Rudolfo would be here at the train station?"

"That's easy. In talking to Angie, she told me that Rudolfo and his cousin Oresto were charging Mrs. Fields five dollars to take her to the train station this afternoon."

"Well, I'll be."

Looking out the window, Nora saw that they were at the corner of Eighth and Monte Verde Street in Carmel. "Stop," she said. "I need to pick up my two pints of milk from the shrine."

Jimmy chuckled. "You don't forget a thing, do you, Nora Finnegan?"

CHAPTER FORTY SIX

Sitting together in the front row of City Hall's upstairs meeting room, William Owens said to Nora, "I wish Doctor Taylor were here. Tonight, only four men will be deciding Carmel's future for years to come. A motion that comes down to a two-to-two tie will be defeated and that won't resolve anything."

"When I was helping Mrs. Owens in the kitchen before supper tonight, she said that you visited the barber shop this afternoon, despite the fact that you didn't need a haircut. Did Trustee Milliken indicate how he was going to vote on the hotel project?"

"I need to be more circumspect. What I can say is that Roland is leaning against using tax money to buy property. He thinks, as I do, that the beach should be developed commercially. That will bring more visitors and revenue to Carmel."

Nora disagreed, but she was determined to remain optimistic about the outcome of the vote. She said, "When I called Keith before tonight's meeting, he explained what the residents' group is offering. When they hear the details from Mr. Newberry in a few minutes, I believe the city Trustees will go along with the residents' wishes."

Owens fidgeted in his seat. "They'll vote for what's best for the city, Honora."

"I think they should listen to the people who live here, sir. Furthermore, they'll have to make sure they consider the women's votes as well."

Checking the wall clock, Board President Ben Fox rapped his gavel on the table to hush the jabbering crowd. He said, "Does anybody know where Doctor Taylor is?"

The three Trustees sitting on both sides of him shook their heads in unison.

One man in the audience stood up. "I saw the good doctor walking on the beach after breakfast. I said hello to him, but he ignored me. He seemed preoccupied."

Fox shrugged. "This meeting's called to order. Being Thanksgiving is the day after tomorrow, I admit it's unusual for us to hold it two days before a holiday. But this is a continued hearing. I want to start it off by taking public comments. We'll listen to all sides. I'll begin with those who think that we should purchase the dunes from the Carmel Development Company to keep the beach free of development. Please come forward, folks, and form a single line."

Nora heard a rustling several rows behind her. A man got up and headed for the podium. Wearing a leather jacket, freshly-pressed shirt and trousers, Perry Newberry had dressed up for the occasion. Smiling at the Trustees, he said, "I have good news tonight." Many in the crowd murmured, as Newberry continued, "Most of you know I'm a member of the artists' group that has fought for years to stop the city fathers from paving Ocean Avenue. We've argued about that issue long and hard, due to the unwanted changes that street paving would bring us. More traffic. More tourists. Now we're involved in a far more important battle, one we believe will have a deleterious effect on our city's future. When we heard that outside developers wanted permission to build a hotel right at the water's edge, over forty of us got together to voice our objections to this ill-advised idea."

"That's not my opinion!" a loud voice shouted from the back of the room.

"Let Perry finish his remarks," Fox yelled. "Your turn will come."

Newberry nodded at the Board President. "Thank you, Ben. Three of us were delegated by the Save the Dunes Committee to negotiate the sale with Mr. Devendorf, who, with Frank Powers, co-founded the Carmel Development Company. We've had several meetings. The last one was held yesterday. We told Devey that we're going to ask the city to purchase the beachfront property. We plan to pay for it by passing a bond of fifteen thousand dollars. I have a petition with me tonight with more than enough signatures to put this critical issue to a vote by all the city's residents — that is, if you Trustees agree."

Whistles and shouts erupted on all sides of the meeting room. Most of the audience was on its feet. Nora was thrilled by the demonstration. She jumped up and applauded, as she watched Newberry walk up to the Trustees' table and present the residents' petition.

Fox rapped his gavel several times to restore order. "Quiet down, please!"

A man behind them tapped Owens on the shoulder. "Did I hear Newberry right? Did he say fifteen thousand dollars? Isn't that too expensive?"

Owens turned around in his seat. "I'm afraid not, Everett. Mr. Devendorf told me himself that the land has been appraised for at least fifty thousand dollars. I can't imagine why he would let it go for so much less."

As the petition was being passed among his colleagues, Trustee Stephen Pringle took a look at it and then said out loud, "It seems like a fair amount of money to pay for oceanfront land."

Owens looked at Nora. "This is the one of the few times that Pringle has spoken up since he was elected two years ago. He's a scientist at the coastal laboratory run by the Carnegie Institute. It seems that he's not in favor of a hotel."

President Fox rapped his gavel again, as several people continued talking to one another. After the room quieted down, he said, "Perry, do you have the Company's acceptance of this low price in writing?"

"I do, Ben. In addition to selling us the beach property, they'll sweeten the deal by throwing in the vacant lot at the eastern end of Ocean Avenue. As you know, that's the lot that is usually a quagmire after every rainstorm. But we can do something with it. Perhaps we can turn it into a public park."

"It seems like the Carmel Development Company is acting in the public's interest," Fox said.

Cheers erupted from the audience.

"That empty field is a mud hole in winter," Owens whispered to Nora. "I've always thought it would make a good site for a new city hall. The Trustees can't keep meeting in this cramped second floor space forever."

Wrinkling her nose, Nora said, "I prefer Perry's suggestion of a public park, sir. The Trustees could always meet in one of the churches."

For the next hour, she and Owens continued listening to the testimony, both for and against the hotel. Nora wrote down comments made by the village businessmen, hoteliers, workers, artists, actors, and writers until her fingers ached. Conspicuously absent were comments by Davey Chatham, Sarah Fields, and, of course, Mr. Fields.

When there were no more speakers, Nora tapped Mr. Owens on the arm and asked, "Do you think the Trustees will decide the matter tonight without Doctor Taylor? Or will they vote to continue the decision until a future meeting?"

Owens shook his head. "The doctor wasn't here to listen to the testimony, which makes it impossible for him to vote. I doubt they're going to put it off. We should have the answer any moment now. President Fox looks like he's ready to call for a motion."

The Board President looked up. "Everyone who wanted to speak has spoken," he said. "I'm going to bring the matter back to the Trustees for discussion and a decision."

Raising his hand, Trustee Pringle said, "Mr. President, I move that we support Mr. Newberry's petition and that we take a stand to prohibit all commercial development on any part of Carmel's beach."

"Is there a second to Trustee Pringle's motion?" Fox asked.

No one spoke for a few seconds. Nora heard the crowd beginning to grumble.

"If not," Fox said, "I'll second the motion for purposes of discussion."

Nora whispered, "This sounds like it might be the two-to-two vote that you predicted could happen, Mr. Owens, which means that the motion will fail."

Owens didn't answer. He was caught up by the significance of the motion.

"I'll second it also," Trustee Roland Milliken said. "I intend to speak in favor of Trustee Pringle's motion and for the petitioners tonight."

The audience came alive with shouts and hoots. Fox had to gavel them to order.

Looking embarrassed, Milliken continued, "Fifteen thousand dollars is cheap for unspoiled beach property with an unobstructed ocean view. It should be in the public's hands for that price. I know everyone worries about the success of their businesses like I do, but if we preserve the beach for future generations, more visitors will find Carmel-By-The-Sea a unique destination."

"I echo Roland's remarks," someone said. The voice came from the end of the table where the fourth Trustee, Hal Smith, a retired educator, was sitting. He'd been silent until now. "I move to make the vote unanimous — that is, if Ben supports the motion, as the rest of us do."

"Well, I'll be darned," a visibly flabbergasted William Owens said out loud.

"I *will* make the vote unanimous," Fox declared, "and I would like to amend the motion with the maker's consent to include placing a bond measure before the Carmel voters as soon as possible. The residents will decide if they're willing to support our decision and pay for the beach. Will the maker of the motion accept that amendment?"

"I will," Trustee Pringle said.

Behind Nora, the audience rose to its feet and applauded. People were yelling and drowning out the "ayes" of all the Trustees. Getting up to join in the celebration, Nora noticed Mayotta Brown and Keith in the aisle a few yards away. They were in the midst of a cheering group that was exiting the room. Nora imagined they probably were going somewhere to celebrate. She looked for Mr. Owens, who had remained seated, his head in his hands. "Are you feeling all right, sir?" she asked.

"One would think that the publisher of Carmel's weekly newspaper would have been able to predict this outcome," he said, as he straightened up. "I'll never know for sure whether Fox was for or against the hotel or why Milliken changed his mind since this afternoon. I incorrectly gauged the pulse of the Trustees and the community."

Nora put her hand on his arm. "I know you're disappointed, but I think it's the right decision. However, you're the one who taught me that a good reporter tells the story as it is and avoids expressing emotion or personal bias — except in editorials, of course. Shall I go over and stand at the exit to get comments on the decision from the departing residents?"

Owens could tell that she was concerned about his reaction to the Trustees' vote.

"Yes, that's a good idea," he said. "And I can accept the fact that a major battle has been won, but only time will tell whether a majority of the residents agree to pay for the beach. After you finish your interviews at the door, I'll be ready to escort you home."

"That won't be necessary, sir," a voice said. Turning around, Nora was surprised to see Deputy Connery. Still in uniform, he was standing in the center aisle.

"I didn't expect you, Jimmy," Nora said. "Are you here on official business?"

"I thought both of you would want to know that Davey Chatham has talked some more. He implicated Doctor Taylor in your kidnapping, Nora. Sheriff Terry sent me to Carmel to pick up the doctor for questioning. I've just come from his sanitarium, where I learned from his nurse that he left town this afternoon. She didn't know where he went. I thought he might have come here to the Trustees' meeting."

"He never showed up," Owens said, as he stood up.

Nora could see that the publisher was drained of energy. She said, "Jimmy, can you walk me back to Pine Log after I get some comments from a few more residents?"

"Sure, if it's all right with you, Mr. Owens."

"If that's the case, I think I'll hurry home before my daughter Sally falls asleep. I've been reading one of the Sherlock Holmes' adventure stories to her. She's eager to hear how it turns out. So am I. I'll say goodnight, and I'm obliged to you, Deputy."

"Thank you again for including me this evening, sir," Nora said. "I'll transcribe my notes and have them on your desk tomorrow. I'll work on them as soon as I get home. I'm far too excited to go to bed."

Owens nodded. "Mrs. Owens and I want you to spend Thanksgiving with us, Honora. You're welcome to join us, Deputy."

"That's kind of you," Nora said, "but I've accepted Miss Morgan's invitation to dinner. She returned from San Simeon yesterday and will be staying for the holiday."

Jimmy spoke up. "Thank you for the kind invitation, sir, but I'm a member of a large Irish family. We spend holidays at my parents' home in Pacific Grove. Like you, I'm the father of a little girl, which brings additional responsibilities, as you know."

"There's one other thing, Mr. Owens," Nora added. "For the past week or so, I've been meaning to ask you something. Would you and Mrs. Owens consider giving Maisie up for adoption?"

Owens laughed. "Consider it? You're reading my mind. I've been thinking of how to get rid of that dog ever since Maisie came to live with us. She's a handful. Problem is, I can't come up with anyone in Carmel who would take her off my hands."

"I know someone who would care for her and love her as much as Carlotta Fleming did," Nora said. "Will you ask Mrs. Owens if she can part with Maisie?"

"I already know her answer, and I'll happily throw in a month's worth of dog food to seal the deal!"

Leaving City Hall, Jimmy took Nora's hand. She didn't object, but she was new at this, and hesitant to express her feelings openly.

"Are you planning to take on Maisie?" he asked.

She giggled. "If you can meet me tomorrow afternoon, I'll give you my answer."

"Tomorrow's my day off. Tell me where and when. I'm eager to find out."

They strolled up the path to Pine Log's front door. Nora turned to say goodnight. Although she had no difficulty talking to people she hardly knew to get a news story, this was entirely different. It would be easier in the dark to hide her innate shyness.

Jimmy took her in his arms. His voice sounded low and husky in her ear. "I think I fell in love with you the minute I noticed you that day in Pescadero Canyon, Nora."

She found herself face to face with him. Bending forward, he kissed her gently. Then he stepped back, releasing his hold around her waist.

"Tonight, I'm sure of it," he whispered.

"Does that mean you're going to kiss me again, Mr. Connery?" Nora murmured.

He did, and this time, more passionately.

She responded and even surprised herself.

CHAPTER FORTY SEVEN

Wednesday

Despite feeling tired from a late night of transcribing her notes on the Trustees' meeting, Nora looked forward to the day. Going to her closet, she selected a tailored skirt coming just below the knees and her favorite long-sleeved white blouse. Her grandmother's brooch — the one with the swirl of pearls and silver filigree — looked perfect on her wool plaid vest.

While she dressed, she considered her new feelings for Jimmy. There was no doubt that she enjoyed his company, but she wasn't sure whether this was the time to become involved with a policeman who had a five year-old daughter. How would their relationship affect her career? Realizing that she couldn't reach any conclusion, she quit daydreaming and left her cottage a few minutes before eight o'clock.

Arriving at the newspaper office, she waved at Mrs. Owens, who was talking on the telephone, and put her pint bottle of milk in the ice box. Sitting at her desk, she read over her account of last night's momentous meeting. Nora hoped Mr. Owens would use her quotes from the residents who overwhelmingly supported buying Carmel beach.

Her thoughts were interrupted when the door to the back room opened and then slammed shut. She expected Mr. Owens to appear, but instead, Maisie ran towards her. Putting out her hand, Nora said, "Come here, Maisie." The dog obeyed.

When she finished with her caller, Mrs. Owens exclaimed, "Well, I'll be!"

"What is it? Nothing bad, I hope," Nora said.

"I can't wait to tell Mr. Owens my news. And by the way, what a pretty outfit you're wearing today."

"Thank you. You look very excited. What's going on?"

"That was Perry Newberry on the telephone. He said he had just come from the fix-it shop, where Ben Fox told him that Trustee Taylor has submitted his letter of resignation from the Board. Ben only found it this morning. It was slipped under his shop's front door. The doctor has left town. Mr. Newberry called to tell William that he's going to file the necessary paperwork to run for Taylor's seat and that he would like William to endorse him."

"Did Mr. Fox find out why the doctor resigned?"

"No, he didn't. All the letter said was that he was selling his medical practice."

Nora feared this new development would likely hamper Sheriff Terry's ability to prove Doctor Taylor's part in her kidnapping. But she had to let that go for the moment. She said, "I'm going to ask Mr. Owens to assign me the story of the next Trustees' race."

On her way to the back room, Mary Lee Owens paused in front of Nora's desk. "He may do that, except for the fact that you've lived here for such a short time. You might be unaware of the depth of Mr. Newberry's civic activism."

"I've learned a great deal about him, Mrs. Owens. I heard him speak at Miss Fleming's cottage and also last night at the Trustee's meeting. I have a strong sense of the man and his dedication to keeping Carmel in a natural state."

"He has a creative side as well, Nora. Did you know that I once had a supporting role in a play he produced and directed at the Forest Theater?"

"No, I didn't. Also, he's a talented house builder. I'm definitely going to ask to be assigned to write a story about the new candidate for city Trustee."

"I hope Mr. Owens gives you the chance, dear."

Nora thought of something. "Do you think he might not support Mr. Newberry?"

"We'll have to wait and see," Mrs. Owens said, as she headed to the back room to deliver Newberry's message to her husband.

The telephone rang. Nora got up and went to Mrs. Owens'

desk. "*Carmel Pine Cone*," she said. "Miss Finnegan speaking. How may I help you?"

"It's Julia, Nora. How are you feeling this morning? I didn't want to disturb you yesterday, knowing that you needed your rest. Everyone here at the hotel has been talking non-stop about your narrow escape from drowning over the weekend."

"I'm fine, honestly, and I have so much to tell you." Nora briefly covered the details involved with her swimming to shore and Sarah Fields' arrest for Carlotta Fleming's murder. "And there's a lot more I want to share with you, Julia," she said.

"I'll look forward to hearing the details. I called you, as I'm about to make our Thanksgiving dinner reservations here at La Playa. How does two o'clock sound?"

"That's perfect. Oh, by the way, how was your drive back from San Simeon?"

"It wasn't difficult and the time passed quickly. You'll be pleased to learn that Mr. King turned out to be a competent chauffeur and an engaging conversationalist. He regaled me with all sorts of stories about the plays he's starred in at the Forest Theater."

"I wish I'd been there to hear them. How did your meeting go with Mr. Hearst?"

"It was tiring. The man is such an energetic individual with so many ideas for his new home. I'll tell you more tomorrow."

Returning to her desk, Nora decided to concentrate on her story concerning Sarah Fields' arrest, since she planned to take the afternoon off. She worked without a break and was startled when she looked at the wall clock and saw that it was nearly noon. Getting up, she placed her article on the counter for Mr. Owens as Jimmy walked in. He was carrying a covered picnic basket.

Smiling at her, he said, "Hello, Nora. Will you join me for lunch on the beach?"

"You're right on time, Deputy, and I'm starved," she said. Seeing Mrs. Owens come out of the back room, she added, "I'll be out of the office for the rest of the day."

"Will you telephone us on Thanksgiving," the publisher's wife asked. "We know you're dining with Miss Morgan, but Mr. Owens and I want to make sure you're fine."

"I'll call you," Nora said, as she put on her jacket and picked up the dog's leash. Smiling at Jimmy, she said, "Come on,

Maisie. We're both ready to go."

The deputy shrugged his shoulders and held open the door for them.

Outside, Nora felt energized. They walked to the end of Ocean Avenue and the beach. The day felt cool, but the sun was shining. Nora removed Maisie's leash and let the spaniel race to the edge of the breaking waves. Other than a few gulls, Carmel beach was deserted.

Jimmy had brought a blanket. They spread it out behind a sand dune to stave off the wind. He said, "I'll open the ginger beer if you make the sandwiches."

"That's an unequal division of labor," Nora teased, "but I'll be happy to oblige."

After they finished eating, they walked along the beach. The dog alternated between barking at the birds and racing back to Nora, who had all she could do to keep the animal's sandy paws from soiling her skirt. She noticed how relaxed she felt in Jimmy's company.

He leaned against her and said, "When are you going to explain your plan for Maisie's future?"

Nora laughed. "All in good time. I've enjoyed this afternoon with you, Jimmy, but we should probably be leaving now."

"I'll gather up our things while you corral and put a leash on that dog — that is, if you think that's a fair exchange of labor," he kidded.

"Let's go. I'm on a mission."

With the dog between them, they hiked up Ocean Avenue to Junipero, where they turned south and headed into the Eighty Acres neighborhood.

Jimmy spotted the welcoming party. "Is that Freddie Woodward?" he said. "What a good idea this is, Nora. That boy will be very pleased to have Maisie."

"That's what his mother said, when I called her yesterday."

When Freddie caught sight of Nora, he waved and jumped off the porch steps. "Is she really going to be mine, Miss Finnegan?" he yelled, as he raced towards them.

Dropping Maisie's leash, Nora let the dog run.

Kneeling down, Freddie hugged Maisie and allowed his face to be licked. Nora and Jimmy were greeted by Claudia Woodward and Rob Jacklin. They made a perfect couple, Nora thought.

"I haven't had a chance to thank you for what you did for me, Nora," Claudia said. "If you hadn't telephoned the doctor when you did, I wouldn't be standing here now."

Nora took her hand. "I'm glad I was able to help. It would have been a tragedy if Freddie had lost you. It would please me very much to have you for a friend."

"I'd like that too."

Rob stepped forward and put his arms around both women's shoulders. "How would you two and Mr. Connery like some coffee?" he asked.

"Let me help," Nora said.

Jimmy sat down on the porch steps, where Rob joined him. Freddie and Maisie romped in the yard.

As Nora followed Claudia up the steps and into the house, she thought it odd, but comforting, that Rob and Jimmy could be friendly, despite their past disagreements.

The two women returned with a tray. Claudia served the men and then joined Nora on the porch swing.

Sipping his coffee, Rob caught Nora staring at him. He said, "It was thoughtful of you to give Carlotta's prized spaniel to Freddie, Nora. He needs a companion, especially when his mother gets preoccupied with her photography work. That happens frequently."

Feigning a frown, Claudia said, "You make it sound as if I do nothing else, Rob."

Nora reacted. "As a career woman myself, I can appreciate how hard it must be for Claudia to work and also care for a child."

Rob stood up. "I have an announcement to make," he said. "You two are the first to know that Claudia and I are getting married this coming Sunday. I'm determined to make her happy and be the kind of father that Freddie needs."

Claudia turned to Nora. "It will be a private ceremony in the Carmel Mission chapel. Rob and I want you to be a witness to our marriage vows, Nora."

Nora hugged her. "I'm honored that you want me to attend."

Looking down at Jimmy, Rob added, "We need two witnesses, Deputy. Given that you arrested me last week, you might think what I say next is unusual. I'd like you to be my best man."

Jimmy jumped to his feet and shook Rob's hand. "I'll

be happy to," he said. "Congratulations, and thank you for not holding a grudge. I'll be there on Sunday."

The four continued chatting, until Nora finally said, "I think it's time for us to leave."

Seeing that she and Jimmy were ready to go, Freddie came up on the porch, followed closely by Maisie. "Thank you, Miss Finnegan. I love my beautiful dog and I promise to take good care of her."

Nora bent down and hugged him. "I know you will, Freddie. I hope you'll bring Maisie by to visit me when you're out walking."

As they left the Eighty Acres tract, Jimmy said, "Rob is a good man. I'm glad to get the chance to know him under better circumstances."

"I'm glad too," Nora replied. "He and Claudia deserve much happiness after their terrible experience with Martin Fields."

They had reached her front door. Nora said, "Promise you'll telephone me after your family's Thanksgiving festivities end tomorrow evening, Jimmy?"

"I'm afraid I can't do that."

Hiding her disappointment, she said, "I guess you'll be much too busy."

"It isn't that." Taking her in his arms, Jimmy whispered, "I'm coming back here to Pine Log afterwards so we can watch the moon come up together."

CHAPTER FORTY EIGHT

San Francisco, California

December 25, 1921

By four o'clock, Nora's Christmas Day was winding down, but not going well. Seated next to her friend Keith at the Finnegan's dining table, she had halfheartedly listened to the conversation and politely responded to her mother and father's questions. Luckily, Keith had taken most of their attention away from her. His easy Southern manners charmed her parents and held off their sly attempts to draw her out.

At one point during dinner, she could tell that she had disappointed them by announcing that she was returning to work at the *Pine Cone* that weekend.

The news had brought a rise from her father. "The crimes that took place in Carmel last month were tragic, Honora. But also, they put you in danger. Your mother and I think you should come home."

"I don't agree," Nora argued back. "Those experiences strengthened my self-confidence and sharpened my skills as a reporter."

He shrugged. "We worry about you, living alone in Carmel."

"You aren't eating well and you look entirely too thin to me," Alice Finnegan interjected. "You still haven't finished your dinner."

"She looks very healthy to me," Helen Simon said. The

Finnegan's housekeeper and Nora's former nanny had come out of the kitchen to clear the table.

Nora was pleased to have Helen's support. She knew that she had lost some unwanted pounds, but she wasn't 'thin' by any means.

"When are we going to be introduced to this young man you've been seeing?" her father asked. "And what is his profession?"

Nora couldn't understand why he was trying to provoke her. She knew that her father was aware of Jimmy's job as a Monterey County deputy sheriff. Moreover, Mrs. Owens had said that he had quizzed Mr. Owens about Jimmy as recently as last week. Controlling her temper, she replied, "Mr. Connery is Sheriff Frank Terry's senior deputy. Police work runs in his family, Father. As to when you and Mother will meet him, I really couldn't say."

She saw her mother's eyes narrow. "You've told us very little about Molly, his daughter. A five year-old child is a responsibility for any woman to assume, especially one who works outside the home."

Trying not to sound too defensive, Nora said, "I'm not looking to becoming his wife and Molly's stepmother. Mr. Connery and I are just friends, Mother."

John Finnegan wasn't convinced. "Keith, you must know this policeman. What's your honest opinion of Honora's beau?"

Nora stretched her foot out under the table and kicked Keith's ankle. He nearly choked on his water, but he managed to say, "I like him very much, sir. He's a steady, hard-working fellow and people think he's very professional." Pulling his feet under his chair, Keith avoided mentioning that he had challenged Connery on several occasions.

Looking at Nora, her father said, "I gather then, that you're settled on remaining a reporter. But what will happen to your career if Mr. Connery asks you to marry him?"

As if on cue, Helen Simon noisily pushed open the swinging door from the kitchen and held everyone's attention. "It's time for our dessert," she announced cheerily.

Nora guessed that the white-haired woman had been eavesdropping. Glad for her support, she said, "I can't imagine marrying anyone now, Father."

Setting a freshly baked pumpkin pie on the buffet, Mrs.

Simon turned to Nora's father. "May I serve you the first piece, sir?"

Putting down her water glass, Nora's mother interrupted, "Before you do, Helen, I want to know what you think. You've known our daughter her entire life. Would you say that Nora is mature enough to realize what's best for her?"

Helen Simon's blue eyes sparkled. "I'd say that she's the best judge of that."

Alice Finnegan raised her eyebrows. "But what chance will she have to define herself in an out-of-the-way place like Carmel, although I admit that her father and I always enjoy our summer vacations there. I think city life offers Nora more possibilities. Turning to her daughter, she added, "Come home to San Francisco as soon as your year's commitment to Mr. Owens is over, won't you, dear?"

Before she could answer, the telephone in the parlor rang. "I'll get it, Helen," Nora said, and jumped up.

Her father looked peeved. "Who can be calling us on Christmas Day in the middle of dinner? Motioning at Keith, he went on, "Since we're postponing our dessert, why don't you and I step outside for a smoke?" Getting up, John Finnegan went to the humidor that sat on a table behind his chair. He selected two cigars and handed one to Keith. "My wife will call us when it's time for pie and coffee." The two men headed for the back porch, as Mrs. Finnegan left the table and joined Mrs. Simon in the kitchen.

Nora reached for the receiver. "Hello. This is the Finnegan residence."

"Merry Christmas, Nora," Jimmy said.

"Merry Christmas yourself, Jimmy. I was hoping it was you. I've been anxious to thank you for my present." Nora looked over at the fireplace mantel, where she had placed the foot-high figurine of Aphrodite. It complemented her mother's arrangement of fresh pine boughs and candles.

"I tore off the Christmas wrapping as soon as I woke up this morning. I could hardly wait to see what you gave me when we said goodbye at the train station. How did you know that I wanted her from the moment I first saw her in Mr. Levy's stock room last month?"

He laughed. "You're forgetting that I'm a policeman and a very good one at finding out things."

"She's so special, Jimmy. Thank you again." Nora kept her voice low, so that no one else could hear what she was about to say next. "I only wish you were here with us today, instead of Keith."

"I'm jealous that he's there with you, and not me."

"You needn't be. When he arrived this afternoon, Keith was quite moody. He confided that he saw Mayotta Brown out walking her Saint Bernard and in the company of a young man whom Keith didn't recognize. He's devastated."

"I'm sure he'll get over her. By the way, I have two pieces of information for you, Nora, and both are far more important than your Carmel librarian's love life."

"Does one of them concern Sarah Fields?"

"Yes. Remember the bloody fingerprints we found on the boning knife?"

Nora thought back to the sad day when she had walked into Carlotta Fleming's garden. "I'll never forget them."

"A second outside expert from New York has just corroborated Deputy Jensen's conclusion that Mrs. Fields' prints are on that knife."

"I suspected it from the moment we confronted her at the train station."

"Now with that evidence, Sheriff Terry said that the district attorney will schedule her trial for the first week in January."

"I'm hoping Mr. Owens assigns me to cover it. But you said that you had two pieces of interesting news. What's the other one?"

"Davey Chatham was sentenced to five years in state prison yesterday."

"I think he deserves it. Now let me tell you my news. Keith said that auditions begin for the brand new play at the Forest Theater early next week. When I get back to Carmel, I'm going to try out for a small part. I hope you'll come to see the play."

He chuckled. "You couldn't keep me away, Nora, no matter how bad your performance."

FORTY NINE

May 23, 1922

Carmel-By-The-Sea, California

At six o'clock in the evening, William Owens followed Nora out the side door of City Hall. They had just left the upstairs meeting room and the newspaper publisher was feeling exhilarated by the momentous decision that the town's new Planning Commission had made moments ago.

Nora paused at the corner of Ocean Avenue. "If you don't mind, sir, I'd like to stop by the office. I forgot my library book."

Owens nodded and picked up the pace.

When they arrived at the door of the *Carmel Pine Cone*, Nora said, "I feel disheartened. I didn't expect this day to ever come to pass."

Owens looked at her. "On the contrary, Honora. The Commission's action has been a long seven years in coming. I'm quite pleased that Carmel's main street will finally be paved — and in concrete, no less." Taking out his key, he unlocked the door and allowed Nora to enter first. He left the door ajar, as the spring weather had been much warmer than usual. His wife, Mary Lee, had closed the stuffy office an hour ago and had gone home. He knew she was expecting the two of them for supper and they shouldn't dally.

Nora went around the counter and retrieved the library book from her desk. She was looking forward to forgetting her disappointment by finishing Mary Austin's novel, *Woman of*

Genius.

As if sensing her mood, Owens said, "Although you've sided with those who want to leave the village as it is, I'll have no difficulty composing my editorial lauding the Commission's action. I've never felt better about being in the newspaper business."

Nora could only imagine the letters that would be written to him, arguing that the Planning Commission's decision had been a terrible mistake. She wished that she could write one too, but that would be inappropriate, given her reporter's status, not to mention the possible withdrawal of the ten dollar raise that Mr. Owens had recently given her.

"I don't share your excitement," she said. "The only thing that gives me any comfort is that the Commission preserved the pine trees in the middle of Ocean Avenue."

Owens came around the counter and faced her. "You know, that only happened because our new city Trustee, Perry Newberry, has been put in charge of the Board's Streets, Sidewalks and Parks Committee. What did you make of the rest of his speech to the Commission? I thought a battle might be brewing when he told them that twenty eight thousand dollars was too much to spend on paving any road, even our main street. Turns out, Perry didn't sway anyone over to his side."

Nora frowned. "At least they came up with a compromise and gave Perry his trees. In my opinion, that was another victory following the one he had last February."

When Owens didn't respond, Nora added, "Remember? It was his persuasiveness that carried the day. We residents bonded ourselves and bought the beach property. Now it can never be developed."

Owens resisted saying anything more about the road paving issue or the beach. He was aware of Honora's convictions. She was self assured, and a different person from the one whom he had begrudgingly hired last fall. Mary Lee had been right. Honora would make a good reporter.

Changing the subject, he said, "So tell me about the new play that's opening soon at the Forest Theater. Is the part you auditioned for going to be challenging enough?"

"I think so. In addition to the maid, it turns out that I'm also the understudy to the female lead."

"Bravo! But that brings me to ask you a rather delicate

question. Does your acting avocation, combined with your job responsibilities, allow you to keep company with Deputy Connery?"

"Only time will tell, sir."

"Fair enough." Taking her arm, Owens headed for the door. "Shall we find out what Mrs. Owens has fixed for our supper?"

Nora laughed. "I already know the answer to that question. Leftovers."

AUTHOR'S NOTE

Murder in the Pines was conceived and intended as a work of fiction. I want to affirm that a majority of the characters who are portrayed in the novel are fictitious, although they have been cast among numerous real persons who lived during those times.

Additionally, one major controversy has been woven into the book's plot that actually occurred in the early 1920s. It proved to be very significant with regard to Carmel-By-The-Sea's future growth and development. The issue centered on preventing commercialization of Carmel beach. An influential group of early environmentalists joined together to convince the city's Board of Trustees to place a bond measure on the ballot, thus allowing the residents to purchase this valuable piece of untouched shoreline from J. Franklin Devendorf and Frank Powers, the two co-founders of the Carmel Development Company. Some of the community activists mentioned in the novel helped to organize the beach preservation effort. These include: Perry Newberry, Fred Bechdolt, Jimmy Hopper, Alice and Grace MacGowan, Mary De Neale Morgan, and George and Catherine Seideneck.

Another critical dispute that has been described in the novel concerns the argument between Carmel's permanent residents and its business owners over whether to improve the condition of Ocean Avenue at the time. This problem was resolved in 1922, when the city fathers finally voted to pave over Carmel's main street with concrete.

Also, Julia Morgan, the first woman in California to set up her practice as an architect, is introduced as the fictional Nora

Finnegan's friend and mentor in the novel. Morgan did visit Carmel on occasion and did design homes for her Carmel clients.

Other real-life characters, whose names appear throughout the book, contributed in vital ways to the cultural history of Carmel-By-The-Sea. Among these individuals are: Perry Newberry, Herbert Heron, Mary Austin, Edward Kuster, Mayotta Brown, George Sterling, Sinclair Lewis, and Robinson and Una Jeffers.

Carmel Chemical Company No. 1 grew out of a volunteer fire brigade effort, and included such residents as J. E. Nichols, Robert G. Leidig, Fred Leidig, Delos Curtis and A. C. Stoney. I feel privileged to be able to acknowledge these men as essential persons who protected Carmel's homes, businesses and residents. Also, Marshal Gus Englund, Carmel's first policeman, contributed to the village's well-being on a daily basis.

In the end, the *Carmel Pine Cone*, which began publishing in 1915, was the vehicle I employed to thread through the story and hold it all together. The newspaper's importance to the community has been a reality, and not fiction, for almost 100 years.

NORA FINNEGAN'S CARMEL

Some of the buildings, structures and locales that existed at the time of the novel can be identified today. To locate them, the reader can refer to the captions below the following photographs.

A typical Carmel milk shrine (Chapter One)
Another example is located in front of the First Murphy House
on west side of Lincoln Street between Fifth and Sixth Avenues.

Original Carmel City Hall (Chapter Three), now a commercial building. Located at northwest corner of Dolores Street and Ocean Avenue.

Hotel La Playa, (Chapter Five)
Located at southwest corner of Camino Real and Eighth Avenue

All Saints Episcopal Church (Chapter Eight), renovated into current Carmel City Hall. Located on east side of Monte Verde Street between Ocean and Seventh Avenues.

Original Carmel Library (Chapter Ten), current site of Harrison Memorial Library. Located on east side of Lincoln Street between Sixth and Ocean Avenues.

The Forest Theater (Chapter Thirty Six)
Located at Mountain View Avenue between Guadalupe and
Santa Rita Streets.